SUDDEN DEATH

Blade brought the SEAL to a stop, turning the transport, angling it across the road, Hickok's side to the fleeing motorcycle.

Hickok hastily rolled down his window and raised his Henry, sighting carefully.

"You can't," Joshua claimed.

"He tried to kill us," Blade reminded Joshua.

"Not in the back!" Joshua protested.

"We have no choice!" Blade declared, watching the other driver speed off. If Hickok didn't fire soon, even he wouldn't be able to make the shot.

"No!" Joshua shouted, flinging himself forward, lunging for Hickok.

Geronimo reacted instantly, clutching Joshua, restraining him.

"No!" Joshua struggled to break free. "He's another human being!"

"Not any more," Hickok said softly. He inhaled, held his breath and squeezed the trigger.

The Wilderness series writing as David Thompson:

ENDWORLD #1: THE FOX RUN

DAVID ROBBINS

LEISURE BOOKS NEW YORK CITY

To Judy, Joshua and Shane

A LEISURE BOOK®

July 2009

Dorchester Publishing Co., Inc.
200 Madison Avenue
New York, NY 10016

ISBN 10: 0-8439-6233-X
ISBN 13: 978-0-8439-6233-8

Visit us on the web at www.dorchesterpub.com.

1

The blasted dog pack still had his scent!

Blade paused, angry, his gray eyes smoldering, his head cocked to one side, listening intently. How long had they been after him now? Sweat soaked his thick, curly hair and caked his green canvas pants and tattered fatigue shirt to his muscular body. At least a dozen were on his trail, their eager baying filling the morning air. They were close, too close, and narrowing the gap rapidly.

Just what he needed!

Blade ran, balancing the deer carcass on his broad right shoulder, hefting his bow in his left hand. The quiver of arrows on his back and the Bowie knife on each hip bounced as he moved. He'd never make it to the Home with the extra weight, and after the three days of tracking it took him to bag the buck, three days with little sleep and less food, he wasn't about to abandon the meat to the dogs.

No way!

Blade knew he was only two miles from the Home, two miles from shelter and comfort, two miles from help. But the others had no idea when he would return, they didn't know which direction he would be coming from, and they wouldn't be this far from the Home under normal circumstances anyway. In short, he couldn't rely on any aid from his friends.

He was up the creek without a paddle. Blade smiled grimly. Who was he kidding? He was up the creek without a canoe.

The howling was louder, closer. The fleetest of the pack had the fresh scent of blood in their nostrils, and the aroma goaded them to increased speed.

Blade ran over the crest of a small hill and paused. A natural clearing was forty yards away, half the distance down the hill. It would be his best bet. He would be able to see them coming. Even better, they wouldn't be able to sneak up on him and nip his hamstrings when his back was turned.

The first dog must have spotted him because a tremendous howl split the dawn.

Blade hurried, running for all he was worth, the buck slowing him down, though, 'impeding his progress, and he knew he was in trouble, knew he wouldn't quite make the clearing, even before he heard the patter of rushing pads on the hard ground and then the ominous, throaty growl from a canine pursuer. He tried to whirl, but he was too late, his movements hampered by the weight of the buck.

The dog hit him squarely in the center of his back, the buck absorbing the brunt of the brutal impact, the force of the blow still sufficient to drive Blade to his knees, and he dropped the deer and twisted, his right-hand Bowie drawn and ready, held waist high, the blade extended.

He's show these bloodsuckers how he got his nickname!

The lead dog was a big one, called a German shepherd in the days before the Big Blast. Huge, hungry, and deadly, it curled its lips back to display long, sharp teeth, its body crouched, its legs tensed for the spring.

The bow had landed to one side. The buck was lying on the ground between them.

"Come and get it!" Blade hissed.

The dog obliged. The German shepherd leaped, snarling.

Blade side-stepped, his right hand flashing, the Bowie slicing into the dog, opening its neck, crimson spurting over the grass.

The dog yelped and landed unsteadily, wavering, stunned by the sudden loss of blood.

Blade put his Bowie in its sheath and scooped up his bow. He drew an arrow and fired in one smooth, practiced motion, the dog dead on its feet before it realized what had happened, and Blade was spinning, another arrow ready, because the pack was on him now, and the second dog was caught in midair, the arrow thudding into the hairy brown chest and toppling the animal to one side.

The pack didn't miss a beat.

Another dog, a mixed breed, came in low and fast and struck Blade in the legs as he was notching another arrow to the bow string.

Blade fell, flinging the bow aside, grabbing his Bowie knives, one in each hand, and he rose to his knees, slashing right and left, frantically cutting and slicing, berserk, and he lost count of the number of dogs he laid open, the fur and the dust and the blood flying in every direction, the barking and snapping and yowling reaching a crescendo.

A Doberman pinscher fearlessly plowed into Blade, slamming into his chest, bowling him over, exposed and defenseless.

The pack expectantly howled with glee and closed in.

Blade managed to bury his left-hand Bowie in the Doberman. I gave it my best shot, he thought, which was small consolation for failing to get the meat back to the Family.

Teeth bit into his left calf.

Another dog had his left wrist in a vise grip.

Blade lunged with his remaining Bowie, ramming the knife into a black dog's throat. He was surrounded by the raging canines.

One of the dogs to his right was abruptly picked up and smashed to the earth, and an instant later the blast from the 30-06 carried to Blade's ears. Another dog, the one gripping his wrist, twisted and dropped away, flesh and blood erupting from its neck.

Hickok, Blade speculated.

A war whoop was added to the din.

And Geronimo.

Blade grinned, relieved, as the 30-06 continued booming.

Four more of the dogs were down now, and the ones still able took off, making for the nearest cover, a stand of trees and dense brush twenty yards to the west.

The rifleman was reluctant to let them go. Two more dogs were dead before the remnant of the pack reached cover.

Had to be Hickok, Blade knew. Hickok was the best shot, and Geronimo would be loath to waste the bullets.

Blade slowly stood, taking stock of his wounds. He was bleeding from a number of bite wounds, but none were particularly severe. His left wrist was throbbing, the bone exposed. He angrily kicked the dog responsible for his wounded wrist.

"I think the critter is dead," someone commented.

"He's obviously not a dog lover," added someone else.

Blade turned, smiling.

"You always gotta do everything the hard way?" Hickok asked.

"He likes to do things the hard way," Geronimo observed. "He thinks it builds his character."

Blade faced his two best friends, grinning.

"We came out of the woods at the bottom of the hill," Hickok said, pointing, "just as the dogs closed in on you. Had to fire and run at the same time. Tricky. I was hoping I wouldn't waste a bullet by accidentally hitting you." He laughed.

"You mean that you were aiming at the dogs?" Geronimo pretended to be surprised.

Blade shook his head at their antics, delighted they were there.

Hickok was examining the shot dogs, insuring that none of them were still alive, his lean frame coiled for action. He held his rifle loosely in both hands, casually sweeping the barrel from side to side. A leather belt was draped around his hips, a holster hanging from each side, his prized ivory-handled .357's loaded and gleaming in the sun, reflecting the meticulous care and attention they received from their owner. And well they should. With a rifle, Geronimo and one or two others in the Family might come close to tying Hickok, but with a handgun Hickok was unequaled in marksmanship, almost uncanny in his speed and ability to hit any target without consciously appearing to aim his revolver. The .357's were his by virtue of his skill, and he was called Hickok because he had selected it on his sixteenth birthday, at his Naming. One of the old history books called *The Gunfighters* told of a man long ago who was a legend with pistols, a man called Hickok, a tall man with blond hair and a sweeping moustache. It was fitting that sixteen-year-old Nathan, already a qualified member of the Warrior Class at that early age, should select as his namesake of the dealiest gunfighter of all time, simply because he, Nathan, was the most proficient gunman in the Family's history.

The Warrior Class was well trained.

While Hickok checked the dogs, Geronimo kept alert, scanning the tree line, prepared for any assault. In contrast to the blond, thin Hickok, Geronimo was stocky and had black hair. Where Hickok had blue eyes, Geronimo had brown. Where

Hickok was tall, Geronimo was short. Where Hickok had long hair and a moustache like his hero, Geronimo wore his hair cut short and his face was clean shaven. And what Geronimo lacked in ability with a handgun, he more tha made up for in other areas. Geronimo was the Family's supreme tracker, a lingering legacy of his Indian heritage. Geronimo was proud of the Indian in his blood, despite the fact that Plato had informed him his blood contained, at most, one-eighth Blackfoot inheritance. Geronimo could hunt, he was immensely strong, and his eyesight was spectacular at great distances. He was their best trapper, his trap line in the winter months often being their single largest supplier of fresh meat and new skins. Even in the worst of weather, Geronimo would return with food.

Blade, his grey eyes twinkling, motioned at the slain dogs. "Don't think I'm not grateful for the timely rescue, but how in the world did you know where to find me? Lucky?"

"Design, Plato would say," Geronimo replied.

"What's that mean?"

"It means," Hickok interjected, "that Hazel told us where to find you. Specifically, which direction you would be coming from. The timing was strictly ours. I'm just glad we didn't stop to relieve ourselves."

Hazel. Blade had experienced the results of her unique power several times in the past. Hazel's official title was Chief Family Empath. The Family was blessed, currently, with six individuals with psychic capabilities. Hazel was the oldest, the one with the most sensitive nature.

"Why was Hazel homing in on me?" Blade asked Hickok.

"Plato asked her to." Hickok had completed his check of the dogs; they were all dead.

"Why?"

"We don't know ourselves," Geronimo

answered. "But whatever it is, it's urgent. Plato sent us to get you back as quickly as we could."

"I wonder what's up?" Blade asked, more to himself than the others.

"Instructions?" Hickok requested of Blade.

Blade paused, pondering. He was the section leader of the Alpha Triad, and as such he was responsible for issuing orders and implementing strategy. The Warrior Class was divided into four triads, each with a designated section leader. Plato had paired Blade with Hickok and Geronimo and appointed him as the leader. Plato had said that their teaming "compensated for individual deficiencies and maximized potential achievement." Plato should know. He was the Family Leader, the wisest man in the Family.

Hickok and Geronimo were waiting.

"We'll take the buck back, even if it does slow us down a bit," Blade directed. "The Family needs the food." Blade rubbed his injured wrist.

"You okay?" Geronimo asked.

"I'll make it back." Blade pressed the torn wrist against his left side, hoping to completely stop the dripping blood. The wound was deep, but the veins had been spared and his blood loss was minor. He bent over and retrieved his Bowie from the dead Doberman and slid both knives into their respective scabbards.

"Think we could use any of the dogs?" Hickok prodded one of the carcasses with his left moccasin.

"Too mangy," Geronimo stated. "Look at their hides. Sores and blisters everywhere. The pelts wouldn't do us much good, and the meat would be too stringy and tough. Who knows what diseases they're carrying?"

"Point taken." Blade nodded in agreement. "Okay. We take the buck and make tracks. Plato wouldn't want us without very good reason. Hickok, take the point but keep in constant visual contact.

Geronimo, bring the buck. I'll bring up the rear."

Hickok was already in motion. Geronimo hefted the buck onto his right shoulder, waited until Hickok was ten yards ahead, then followed.

Blade fell into place behind them, speculating on the explanation for Plato's summons. He drifted back in time to his first meeting with the remarkable scholar and philosopher. Of course, nineteen years ago Plato wasn't so old, nor was he leader of the Family. He had been elected to that post only four years ago, after Blade's father had been killed by a mutate. Blade remembered his first impression of Plato was one of extreme kindness, conveyed in the gentle blue eyes, the perpetually wrinkled brow, and the long hair and beard, now gray but then brown.

"So this is your pride and joy?" Plato had said to Blade's father. "And he's only five? Big for his age. I see he has his dad's dark hair and abnormal gray eyes." Plato had knelt and studied Blade's youthful, earnest face. "There is character here. He will be a tribute to both his parents." Plato had stood, toying with the hairs in his beard as was his habit when deep in contemplation. "Have you noticed that since the nuclear war our records indicate each generation contains a proportionally higher percentage of offspring with hair and eye pigmentation of an unusual coloration and combination?" This fact, apparently, had greatly impressed the sage, and Blade had wondered why. Nineteen years later he still didn't know.

Blade's reverie was shattered by a low, piercing whistle from directly ahead. The danger signal. He dropped, flattening on the rough ground, ignoring a stabbing pain in his left wrist, and glanced at Geronimo.

Geronimo was prone too, the buck lying to one side. He was watching Hickok.

There was a small rise in front of them, covered

with bushes. Hickok was crouched behind one of the
larger shrubs, intently watching something on the
other side of the rise. He turned and motioned for
them to approach, but he placed a finger over his
lips in cautious warning.

Blade followed Geronimo, crawling on his
elbows and knees, his left wrist now starting to
throb. They reached Hickok.

"Mutate," Hickok whispered, and pointed.

Every time he saw one, Blade felt an instinctive
urge to puke his guts out. They were disgusting,
repulsive, an aberration of nature, the consequence
of man tampering with cosmic forces better left
alone.

This one, once, must have been a black bear.

"Ugly sucker, isn't it?" Hickok asked softly.

An understatement, Blade thought.

The mutate was standing on the eastern bank of
a small stream, the water not more than a foot deep.
There was a large pool below the small rise, about
twenty feet in diameter. The mutate was concentrating on the pool, apparently hunting for fish. The
general shape and size of the creature was that of a
bear, and the snout resembled that of a black bear,
but the remainder of the beast was deformed and
distorted, grotesque and bizarre. The black hair was
all gone, replaced by huge, blistering sores, oozing
pus from a dozen points, and cracked, dry, peeling
brown skin. Two mounds of green mucus rose in
place of the ears. The mutate breathed in wheezing
gasps, the mouth open, the tongue slack and dis-
tended. The teeth were yellow and rotted. The
stench was overpowering, and Blade could feel his
stomach beginning to toss.

"We'll swing wide to the south and avoid it," he
whispered to the other two and began to back away.

Hickok was still watching the mutate, and he
saw it suddenly rear upright and sniff the breeze.
The wind was blowing from the thing to them, so it

shouldn't be able to detect their scent. Then he remembered the buck, and he wondered if the deer smell could carry to the mutate without any strong gust.

The mutate was still smelling, eyeing the rise suspiciously.

Hickok placed his hands on his Colt Pythons.

The mutate shuffled forward and entered the stream, still on its two rear legs. The massive head was swiveling from side to side, the beady eyes searching.

A hand dropped on Hickok's right shoulder.

"Think it has our scent?" Blade asked.

"I reckon," Hickok laconically responded.

"Let's move."

They carefully edged backwards and rejoined Geronimo, patiently waiting with the buck draped over his shoulder.

"It knows we're here," Geronimo said, immediately assessing the situation.

"Think so," Hickok said.

They hurried, Blade leading, Geronimo in the center, Hickok bringing up the rear. They had been heading in a southeasterly direction. With the mutate blocking their path they were forced to bear south, hoping to strike an easterly course later on. The Home was only a mile and a half distant.

That fact worried Blade.

A mutate this close to the Home was disturbing and a potential danger to the Family, a very real and extremely deadly menace. Thank the Spirit that the Founder had erected the walls! Without the encircling protection afforded by the twenty-foot-high brick walls, the Family would have long since been overrun by the proliferation of wild animals evident in the area in recent years. The surge in wildlife was inevitable with the decline of man.

"Maybe we've lost it," Hickok suggested.

The underbrush behind them crackled and

snapped and loud snorts punctuated the mutate's determined advance.

"Damn!" Blade fumed, enraged. He thoroughly detested the mutates, in all their varieties and manifestations. An ordinary black bear would usually avoid contact with humans, fearing the two-legged horrors as if they were walking death. But mutates, in whatever form, deviated from the norm. Every mutate, whether it had once been a bear, a horse, or even a frog, inexplicably craved meat and stalked living flesh with an insatiable appetite. No one, not even Plato, knew exactly what caused a mutate. Plato was particularly desirous of locating, capturing, or killing a young mutate, a mutate not in adult stages of growth. No one had ever seen any but an adult mutate. Plato had speculated, many times, that mutates were the result of the wide-spread chemical warfare initiated during the nuclear conflict. If radiation alone was the cause, then logic would dictate that humans would be affected, and there was not a single report in the entire Family history of a solitary human mutate. Plato had emphasized over and over that discovering the reason for the mutates must be a Family priority. Within the past decade the mutate's population had increased drastically—apparently by geometric proression, according to Plato—and this fact was fraught with devastating implications.

Blade paused, considering his options. If they continued on their course, even if they reached the safety of the Home, the mutate would follow them to the walls, would know where the Family was based, and it might linger outside, waiting for someone, anyone, to venture outside. Or it might return from time to time, hoping to catch a human out in the open, exposed and vulnerable. Blade couldn't allow that to happen.

Hickok and Geronimo were standing still, watching him.

Blade surveyed their surroundings. They had stopped in a small ravine, no more than a shallow depression, encircled by trees on every side. The Spirit smiled on them.

"We make our stand here," Blade announced.

Hickok smiled.

Geronimo, knowing what was expected, dropped the deer carcass in the middle of the ravine.

"Find your spots," Blade advised.

"You better take this," Hickok said, and tossed Blade his rifle.

Blade caught it with his right hand.

"At this range," Hickok went on, "my pistols will be just as effective as the long gun. Besides, your bow wouldn't hardly scratch a mutate that big."

Blade grinned and nodded. If the mutate followed their path into the ravine, and there was every reason to believe it would, then it would enter from the north, as they had done. That left three points to fire from.

Geronimo was already climbing the west wall, his sturdy legs pumping. He reached the top and glanced back, his green pants and shirt, sewn together from the remains of an old tent, making excellent camouflage. Geronimo disappeared into some trees.

Hickok started up the east slope. "Aim for the head," he said over his shoulder.

Blade nodded. Frequently, whenever Warriors were socializing, the subject turned to killing, to the best techniques for downing prey or foe alike. Some advocated the heart shot, a few the neck, but Hickok was adamant in his defense of the head shot as the only viable shot to take, whether with a firearm, a bow, or a slingshot. "If you're aiming to kill," Hickok had said one night when the Warriors were gathered around a roaring fire, "then aim to kill. Any shot but a head shot in a waste of time, not to mention a danger to yourself and those you're protecting. If you hit a man or an animal in the chest or neck, or anywhere else except the head, they can still shoot back or keep coming. It takes several seconds, sometimes, for the shock of being hit to register, and those seconds can be fatal for you. But when you hit them in the head, on the other hand, the impact stuns them immediately, and if you take out their brain, you snuff them instantly. No mess, no fuss."

Sometimes, Blade reflected, Hickok could be as cold as ice.

Hickok was perched on the rim of the depression, his buckskin-clad frame hunched over as he intently studied the back trail. He motioned for Blade to hurry, then vanished behind a boulder.

The mutate must be getting close.

Blade slung his bow over his left shoulder, gripped the rifle in both hands, and ran up the south slope, the lowest. Dense brush covered the slope, right up to the tree line. Blade swung behind the first tree and crouched.

Not a moment too soon.

The mutate appeared at the north end of the ravine. It hesitated, scanning the terrain, uncertain. Its eyes rested on the dead buck.

Come and get it, gruesome! Blade hefted the rifle, eager for the kill. Mutates gave him the willies!

This one ambled forward slowly, cautiously, not satisfied with the setup, raw animal instincts warning it that something was wrong.

Eventually, Blade knew, the thing would approach the deer. Mutates, like those tiny terrors, shrews, could never get enough to eat. They even ate one another. That fact, Plato maintained, was the primary reason the mutates had not taken over the land. Yet.

The thing grunted, evidently deciding it was safe after all, and it lumbered towards the buck.

Blade silently debated the wisest course of action. He only had seconds to decide. If he waited for the thing to reach the dead buck, they would have the best, clearest shot. But if the mutate touched the deer, came in contact with the meat in any way, it would be useless as food for the Family. The carcass would be irretrievably contaminated. Anything a mutate handled had to be destroyed or removed from all possible human proximity. Could the Family afford the loss of this meat?

No!

The thing was five yards from the buck, head held low, concentrating on its meal.

Blade stood and raised the rifle to his shoulder, quickly sighting, aiming for the head as Hickok advised.

A glint of sunlight on the barrel of the 30-06 alerted the beast, and it immediately threw itself to the left, sensing an ambush, making for cover. For its bulk and size, the mutate was lightning fast.

Blade was forced to hurry his shot. The gun bucked and boomed, and his shot ripped into the mutate's neck, blood and yellowish-green pus spurting every which way.

The mutate twisted, snarling, and Geronimo opened up from the west rim, his bullet tearing a furrow out of the top of the mutate's head.

The thing was furious! It wanted to attack, to rend and tear and crush, but searing pain racked every cell in its body, and it elected to run, to seek cover, then circle and pounce when its quarry would be off guard. The mutate charged up the east wall of the ravine, bellowing with rage and frustration.

That was when Hickok closed the trap. He calmly came into view, his feet firmly planted, his hands on his Colts.

The mutate was twenty yards from Hickok and it roared when it spied him blocking its escape route.

Hickok did not draw his .357's.

The mutate was closing, the mouth wide open, the horrible teeth exposed.

Hickok remained immobile.

The mutate was pouring on the speed.

"Now!" Blade screamed, wondering why Hickok was waiting and knowing the answer, knowing that Hickok thrived on excitement, that he reveled in danger and adventure, and dreading that, this time, Hickok had gone too far, that the gunman had overestimated his ability.

But he was wrong!

Hickok drew, the Colts clearing leather simultaneously, the two shots as one, the slugs striking the mutate's forehead, and the thing stumbled, recovered, and continued to charge, even as the Colts cracked again, and a third time, and the mutate was dead on its feet, carried forward by the force of its own momentum, up and over the top of the east wall.

Hickok leaped to one side.

The mutate plowed into a large tree and dropped on the spot. There was a final, wheezing gasp, then silence.

Hickok stared at the dead creature for a moment, smiling. He casually twirled the Colts and replaced them in their holsters in a quick, fluid motion.

Blade and Geronimo were running towards the buck. Hickok joined them.

"That was a stupid thing to do," Blade snapped when they regrouped. "Were you trying to get yourself killed?"

Hickok simply shrugged.

"You take too many chances," Geronimo asserted.

"Why do you do it, Nathan?" Blade asked, suppressing his anger. "Don't you realize that one day your grand plays will be the death of you?"

Hickok glanced at the mutate, at the ground,

and at his friends. "Can you think of a better way to go? I'd rather die in a fight, with my guns in my hands, than old, sick, and decrepit." Hickok lowered his voice, and his companions were surprised by an insight into his character they'd never glimpsed before. "You both heard Plato. About six or seven months ago. The Family records show that each generation is not living longer, like it used to be in the old days, before the Big Blast. Each generation has a shorter life expectancy now. Plato said it's more than our constant fight for survival, more than our lives being a lot harder than life was in the old days. He said he wasn't sure what was causing our shorter life spans, our aging earlier and earlier in each successive generation. He suspected some form of radiation-induced genetic imbalance just might have something to do with it, but he doesn't have the equipment he needs to be certain."

Hickok absently drew a circle in the dirt with the toe of his right moccasin.

"Don't you see?" he continued. "Look at Plato. He's a prime example. He's . . . what? Not quite fifty? And look at him! Already he's gray and wrinkled, old way before his time. I went and did some checking in the library. I've compared pictures in the different books. Plato looks the way a man of seventy or more would have looked before the nuclear war. And that's going to happen to us, sure enough."

Hickok angrily slammed his right fist into his left palm.

"Well, I'm not about to let it happen to me!" he brusquely declared. "I'm going to go out while I've still got my senses about me!" He fell quiet for a moment, then resumed. "Besides, it really doesn't matter how we go. Plato's convinced me that we'll survive this world, that there is a higher plane of existence. It isn't important how we get there, just so we get there."

Blade was disturbed. He could see the logic in Hickok's argument, and it bothered him, but he completely disagreed. "What if you marry some day?" he asked Hickok. "What then?"

Hickok shrugged. "Cross that hill when I get to it."

"And when you do," Geronimo chipped in, "I predict you'll change your tune."

"We'll see," was as far as Hickok was willing to commit himself.

Blade wanted to change the conversation and dispel the moodiness settling in.

"My wrist is bothering me," he announced, and it was. "I better have it tended before dirt gets in the wound and it becomes infected."

"Yeah." Hickok drew his right Magnum and began reloading the spent cartridges from his cartridge belt. "And the old man did say he wanted us back as soon as we could manage it."

"I wish you wouldn't refer to him like that," Blade said stiffly.

"The old man?" Hickok grinned. "I like Plato, sure. But he's not my favorite person like he is yours. I don't mean anything personal by it."

They had discussed Hickok's apparent lack of respect for Plato before, and Blade was about to wade in again, to defend his mentor, when Geronimo sighed.

"Why am I doing all the carrying today?" he demanded. He slung his rifle over his left arm, stooped, and lifted the buck onto his right shoulder. "Glad you're not much of a hunter, white man." He smiled at Blade.

"And what do you mean by that?"

Geronimo started walking. "Look at this buck." He gave the carcass a whack. "All skin and bones. Not much more than a year or two old."

"We need the meat and the hide," Blade reminded him, following.

"I'm not complaining," Geronimo said. "Makes it easier for me. If this thing was full grown, you'd be helping me right now, sore wrist or not."

"You want me to lend a hand, pard?" Hickok had loaded his revolvers.

"I can manage," Geronimo snapped indignantly. "And why do you persist in using that phony Wild West talk? You were taught in the same school we were, by the same teacher. So where do you get off talking like you really were Wild Bill Hickok?"

Hickok pretended to be hurt by the rebuke. "What is this? Pick-on-Hickok Day or something?"

"Now that Geronimo mentions it," Blade interjected, "I've often wondered about the same thing myself. Why do you talk that way sometimes?"

"Just count your lucky stars I'm not partial to that Shakespeare dude," Hickok replied. "What a loser! Imagine anyone talking like that! As for me . . ." He paused. "I feel comfortable dressing like Hickok and talking like Hickok. . . ."

"Like you think he talked," Geronimo corrected.

". . . and if it makes me feel good, what's wrong with that? Maybe it helps me forget."

"Forget what?" Blade wanted to know.

"Forget who I am, and where I am, and the utter senselessness of it all."

Blade was sorry he had asked.

2

The Founder, as the Family called him, had built well.

Kurt Carpenter, as revealed in his other legacy, the diary he left behind, had been a filmmaker, an environmentalist, yet practical, an idealist and a visionary, all the while retaining a mature, firm grasp on reality. When others had said that the world's leaders would never blow up the planet, Carpenter had smiled and shook his head in disagreement. When the talks had broken off and the media had offered hope that peace could still be maintained, Carpenter had known better. When his many friends had gently derided im for spending so much time and his considerable fortune on his pet project, Carpenter had wisely ignored their barbs and proceeded anyway.

Yes, Kurt Carpenter had been extraordinary and, like the majority of forward-looking individuals in the course of human history, he had been ridiculed and sneered at, castigated behind his back, and mocked to his face.

Ironically, Carpenter, in a sense, had had the last laugh.

When World War Three finally had erupted, when the misguided political madness known variously and collectively as government had attained inevitable fruition, Carpenter and those relatives and friends he had gathered about him at his carefully selected survival site actually had outlasted his many detractors.

The horror of the aftermath of global nuclear devastation had precluded any urge to gloat; conversely, Carpenter had often wished he had perished in the holocaust, that he had not lived to see the world as he knew it come to an abrupt end. Living had become a bitter experience, an excruciating conflict for the simple basic necessities. The world had done a radioactive flip-flop, and the terrifying results were worse than anyone had predicted they would be. For instance, Carpenter had never anticipated chemical warfare would be extensively employed, never envisioned the outcome, and had failed to include chemical contingencies in his master plan. In the end, one of the clouds had gotten him.

Still, all in all, Carpenter had built well.

The Home, as Carpenter dubbed his survival site—and the name stuck—was built on a thirty-acre plot. First, he had surrounded his site with sturdy brick walls, twenty feet high. Later, his followers would string barbed wire all around the top of this first fortification. Next, along the inside of the wall, he had dug a twenty-foot trench. A large stream flowed across his property, entering from the northwest and exiting towards the southeast. Using aqueducts, the walls had been constructed over the stream. He had diverted part of the flow to the inside trench, creating another effective barrier, a moat. He knew human nature, knew that with the decline of civilization, culture, and law, society would revert to primitive, bestial levels, and he wanted his Family, as he affectionately called his followers, to be prepared to defend itself if the need arose.

Carpenter's buildings had been fabricated with strength and durability in mind, from reinforced concrete. The Home would have never survived a direct nuclear hit, or even a near miss, but he had selected his isolated site with that possibility in mind. He had located his survival site as far as possible from primary military targets, and the nearest civilian metropolis had been hundreds of miles distant. His buildings, both above and below ground, had been built according to scientifically calculated specifications for optimum impenetrability. He had been confident the Home would not be destroyed in the initial attack.

Carpenter's main worry had been the fallout. He had realized the pattern of fallout would be dictated by the targets hit, the number and type of weapons used, and, more importantly, the prevailing wind currents and other weather conditions. His fear of fallout had been his reason for building the underground chambers, well stocked with provisions, oxygen tanks and masks, an internal ventilation system, and the special equipment required for the monitoring of gamma rays. Fortunately, the direct fallout the site received had been minimal, and within a month of the nuclear war the Family had been able to come above ground again.

All these facts, and more, Kurt Carpenter had detailed in his diary. They were taught to every child in the Family during their schooling years.

Blade was thoroughly versed in the story of Kurt Carpenter's life and lasting triumph, and he ruminated on the implications as the Alpha Triad descended the hill west of the Home.

A strident horn sounded inside the Home.

"They've seen us," Hickok commented.

They could distinguish figures scurrying along the rampart on the upper level of the wall. Most of them were congregating above the drawbridge placed in the center of the western wall. The fields surrounding the Home were kept cleared of all vegetation except grass, a necessary precaution against surprise attack for human and bestial foes.

As they crossed the field nearest the draw-bridge, Geronimo scanned the people on the wall. "Jenny is waiting for you," he said to Blade.

Blade squinted, compensating for the glare of the bright sun. "Where. . . ?" he began.

"I see her," Hickok confirmed. "Just to the south of the drawbridge."

Blade spotted her too. Her blonde hair was swaying in the breeze, and she waved at him.

Blade returned her wave.

"So when are you two binding?" Hickok asked.

"When we're damn good and ready," Blade snapped.

"Touchy." Hickok grinned.

"You know how he is about his personal affairs," Geronimo said. "Why bait him?"

"It's just his nature," Blade responded before Hickok could reply.

"And it keeps you from getting a swelled head," Hickok cracked. "Our future leader should maintain a firm grasp on humility, and not distort his importance out of all proportion."

Blade stopped. "What do you mean by that?"

Hickok and Geronimo were still walking.

"I said," Blade emphasized, "just what the hell do you mean by that?"

They halted and faced him.

"I was just quoting Plato," Hickok said. "No need to lose your temper, Red."

"You know what he meant," Geronimo offered.

"Do I?" Blade retorted.

"Don't play the naive innocent with us," Hickok stated sharply. "Whether you like the idea or not, pard, the fact is that Plato wants you to become leader after he kicks."

"What if I don't want the responsibility of leadership?" Blade countered.

"Tough," Hickok said.

"Why must we go over this again and again?" Geronimo asked Blade.

"Because I'm not sure I want to be leader," Blade replied honestly.

"Why not?" Hickok demanded. "Too good for us?"

"Maybe I don't want over six dozen lives dependent on decisions I would be required to make."

"The Family must have a leader," Geronimo reminded Blade. "And you have the natural aptitude and ability a leader should have. It's in your blood, Plato says. Your father had it."

"And look where it got him!" Blade rejoined.

"Now is not the time and place for this." Geronimo waved his left hand in the direction of the Home. More members of the Family were gathered for their homecoming.

"Let's go." Blade glared at Hickok, who laughed, and led the way.

The drawbridge was being lowered and a reception committee was forming on the other side of the moat.

Blade scanned the rampart, but Jenny was gone. A moment later he saw her come into view on the drawbridge. She waved again and ran towards him.

The horn blasted again.

Blade glanced up at the lookout post on the northwest corner of the wall. Whoever had duty had already spotted them and sounded off, so why was he blowing the horn again?

The lookout blew twice more, paused, then three more times.

"Damn!" Hickok exclaimed.

"Where?" Blade was turning, searching the horizon.

"There!" Geronimo pointed.

Three quick notes, a pause, then three more. It could only be one thing.

Blade saw it, and his skin crawled.

The cloud was creeping over the hill behind them, shrouding the forest in a peculiar greenish mist, traveling slowly, borne by the breeze.

"Blade!" Jenny screamed, running faster.

"Make for shelter," Blade directed his friends.

Hickok obeyed, running. Geronimo, fatigued from carrying the buck for two miles, started to shuffle off.

"For God's sake," Blade yelled, "drop the carcass!"

"But the food . . ." Geronimo started to protest.

Blade grabbed the deer by a rear leg and yanked, toppling the buck to the ground. "You're more important! Move!"

Geronimo sprinted towards the Home.

Blade looked back. The wind was picking up, it had shifted since the mutate incident, and was now coming from the west, bearing the cloud right down on them. It was coming fast, too fast!

"Blade!"

Jenny was by his side, gripping his right hand, squeezing hard. There was a hint of panic in her voice, in her wide green eyes. Her white blouse was heaving, her breathing labored, from her exertion.

"Let's go!"

They fled.

The cloud was at the border of the field, sweeping in. A faint hiss carried through the air.

Jenny stumbled in a rut and fell on one knee, tearing a hole in her already faded and patched jeans, stifling a cry.

Blade heaved her to her feet. "Hurry, honey!"

How could the damn thing move so fast? No wonder the clouds had claimed so many lives over the years, including that of Kurt Carpenter.

Blade and Jenny ran all out, breathing hard.

They crossed the drawbridge and Blade spotted one of the Family striving to raise the massive mechanism by himself.

"Leave it!" Blade ordered.

"But . . ." the man protested, knowing his duty was to always insure the drawbridge was promptly closed after any opening.

Blade recognized him. "It won't keep the cloud out, Brian! Want your wife to become a widow? Move!"

Brian fastened his brown eyes on the approaching cloud, nodded, and ran for shelter.

The green cloud had consumed half of the field.

Blade drew Jenny with him. Ahead, Hickok and Geronimo were entering the C Block. Smart choice.

The hissing was louder.

The compound was nearly deserted. The Family had taken shelter in the underground chambers. Those chambers were the last refuge in case of an attack by human, or inhuman, sources. Provisions were continually replenished. There were six concrete buildings within the brick walls, each one in reality a reinforced bunker. Below each building, called a Block after the customary military fashion, was a survival chamber. Access was gained via a hidden trap door, and every door was practically impregnable, consisting of alternating steel plates and insulation designed to filter any harmful particles, such as fallout, and reduce the penetration of ionizing radiation.

Blade and Jenny reached the doorway to C Block. Blade saw the trap door, in the northeast corner, open and beckoning.

Behind them, a woman shrieked in terror.

Blade whirled.

An infant, a toddler, was wobbling on unsteady little legs toward the drawbridge, towards the cloud, now only fifty yards from the Home.

"Mark!" the woman, Nightingale, screamed.

"Come back!" She was standing fifteen yards away, trembling, wanting to rescue her offspring but too petrified to make the attempt.

The small boy was still moving in the direction of the cloud.

Blade released Jenny and headed for Mark.

"Blade!" Jenny called after him.

"Stay there!"

The green cloud was only forty yards from the drawbridge, wispy, vaporous tentacles probing ahead of the main mass, reaching, searching, seeking flesh. Inexplicably, the mysterious clouds left vegetation unaffected by their passage. Any humans or animals, however, were never seen again if consumed by a cloud.

Blade knew the child was fascinated by the cloud, dazzled by a sight unlike any other the boy had ever seen. In a matter of moments, it would become the last sight the boy ever saw.

The creeping menace was closing on the draw-bridge.

The boy had stopped just yards from the draw-bridge, gaping.

Blade was running full out, straining his leg muscles to their limit.

"Mark!" the mother screamed again.

Mark twisted, glancing over his right shoulder.

The breeze slackened just a bit, and the cloud slowed.

Mark smiled at his frantic mother and returned his wondering eyes to the cloud, marveling.

Blade could feel his blood pounding in his temples, the toll on his leg muscles causing sharp pain in his thighs. He had gone too long without adequate rest and proper nourishment.

The cloud was almost at a standstill.

The boy ambled onto the drawbridge.

No! Blade lacked the energy to voice his warning. He concentrated on moving, on maintaining his speed. Speed was everything.

The preternatural hissing filled the air, resembling the sound of a pan of frying turtle amplified a thousand times. The wind suddenly picked up and the cloud resumed its advance.

Blade reached the boy. He scooped Mark into his arms and hugged him to his chest. For an instant he paused, riveted, watching the opaque cloud eat up the distance.

"Blade!" he heard Jenny yell.

Blade spun.

"Mommy!" the boy shouted, beginning to cry, suddenly terrified.

"We'll make it!" Blade assured him.

But would they? Blade could not afford a backward glance as he made for C Block. He saw Nightingale and Jenny were standing side by side near the doorway. Nightingale had apparently run to Jenny for comfort, for support. Jenny's right arm was around Nightingale's shoulders, their expressions ashen, their eyes wide. Mark was bawling, and Blade felt several warm tears spatter on his neck.

The hissing crackled in his ears.

To his right, out of the corner of his eye, Blade caught movement. He risked a quick look-see and his breathing increased.

A finger thin green tentacle was coming at him. Thin, yes, but just one whiff and he was instantly dead.

"Mommy!" Mark squealed.

His attention still focused on the approaching tendril, Blade missed spotting a small hole in the ground in front of his churning feet.

"Mommy!" the instinctively horrified child screeched.

Blade hit the hole and went down.

The tentacle was ten yards away, closing in, as if sensing warm blood.

Blade jammed his left elbow trying to absorb the force of the fall and protect the infant. The boy's knees dug into Blade's stomach, and Blade's vision whirled and danced, his midriff lanced with intense agony.

Blade tried to rise, to keep moving, but he couldn't seem to catch his breath and his limbs felt like mush.

"Blade!" came from Jenny.

Jenny. He wanted to go out thinking about her, his first and only love, sweethearts since they were ten. Jenny. His precious beloved.

Strong arms abruptly gripped him by the armpits and hauled him to his feet.

"You sure pick the damnedest times to take your naps, pard."

Hickok and Geronimo were literally carrying him, propelling him towards C Block.

"Hold your breath," Geronimo advised. "It's too close!"

Blade felt life returning to his legs and he pumped them, doing his best to keep up.

"Mommy!"

Nightingale came out to meet him, grabbing Mark, hastening for the doorway.

Jenny waited for Blade and moved in, taking Hickok's place, supporting her man. "Hang in there," she encouraged him.

They reached the trap door. Nightingale and Mark went down the steps first. Jenny followed. Hickok and Geronimo assisted Blade in descending to the underground chamber.

"You ever consider going on a diet?" Hickok asked Blade.

Blade was too tired to respond. He heard the trap door clang shut and knew they were, for the moment at least, safe.

"Is he okay?" Jenny was asking.

Blade tried to focus, but his vision spun,

dizziness overcoming his mind. He wanted to thank them for saving him, but he couldn't keep his eyes open and his mind alert.

"Did he inhale the vapor?" someone was inquiring.

That was all he remembered.

3

The scene was shrouded in mist, the images clouded, but he could discern the mutate perched on a boulder ahead of him, crouched and prepared to spring. This monstrosity was once a mountain lion, now a deformed, demented demon.

He wanted to scream! His legs were carrying him towards the mutate on a path that wound below the boulder on which the horror was perched, and try as he might, until sweat beaded his brow, he could not force his legs to stop. They seemed to be endowed with volition of their own. What was wrong with him? Did he want to suffer the same terrible fate as his father?

The mutate growled and licked its lips.

He shivered as an intense sensation of chilling numbness pervaded his soul. Again and again, over and over, he attempted to will his legs to stop, to turn and flee, but without any hint of success.

The boulder was only feet away, the mutate pressed against the top of the rock as its hind legs searched for a firmer grip.

Stop! He shouted at his legs, to no avail. Stop! Stop! Stop!

He recalled the day a runner came and informed him that his father had been attacked while on a hunting foray. They hastened to the death scene, but arrived too late. His father had passed on only minutes before his arrival. Blood was still flowing from a gaping tear in his father's throat, and the stomach area was torn to shreds, strips of ragged flesh splayed outward from the body. He knelt in the grass and held his father's hand and felt tears streak his cheeks. His mother had died in childbirth, his birth. Now his father was killed, and loneliness filled his grieving heart.

The two men on the expedition with his father blamed themselves for his death. One of them had stopped to remove a stone from his boot, and the other waited with him, the two idly engaged in conversation. His father was thirty yards ahead of them when the mutate charged from the brush, bearing him to the ground, clawing and ripping and snapping. The two men rushed to his father's aid, too late. The mutate whirled at their approach, snarled, and bounded into the woods. Strangely, the two men swore that this mutate was different from any other they had ever seen. They claimed this particular mutate was wearing a leather collar. The men were honest and fearless, respected by everyone, but not one member of the Family really believed their story about the collar. A popular assumption was that the two men had mistaken a shadow under the mutate's neck for a collar. Imagine! A collar on a mutate! The very idea was patently ridiculous.

He glanced up at the mutate on the boulder, petrified, because this mutate was wearing a wide leather collar decorated with silver studs.

No! It couldn't be!

The mutate roared and pounced!

He screamed.

"Blade!"

He opened his eyes, his vision briefly blurry. A cold, clammy sweat caked to his skin.

"Blade? Are you okay?" It was Jenny.

Blade tried to respond, but his tongue felt swollen and awkward, his throat parched, and the room appered to be spinning around and around.

"Blade? Can you hear me?" Her tone conveyed her concern.

Blade wanted to say yes, but couldn't. He noticed his vision beginning to clear.

"Permit me," someone said, and a shadowy figure loomed over his face, obstructing the light from the nearby candle. "Blade, concentrate on my voice, on my directions. If you can hear and comprehend, nod once."

Blade recognized Plato's voice. He nodded.

"Thank the Spirit!" Jenny happily exclaimed.

"Quiet!" Plato ordered her. "No distractions. Blade . . ." He placed his weathered, wrinkled right hand on Blade's forehead. "Did you inhale any of the cloud? Any at all? Nod once for yes, twice for no."

Blade nodded twice. At least, he couldn't recall doing so.

"Good. Nathan and Geronimo agree with that assessment. A stray vapor possibly penetrated into your lungs, but not in sufficient quantity to cause your earthy demise. You must clear your respiratory system. Breathe deeply, in and out, in and out."

Blade's vision was restored to normal, but his throat was still congested. He followed Plato's suggestion, inhaling slowly and exhaling carefully, settling into a rhythm, sensation returning to his numbed senses and limbs.

"Excellent!" Plato commented. "Continue until I instruct you to desist."

Blade complied, taking in his surroundings. He was lying on one of the dozen cots set up in the chamber below C Block. A score of candles provided the illumination. Fourteen of the Family had sought sanctuary in this chamber. The other Family members would be scattered under the other Blocks, each having run to the nearest shelter when the alarm was sounded. Supplies were stacked against the walls: food, clothing, medical necessities, weapons, and the other essentials the Family might require if confined to the chamber for any protracted period.

Hickok and Geronimo were sitting on another cot, engaged in animated conversation.

Jenny and Nightingale were comforting the still-distraught Mark.

Plato was standing, staring down at Blade, his kindly blue eyes probing.

Blade raised hmself on his elbows. He noticed that his injured wrist had been cleaned and bandaged while he was unconscious. Jenny or Nightingale, or both? They were two of the four Family Healers.

"Is your biological equilibrium restored?" Plato inquired.

Blade's throat felt better. "I feel fine," he acknowledged.

"Sit up then, but don't push yourself," Plato directed.

Blade obeyed. The others were all watching him now, alert for any indication of remission. "Really, I'm okay," he reiterated.

"I certainly pray you are," Plato said. "The Family has need of your particular skills."

"Why did you send Hickok and Geronimo after me?" Blade asked.

Plato raised his arms and swept the survival chamber with his gaze. "Dearly beloved, attend me! We have a matter of grave import to discuss." The others present clustered closer, forming a circle around their leader.

"You make it sound so serious," Jenny stated.

"It is," Plato responded. He stroked his gray beard. "I had planned to address the entire Family tonight after the evening meal. Events, however, preclude that possibility. I will share my misgivings

with those present now, and later, while those
selected prepare, will inform the rest of our loved
ones. Time is crucial to the success of the project
I'm about to detail. I might be presumptuous, but I
believe in my heart that a majority will agree with
my assessment of our situation and the proposed
remedy."

Everyone was attentive to his every word.

"You are aware I sent two of our Warriors to
retrieve their Triad leader. I intend to send the
Alpha Triad on a mission, a potentially dangerous
errand from which they might never return."

"At last! Some action!" Hickok exclaimed.

"Why?" Jenny demanded, casting an apprehensive glance at Blade.

"Because I have reason to believe that unless
drastic action, as Mr. Hickok so enthusiastically
refers to it, is taken immediately, the Family is
faced with the bleak probability of impending
extinction."

Mark's sniffling was the only sound in the
chamber.

"Extinction?" Nightingale finally inquired.

Plato clasped his wiry hands behind his stooped
back and grimly surveyed those around him. "Precisely. All of you are aware that our life spans are
decreasing with each generation. Family records
verify this. Those fortunate enough to attain
advanced years are displaying the symptoms of
aging earlier and earlier in each succeeding
generation. My personal calculations indicate that
in another twenty or thirty years the elders in the
Family will reach what was once termed old age by
the time they are thirty-five. The prospects are
evident and terrifying. We must take the necessary
steps, now, to insure that this mysterious process
can be reversed and eradicated."

"What is causing this?" someone asked.

"I don't know," Plato admitted. "I pray to the

Spirit that the reason can be determined before it is too late. Six months ago, when I initially confirmed this phenomenon, I hypothetically assumed the cause to be transient, attributable to the cumulative effects of negligible long-term radiation exposure. Now I have reason to suspect otherwise, and I want Family approval to send the Alpha Triad after equipment that can settle the issue once and for all. I want to send the Alpha Triad out into the world.''

Over the years since the war, the expression "the world" had become a Family euphemism for whatever existed beyond the boundaries of the Home. Hunting forays seldom penetrated further than twenty miles in any given direction. Not since the Big Blast, as many Family members preferred to refer to World War Three, had anyone departed the Home on an extended trip. In his diary, Carpenter advised the Family to stay put until such time as it was sufficiently strong in numbers to withstand any attack by a hostile force, or until it was certain that stability was restored to a disrupted, chaotic world.

"Are any of you aware of the importance of the date?" Plato asked. "Today is June fourth."

There was a moment's hesitation on their part. Time, the consciousness of elapsed intervals frenetically followed by prewar society, was no longer relevant. Instead of dominating and dictating individual behavior, time was now ignored or savored in slow, spontaneous spurts. The Family's generators Carpenter had wisely provided to make the transition from prewar to postwar culture easier had worn out decades ago. With the demise of electricity, the Family's entire mode of living had altered, reverting to simpler ways and austere means. Calendars were still used, though, primarily by the Tillers for farming purposes.

"It is appropriate that we should send out our first expedition now," Plato said. "We don't enjoy being reminded of the war, but if you consult the records you'll discover that in two days an historic anniversary occurs. It will be exactly one hundred years since World War Three."

Plato paused, noting the frowns and sad expressions on his loved ones, on those he mentally referred to as his "children." Could any of them properly appreciate the profound significance of the loss the war had inflicted on humanity? Of the gains?

"The Founder planned and stocked well," Plato continued. "He stockpiled huge quantities of provisions, of every conceivable type, most of which have since been used. Over the years we have adapted as supplies in any area were depleted. We grow and preserve our own sustenance, we construct our own clothing and build our own furniture. Although most of our original medical supplies have been utilized or outlived their effective potency, we have used certain reference books from the library and our own experience to achieve a consistent level of natural healing that is remarkably efficacious. In short, the Family has persevered. But, if we could locate new medicine, find other material we can use, and replenish our stockpiled reserve of ammunition for our firearms, I'm sure we would all rejoice. This brings me to the second reason I want the Alpha Triad to go out."

Plato stared at Blade.

"I want the Alpha Triad to retrieve as many items as they can from a list I've compiled of scientific, medical, and other supplies and basic provisions and equipment the Family requires."

"We gonna carry this stuff back in a knapsack?" Hickok interrupted.

Plato grinned. "No. The load would strain even your broad shoulders. We'll get to the method of transportation in a moment."

Blade wondered what Plato could be referring

to. The Family owned nine horses, but they were exclusively used in the fields for tilling the soil and other farm uses. Taking them beyond the limits of the Home would be exposing them to almost certain death.

"Before I do," Plato resumed, "I want to stress the third and final reason for sending out the Alpha Triad. Pardon me." He moved towards the west wall and a path was cleared for his passage.

The west wall was adorned with over a dozen maps, most frayed and worn from use and age. In the center of the wall was a map of the former state in which the Home was located, Minnesota. A bright red dot in the northwestern corner indicated the Home site.

Plato reached out and tapped the red dot. "The Home. In the one hundred years since the war, the Family has not extended its boundaries beyond the original limits. We are ignorant with respect to whatever is transpiring in the world around us. We own several radios, long since useless. Even when the generators were functional and we had a store of batteries, the atmospheric disturbance was too great to permit reception or broadcast on the short-wave bands. The crucial point to stress is that we have survived, and if we have, then there is a distinct possibility that other groups have too. Remember those scavengers? Where did they come from? We must determine if populated centers are existing in the world, and the Alpha Triad must learn if they are any threat to the Family."

Plato stopped and searched the faces nearest him. "Any objections to my proposal?"

"I have one," Jenny spoke up.

"Yes?" Plato glanced at Blade.

"The Family has survived, true," Jenny began. "But we were not near any nuclear impact points, thank the Founder! We do know, from the early records made when the Geiger counters and the other equipment was working, that the radiation level in the atmosphere rose dramatically after the Big Blast, then tapered off to near normal within five years. But what about hot spots, strike sites? Are they still radioactive? Will the Alpha Triad expose themselves to some unknown form of nuclear or chemical horror and seal their doom? Can we take that chance?"

Plato cleared his throat. There was an evident sadness in his eyes when he answered her. "We can not guarantee that they will not encounter danger on this expedition, which is why it is up to them to determine if the trip is made at all. They are well aware of the dangers. But I want to show you something, Jenny, and the rest of you, that may allay your fears."

Plato touched the red dot again.

"The Home. Located in northwestern Minnesota, on the outskirts of the former Lake Bronson State Park. Not a major metropolis within hundreds of miles. Scant chance to find supplies we require anywhere else but a major city. And there is one here."

Plato lowered his hand to the southeastern section of Minnesota. "Formerly known as Minneapolis and St. Paul, the Twin Cities."

"That's so far!" someone protested.

"How do we know the Twin Cities are still there?" another person asked.

Plato was studying the map. "To take your questions in sequence, the Twin Cities are, according to my calculations, three hundred and seventy-one miles from the Home, give or take a mile or two. . . ."

Hickok laughed. "Shouldn't take us more than a year to get there and back!"

"I'll get to that in a moment," Plato repeated. "First, someone wanted to know if the Twin Cities are still there. As far as we know, yes. Sporadic reception was possible until several weeks after the nuclear conflict. The journals clearly state that Minneapolis and St. Paul, lacking any strategic importance, were spared a direct hit. One entry notes that a commercial radio station, WCCO, was received, broadcasting governmental orders to evacuate. I believe the Twin Cities still stand, although in what condition is anyone's guess."

Plato faced them.

"I also believe the Alpha Triad has a reasonable probability of success in attaining their goal." He slowly gazed at Blade, Hickok, and Geronimo in turn. "You will face untold hazards. Mutates. Clouds. Hostile humans. Who knows what else? But the benefits to the Family outweigh your personal risks. You are caught in a vicious paradox. If you do make the journey, you might not survive. If you don't make the journey, the Family will not survive for much longer. Oh, we might persist for several more generations. Eventually, though, the creeping senility will eradicate the Family at an excessively early age. Mark my words! That is inevitable unless we are willing to do something about it now. Take all the time you require to discuss it amongst yourselves."

Hickok stood and stretched. "Who needs time, old man? I'm bored to tears sitting around here all the time. I say we go."

"Don't be hasty," Plato advised him.

Hickok patted the ivory handles on his Pythons. "Hasty is my middle name. Besides, the way you present it, we don't have that much of a choice, do we? What do you say, pards?"

Geronimo stood. "Fortunately, I don't have a wife and family or I might decline. But I'm for going, if only to satisfy my curiosity. Blade?"

Blade could almost feel Jenny's eyes boring into him. He knew she was looking at him, but he refused to return her stare. He mustn't waver now. He rose to his feet, pleased that his strength had returned. "I agree with you. We don't have a choice. The Family's welfare comes before our own. We'll go."

"Good." Plato smiled at them, nodding his head.

"On one condition," Blade amended.

"Oh?" Plato's eyebrows arched.

"That if we do not return, if you should never hear from us again," Blade said, deliberately continuing to avoid gazing at Jenny, "you will pledge to deny anyone permission to come looking for us, and will restrain anyone who might be so inclined."

Everyone in the chamber knew whom he had in mind.

"Ahhhh. Agreed." Plato grinned. "Although it has been my experience that a determined individual and a flash flood have considerable in common. They are both well-nigh irresistible if you are caught in their path."

Blade expected Jenny would strenuously object and was relieved when the protest failed to materialize.

"I hope you will agree to a condition of my own," Plato casually mentioned.

Too casually! From long experience, Blade recognized the tone Plato used. Their leader was about to make a suggestion that might not go over too well with some of those present.

"I want you to take Joshua with you," Plato stated.

"What?" Geronimo asked, surprised.

Hickok laughed.

"Joshua? Are you serious?" Blade demanded incredulously.

"Quite," was Plato's simple response.

Hickok laughed again.

"I refuse to take Joshua along with us," Blade said.

"On what grounds?" Plato inquired.

"Grounds? I'll give you grounds!" Blade's voice rose with his growing annoyance.

"Go get 'im," Hickok chipped n.

Blade ignored him. "I fail to see where Joshua would be of any benefit on this mission." He stepped up to Plato. "He's not a fighter, he's not a hunter, and he's not trained in any of the sciences. . . ."

"Are you trained in any of the sciences?" Plato interjected.

"No," Blade confessed, "but I'm a Warrior, and Joshua is not. He's not a Healer. He isn't qualified in any area to accompany us on this mission. He would hinder us more than he could conceivably aid us. I'm surprised you would even mention him as an addition for this trip." Blade thought of one more reason. "You said that this will be dangerous, that we might not return. How could you send Joshua with us? Send a man who has vowed never to take a life? Who wouldn't defend himself if attacked? We can't take him."

Plato sighed and sat down on the nearest cot. "Bear with me a moment. Much of what you have said is true. Joshua is devoted to the concepts of love and peace. He's not a scientist, although he is as adept and knowledgeable in technological areas as you are. After all, you had the same teacher. Me. Joshua is not designated an official Family Healer, but you will concede he is talented in the restorative arts, exceeding your ability by far. And he has two strengths, two remarkable aptitudes, qualifying him or this enterprise. First and foremost is his spiritual nature, a definite counterbalance to a Warrior's inherent and cultivated aggressive attitude. Secondly, he is an Empath. The youngest, to be sure. Still, his psychic capabilities could be of distinct advantage. Think about it. I can't compel you to take him, but I strongly advise it. Do you have a specific reason I haven't addressed?"

"I think old Josh is a bit strange," Hickok cracked.

"You have room to talk?" Geronimo countered. He nodded at Plato. "I think I understand what you're saying. You want him to serve as a balance."

"A balance for what?" Hickok asked.

"For your Warrior natures," Plato answered. "You are more inclined to shoot first and ask questions later. On this mission, our first determined effort to establish outside contact, we require someone who will reach out in friendship to strangers, someone who will put any fears or suspicions these outsiders might entertain to rest. Joshua is capable in this respect, eminently so."

"And I'm not?" Blade asked, the implications disturbing him.

"You have achieved a commendable balance," Plato acknowledged, smiling, "but you must admit you have considerable to learn when it comes to spiritual realities and brotherhood."

"And Joshua is to be our teacher," Geronimo concluded.

Plato rubbed his right knee. The joints were bothering him again. "Yes," he answered Geronimo. The quiet one. In some respects, not initially evident in his laconic nature, Geronimo was more intellectually perceptive than either of his Alpha associates. He glanced at Blade and noted his furrowed brow, his thoughtful expression. Should he tell the youth the entire reason for sending Joshua, a motivation previously discussed and agreed to between the two of them when the idea first occurred to Plato? Joshua was willing, even eager, to comply with Plato's wishes. If Blade was to ever assume the mantle of Family leadership, then certain aspects of his personal development must be rigorously attended to. Close association with Joshua could open Blade up to new horizons of spiritual awareness.

"I'm still not completely convinced," Blade said. "I see part of your reason, but I believe it's a mistake. Still, if you think it wisest, then Joshua goes with us."

"That's what I call standing by your guns," Hickok quipped.

"Is anyone else going?" Jenny joined their conversation.

Plato shifted to face her. "No."

"They should take a Healer long," she suggested. "They might be injured on this trip."

"As I mentioned before," Plato patiently stressed, "Joshua will act in that capacity."

"But Joshua is not certified as an official Healer," Jenny protested.

"He will suffice on this venture." Plato began rubbing his left knee. "Besides, Jenny, would you deprive the Family of one of our four Healers?"

"The Family could make do with three," Jenny replied.

"Possibly." Plato paused. What could he possibly say to influence her? She was profoundly in love with Blade, and she was displaying a very natural reluctance to allowing him to leave the Home without her. Plato remembered his one and only love, his binding to a beautiful, intelligent woman filled with an overflowing joy of life. Nadine. They married, joyously living as mates for eleven years, until that fateful day they left on an exploratory expedition. Plato wanted to familiarize himself with the terrain to the east of the Home. He had discovered a reference in the records to a small lake due east and he wanted to ascertain the veracity of the report. They departed in early morning, and by late afternoon they still had not discovered any trace of the elusive body of water.

By evening they decided to call it quits. Plato advised building a raging fire to deter any hostile animals. Even the horrid mutates avoided fire. He went for timber in a stand of trees fifty yards away. Nadine busied herself preparing their campsite. She was armed and an excellent shot and he had not feared for her safety. He took his time, pausing often to examine interesting flora. Eventually, his arms laden with dry wood, he returned to the camp.

Nadine was gone.

Plato assumed she was heeding nature's call, and went about starting their fire. When it was lit, and the kindling was snapping and popping and filling the air with smoke, he stood and called her name several times.

No response.

Plato began circling the camp, increasing his radius with each sweep, shouting for her. He couldn't understand it. If there had been trouble he would have heard her fire a shot or scream. What could have happened?

After hours of fruitless searching he returned to the flickering flames and collapsed, an emotional wreck. She was gone! Nadine had vanished from the face of the earth without a trace.

Plato never did find her. He returned to the Home and organized a search party. They returned and scoured the countryside for sign, any trace of what might have transpired. Not a hint. Plato remained despondent for the better part of a year. In his heart he never recovered from her loss, and he could not bring himself to reach out for another woman after the tragedy.

Plato sighed. Yes, he could sympathize with Jenny. But he could not permit his personal feelings to inhibit his deductive reasoning. He stared up into her green eyes. "I'm sorry. I will oppose any motion to send a Healer with the Alpha Triad. With them gone, we will require every able-bodied man and woman to assume additional duties. Our security forces will be seriously depleted. We can't spare another person to accompany them."

Jenny slowly nodded her head in silent agreement, turned, and walked to a far corner of the chamber. She sat down on the farthest cot and placed her face in her hands.

Plato looked down at the cement floor. If anything did happen to Blade, if the Alpha Triad did not return, he would never be able to forgive himself. He doubted too whether Jenny would ever forgive him. Sometimes, he reflected, the trials of leadership were an oppressive burden.

"This is great, pard," he overheard Hickok saying to Geronimo. "Just think of it! The first of the Family to see the world! Who knows what we'll find out there!"

Quite probably, Plato reflected, your death.

4

Funny thing about clouds. They swept in out of nowhere, passed over the countryside devouring all living flesh in their path, and then disappeared as mysteriously as they materialized. Their passing was swift and deadly. Family records of the clouds, kept since that first cloud had killed Carpenter and nearly decimated the Family, indicated that the clouds would completely pass over the Home within two hours of their first sighting. Add another two hours as a safety cushion, a precaution against a break in the breeze, and invariably it would be safe for the members of the Family to emerge from their shelters and resume their daily lives. Slightly over four hours after the cloud was first spotted, Plato led those in C Block above ground.

The latest cloud was gone, the sky a clear blue, birds singing, the trees wafting in the wind.

Plato sent two Family members to inform the other Blocks that it was safe to come up.

"So when are you going to tell us," Hickok asked Plato, "about this secret way we're going to bring all of the supplies back from the Twin Cities?"

"As soon as the entire Family is present," Plato answered. They had badgered him for the better part of two hours, demanding to know. He had refused to divulge the information, preferring that the whole Family should experience the thrill and the surprise together.

Within ten minutes the Family was assembled. Plato raised his arms to draw everyone's attention; then, for the benefit of those who had sought shelter in the other Blocks, he reviewed the details of the plans he had unveiled in C Block. He closed with: "It is imperative that the Family permit these four men to endeavor to reach the Twin Cities. The future, our future, depends on what they uncover."

"I agree with you, Plato," a lean, elderly man said. "But there is one point you've neglected. How will the Alpha Triad bring back the equipment you want? You can't be intending to send some of our horses with them."

There was a murmur in the group. The horses were among the more valuable Family possessions. They were carefully tended to and kept in prime health. A special ramp under F Block, the Block nearest the fields, enabled the Tillers to hasten the horses to safety at the first hint of danger from an approaching cloud or any other source. The horses were the only domestic animals the Family retained. The few dogs, cats, cows, and chickens Carpenter had stocked and intended for his progeny to continue raising had long since perished.

"We are not using any of the horses on this enterprise," Plato assured them.

"Then how . . .?" someone began.

Plato waved for them to follow and walked to E Block. The Blocks were clustered in the western half of the Family plot. They were arranged in a triangular fashion. Furtherest south, the point of the isosceles formation, was A Block. In a northwesterly line, one hundred yards distant, was B Block. C Block was one hundred yards northwest of B Block, and the closest Block to the drawbridge in the center of the western wall. D Block was one hundred yards due east from C Block, and E Block another one hundred yards due east of D Block. Turning abruptly southwest, F Block was one hundred yards distant, and the triangle was completed one hundred yards further by A Block. The eastern half of the Home was devoted exclusively to agriculture and was maintained in a natural state where the soil wasn't tilled. Just east of the Blocks were several rows of small log cabins, the individual domiciles of the married Family members. The outer wall, and the moat, encircled the entire Home. Plato stopped at the southern entrance of E Block.

"What are we doing here?" a woman asked. "It's the library."

On ground level, each Block was utilized in a specific capacity. A Block was the armory, B Block the sleeping quarters for single members, C Block the infirmary, D Block was the carpentry shop and general construction area, and F Block was devoted to preserving and preparing food and storing farm supplies.

"The library and more," Plato said, pointing at the ground.

"Yeah," agreed one man. "A survival chamber."

Plato smiled. "I am not pointing at the ground directly under E Block. I am indicating the ground directly in front of this doorway."

"What for?" someone asked.

Plato was enjoying himself. He saw their puzzled, perplexed expressions and restrained an urge to laugh. He wondered if it would still be useable after all this time, after being stored for a century? Carpenter had had top engineers work on the special room. Their job had been to insure that it remained airtight, that the contents would be operational whenever the Family needed what was in there. "Will several of you go to F Block and bring back a half-dozen shovels?" he requested, and ten Family members hastened to comply.

While they waited, Plato leaned against the wall and rested. He spotted Blade in the crowd. The

Alpha leader was staring at someone else. Plato followed Blade's line of vision, expecting it would be Jenny, wondering if she was still distraught. Instead, Blade was watching Joshua! Joshua, attired in his usual faded brown pants and green shirt, was standing quietly in the midst of the crowd, his hands folded in front of him. His brown eyes were downcast, his facial expression serene. His brown hair, grown long, draped across his shoulders. He had adorned his face with a full beard and moustache. Plato knew the identity of Joshua's childhood hero, and he understood why the sixteen-year-old Robert had adopted Joshua at his Naming. That thought provoked memories of Plato's own Naming.

None other than Kurt Carpenter had instituted the Naming ceremony. At the age of sixteen all Family members were formally christened. They were permitted to retain the name bestowed on them at birth by their parents, or encouraged to select a new name, any name they wanted, hopefully from prewar history. Carpenter had worried that subsequent generations would eventually forget their historical antecedents, that they would shun any reference to World War Three and prior eras. This conviction was partially borne out by the reluctance of Family members to refer to the holocaust as exactly that; most preferred the colloquialism "Big Blast" instead. Carpenter had wanted to insure that Family members never lost touch with their roots, with the causes and circumstances resulting in their current predicament. He had urged his followers to have their children search through the history books and choose the name of any historical figure they so desired as their very own. Henceforth, they would be known by that name. Family members were not forced to subscribe to this practice, but most adhered to it. A few kept the names given to them by their parents. Even fewer selected an entirely new name. To discourage formality, Carpenter had dictated that surnames were taboo. In his eyes, last names bred a sense of false respect and fabricated civility. Family members were entitled to one name, and one name only. The practice persisted. Sixteen-year-old Nathan, the budding gunman, chose Hickok. Sixteen-year-old Lone Elk selected Geronimo. Dark-haired Michael picked an entirely new name, consistent with his affinity for edged weapons, and became Blade. Robert, already envincing a decidedly spiritual nature, was designated Joshua. And an inquisitive sixteen-year-old formerly known as Clayton became Plato. The Naming became a ritual, the cognomen chosen predicated on personal preference.

Titles, however, were another matter. While Carpenter considered surnames hypocritical, he viewed titles as socially significant. Every member of the Family received an official title, whether it be Tiller, Empath, Healer, Warrior, or another. The title received was based on the area in which the greatest ability was demonstrated. Carpenter had detested the servile attitude adopted by many of his peers towards "Mr. President" or "Mr. Senator" or "Your Honor." Every individual in the Family was to receive equal social status, and to insure this belief Carpenter had decreed that every Family member would receive a title. Titles were badges of social distinction, and everyone had one. This tended to preclude any inclinations towards lording it over one another. As an added safeguard, Carpenter had prohibited the existence of professional rulers, or politicians. If any member exhibited a craving for power, an eagerness to rule, that member was to be immediately expelled from the Family, never to return. Those designated as Family leaders must receive a vote of agreement from a majority of the Family before any decisions could be implemented. One of the few exceptions concerned life-threatening situations, during which the Warriors could order others for their own safety and the defense of the Home.

This review passed through Plato's mind while he waited for the digging equipment.

"Here they come," someone announced, shattering his reverie.

The shovels and several picks were distributed, and Plato directed them to the proper spot for excavation. At least, he hoped it was the correct spot. This was one of the few secrets Kurt Carpenter had kept from his friends and followers. His diary did not contain any reference to it. The Family Leaders passed on the information from one to another verbally. Fortunately, Blade's father had relayed the information to Plato before the mutate claimed his life. Leaders were required to select their successors within three months of their installment as head of the Family, a practice designed to insure a smooth transition should the Leader be unexpectedly terminated. The Family was not obligated to vote the hand-picked heir in as the new Leader. It could pick another candidate if it wished, but in the one hundred years of Family history not one successor had been rejected. Plato had already made it public knowledge that his desired replacement was Blade, and he knew Blade resented the prospect. Plato suspected Blade recalled the turmoil and stress, the constant pressure his father had been under. Leadership necessitated numerous daily decisions, many of which placed the entire Family's welfare at stake.

Plato had been Family Leader for four years. Shortly after his official installment, he had taken Blade aside and cryptically informed him, in case it should become necessary to travel an extended distance from the Home, to dig in front of E Block. Blade wanted to know more, but Plato hedged, a trifle uncertain. Blade was young, and youth was prone to hasty, impetuous action. The temptation might be more than Blade could resist. Plato wondered if Blade remembered his instruction. He glanced at the Warrior and was pleased to detect the glimmering of dawning understanding reflected in Blade's facial features.

The Family was denied knowledge of the secret for the same reason Plato had refused to completely confide in Blade: fear that the temptation would be irresistible, that someone would be compelled to use it before the proper time.

The digging was continuing at a frantic pace, the Family excited and intrigued by what might lie below the surface. When one member tired, the shovel or pick was passed to another.

Plato gazed upward at the late afternoon sun, squinting. Yes, if they continued at this rate, they would uncover the hidden chamber with an hour or so of daylight left. Ample time to open the door and inspect the contents.

Blade approached Plato. "What's under there?" he asked.

"Wait and see," Plato answered, his eyes twinkling.

Blade stretched, his huge biceps and triceps bulging. The day was hot, and he was wearing a torn, faded brown shirt, short-sleeved, his usual green pants, patched together from the remnants of a torn canvas, and the typical Family footwear, moccasins. His finely muscled body glistened in the sun, his brawny development the result of a rigorous dedication to a daily exercise regimen. Only two or three others came close to matching his superb physique. Twin Bowies hung suspended from either hip.

"It's a vehicle of some sort, isn't it?" Blade inquired.

"You'll see," Plato said.

"You're enjoying every second of this," Blade commented, grinning.

"Wouldn't you?" Plato smiled. "I haven't seen them this enthused in ages!"

"They're not the only ones," Blade said. "Hickok is chomping at the bit to be off on this great adventure."

"Which reminds me," Plato mentioned. "Perhaps you should find Hickok and Geronimo and select your provisions. You'll require sufficient firepower and ammunition to defend yourselves, food, and water. We possess several compasses that are functional. Take one, and whatever else you feel you need."

"Let's see," Blade deliberated. "A Block and F Block should contain most of it. We'll get right to it." He walked off, scanning the crowd, searching for the other two-thirds of his Triad.

The minutes pased, turned into another hour.

Joshua came up to Plato, the gold chain and cross he always wore gleaming in the sun. "Did you broach it to Blade?" he asked.

"I did," Plato confirmed.

"And the result?"

"You will be leaving with the Alpha Triad tomorrow, probably around midday."

"Then I will spend tonight in prayer to the Spirit that our expedition will be a successful one," Joshua said in his quiet, reserved style of speech.

"Just pray you all return to the Home safely," Plato amended.

"If we should perish, don't blame yourself," Joshua advised. "Remember, even if our bodies are torn to pieces, our souls will still depart this world to where we go from here."

Plato made a snorting sound. "Small consolation for the guilt I'd bear for the remainder of my earthly life."

"The Spirit will guide us," Joshua confidently

stated. "If we do not return, simply consider it the
will of the Supreme."

"There is nothing simple about he will of the
Supreme," Plato corrected. "Who among us can
presume to perceive the purpose of the Spirit?"

"At times we can," Joshua replied. "If we
remain loyal to the Spirit and apply our souls to
acquiring the perfection we were instructed to
attain, we can periodically glimpse the outworking
of the Spirit in our daily lives. Not frequently, at
first, but more clearly as we become more spiritual.
Surely you have enjoyed moments where the will of
the Spirit seemed startlingly apparent?"

"There have been moments. . . ." Plato agreed,
marveling, again, at the wisdom Joshua constantly
displayed, belying his evident lack of years and
experience.

"I think the Egyptian summed it up best,"
Joshua said.

"Egyptian?" When it came to religion, not even
Plato was as sagacious and profound as Joshua.
Plato's expertise embraced philosophy and ex-
tended to the sciences, all of them.

"The Circles in the library makes reference to
one called Amenemope, a sage in an ancient time.
He believed that consciousness of the Spirit within
us should be our paramount concern, eclipsing all
others."

Plato remembered perusing the book, years ago.
"I'd wager Amenemope enjoyed sufficient leisure to
augment such an achievement. Unfortunately, our
continual struggle for our very existence precludes
adequate opportunity for strictly spiritual pursuits.
Most of the Family, although devoted to the Spirit,
can't find the time to spend in worship and prayer
on a daily basis."

"A little water, each day, is better for the
nourishment of a plant than a sudden deluge,"
Joshua stated.

"True. But how little is sufficient? Blade is a case in point."

"Is he aware of your motivation for sending me with the Alpha Triad?" Joshua asked.

"I endeavored to explain my reasoning, but he doesn't completely comprehend. He doesn't fully appreciate that an aspect of his character is inadequately developed. I'm hopeful that prolonged exposure to your beliefs might influence his thinking, might ameliorate his harshness." Plato stared into Joshua's eyes. "Do what you can with him."

"What about Geronimo and Hickok?" Joshua inquired.

"Hickok?" Plato chuckled. "I seriously doubt whether Hickok is at all concerned with his spiritual growth. That one is a fighter. I expect he will remain a Warrior as long as he lives."

"And Geronimo?"

Plato's brow furrowed. "Geronimo is a puzzle. There is more to him than is initially apparent. He prefers to be a Warrior, but he occasionally displays aptitude for a higher calling. I don't know what to make of him. Do you?"

Joshua shook his head. "He doesn't talk much, and keeps to himself most of the time. He's polite when approached, but he seldom initiates a conversation with me. I've noticed he is quite open with Blade and Hickok."

"They're his best friends and his Triad partners. It's to be expected that they would be close." Plato watched the diggers fling the dirt to one side of the now-gaping pit.

"Do you suppose the reason they relate so well is because all three of them have lost both parents? They're the only Triad who've experienced such a profound personal loss."

Plato was surprised by Joshua's observation. "It never occurred to me," he admitted. Wasn't it amazing how things right in front of your nose could escape your notice?

A sudden commotion commenced at the pit.

"We've hit something hard!" someone exclaimed.

So soon? Plato hurried to the edge and looked down. They had indeed reached the surface of the entrance ramp.

"What is this?" a Family member asked.

"It is an opening," Plato answered. "You must completely uncover it. The dimensions should be approximately thirty feet by thirty feet. After it is clear of dirt, search for three iron rings encased in the concrete. In the interim, someone fetch as much stout rope as we can muster. We will require it when the rings are found."

The digging continued at a faster clip. The rope was brought and piled near the hole.

Plato remained at the edge of the pit. He glanced around, noting Joshua had departed. Blade, Geronimo, and Hickok were also gone, probably still collecting their supplies for the journey. Plato gazed at the entranceway. He speculated, again, on whether the thing would function after all this time. Had it been preserved in serviceable condition? If otherwise, it availed them naught. Top scientists, brilliant men and women, had erected this chamber. If it was humanly possible to accomplish the task, they would have succeeded.

"We've found one of the rings!" someone shouted. Others clustered around to catch a glimpse of the iron imbedded in the concrete wall.

The Family was visibly excited, the diggers renewing their strenuous efforts, the spectators goading them on.

"Here's another one!"

The second ring had been discovered.

Plato studied the rings. The first was in the center of the northern rim of the wall, the second in the center of the eastern edge. That left only the ring in the western edge. The southern edge did not include a ring; it was the hinge by which the door would swing open.

The sun was still ninety minutes from the far horizon.

Plato gazed over the compound. The Omega Triad had closed the drawbridge after the Family emerged from the survival chambers, and they now manned the lookout positions on the wall. All three of them, despite an obvious temptation to watch the excavation, were scanning the surrounding country-side for possible enemies. Vigorous Warrior training eventually resulted in ingrained reflexes, in strict adherence to duty and discipline. Security was a paramount Family concern, and only the ablest members were designated as Warriors, as guardians of the Family welfare.

"Here's the third one!" came the cry.

All three rings had been revealed, and the diggers hastened to completely uncover the opening.

Soon, Plato knew, it would be soon. They were about to ascertain if the Family had any hope for continued survival, or whether they were doomed to bleak extinction, a minuscule dot on the passing page of human history.

Plato felt his stomach muscles tighten.

5

After his conversation with Plato, Blade located Geronimo and Hickok in the crowd and led them to Block A, the Family armory.

"Hickok, you're our firearms specialist. Any suggestions on what we should take?" Blade asked.

The gunman surveyed the huge chamber, the walls lined with rack after rack of assorted weaponry, rifles and shotguns, pistols and revolvers. Crates of ammunition were piled up to the roof. Kurt Carpenter had known his precious Family would become engaged in a desperate struggle for existence after the nuclear holocaust, and he had prudently recognized that their ability to defend themselves, to persevere in a world where survival of the fittest was the norm, would be predicated on the firepower they possessed. Unlike food and medicine and even clothing, weapons, if kept sheltered from the elements, would endure the test of time and last generation after generation. Carpenter had selected arms of every sort, stock-piled ammo, and provided the equipment for gun repair and cartridge reloading.

"There's no telling what we'll go up against," Hickok said thoughtfully. "And we can't afford to come up short where it counts." He walked over to a rack of automatics, the guns neatly arranged and freshly oiled and cleaned, although seldom used. Utilizing the automatics to hunt game would be a case of drastic overkill, and was frowned upon. There was a colossal collection of rifles and shotguns suitable for hunting and most other Family purposes. The automatics were reserved for special occasions.

"Let's see," Hickok studied the rack, running through the hardware. "The AP-74, the FNC, the AR-180, the 27 A-1, the Uzi, and . . ." He reached for one of the guns. "Ahhh. Here it is. Should do nicely."

"Which one did you pick?" Blade inquired, his view blocked by Hickok's right shoulder.

Hickok swiveled, displaying his first choice. "This is a Commando Arms Carbine, fully automatic or semi-automatic capability, weight about eight pounds or so." Hickok hefted the Carbine. "And about three feet in length. Uses 45-caliber ammo. This magazine holds ninety shots. A neat piece of firepower, if I do say so myself." Hickok grinned, appreciating the weapon.

"Reminds me of one of those machine guns used back in what were called the Roaring Twenties," Geronimo commented.

"A Thompson?" Hickok nodded. "Guess it does at that, pard, but we do have a Thompson reproduction around here, somewhere." He began searching the racks.

"Who gets this Carbine?" Blade wanted to know. As if he had to ask.

Hickok tossed him the gun. "Three guesses. You're the worst shot, so you should have the automatic. This way, if we're attacked, just point it in the general direction of the attacker and press the trigger and keep it pulled. You're bound to hit something."

Geronimo laughed.

"Thanks a lot," Blade said to Hickok.

"Hey, pard, don't blame yourself," Hickok stated matter-of-factly. "We've each got special skills. I wouldn't want to tangle with you one-on-one with knives, that's for sure."

"What about me?" Geronimo asked.

Hickok walked to another rack. "Way I figure it, we need to diversify our armament, try to accommodate as many possibilities as we can. We've got our automatic, so I think we should pick a shotgun next."

"Why?" Geronimo questioned.

"For a combination of power and accuracy," Hickok answered. "At close to medium range, a shotgun can tear apart anything that comes at you. Here's the one I want." He picked one gun from the shotgun rack. "This is a Browning B-80 Automatic Shotgun. Twelve gauge, thirty-two inches long, about seven pounds. Easy to handle."

"I haven't used a shotgun too often," Geronimo observed.

"Here, pard." Hickok handed the Browning to Geronimo. "Don't worry about it. You're a good shot, and we'll need the stopping power. We'll use buckshot, double aught."

"What's that leave you?" Blade inquired, facing the rifle racks.

"You got it." Hickok stepped in front of one case. "We'll need a long gun for distance shooting." He grabbed one of the rifles. "A Navy Arms Henry Carbine, 44-40 caliber. The accuracy you can achieve with this rifle is amazing. I prefer the lever action over a bolt job. Levers keep your fingers closer to the trigger, where they belong. This Henry is a reproduction of a gun that was used back in Wild Bill Hickok's time."

"I should have guessed," Geronimo said.

Hickok ignored his friend. "Now to our handguns. I'll stick with my Pythons. For you, Blade . . ." Hickok walked to one of a dozen cabinets containing the Family's pistols and revolvers. He leaned his Henry against the wall and opened the cabinet. "This should do you just right."

Blade recognized the style of gun. "Another automatic?"

"One of us should carry one. Or two. I reckon you'll be keeping those Bowies at your hips?"

Blade nodded his head.

Hickok sighed. "Never could understand what you see in those big knives. No problem, though. You can wear two of these in shoulder holsters."

"What are they?" Blade took one of the handguns from Hickok.

"It's a Vega 45 Automatic, and it's a lot like the Colt Automatic."

"I'm surprised you don't recommend the Colt," Geronimo said.

"I've got mine." Hickok patted his Pythons. "And I don't want to be accused of bias. Besides, the Vegas have never been used and we have plenty of ammo. Do you like the stainless steel and checkered walnut?"

"It's a pretty gun," Blade admitted.

"Pretty?" Hickok snorted. "Women are pretty! Guns are a work of art! When I look at a fine firearm, it's like I'm looking at a Michelangelo or a Van Gogh."

"And you were the one who called Joshua strange?" Geronimo was grinning from ear to ear. "You don't have room to talk."

"You know what I mean," Hickok retorted.

"Okay," Blade interjected. "I'll carry two of these Vega Automatics in shoulder holsters."

"Leaving me," Geronimo stated. "I'd prefer something a bit more basic."

"Let's see," Hickok said slowly, studying the cabinets and racks. "We've already got stoppin' power, and we've got the Vega for Tarzan, which means we need something combining accuracy with versatility. Ever use an Arminius?" he asked Geronimo.

"No."

"Real basic, like you want." Hickok selected the revolver he was referring to. "We have two models, one in .357 Magnum, the other a .38 Special. How many handguns you plan on packing?"

"One."

Hickok shook his head. "Up to you, but you'd be smarter to take two. What if it malfunctions?"

"I'll still have the Browning," Geronimo said. "Besides, you're taking two Colts and Blade is taking along two Vegas. Mine will make five handguns the Family might never see again. I know we have plenty of guns, but why take more than we'll really need? I'm taking other weapons for close range, so just one Arminius will do for me."

"The .38 or the .357?" Hickok asked.

"The .357 Magnum," Geronimo responded.

"There's still hope for you yet, red man." Hickok smiled.

"Which is more than I can say for you, white boy," Geronimo rejoined.

Hickok handed the .357 Arminius to Geronimo. "That's it for me. Pick whatever other weapons you want to take."

They separated, walking to different sections, each preferring weapons from their particular speciality.

Hickok stood in front of the cabinet containing the small handguns, the derringers and other palm guns. He studied the selection and finally picked two. First, to wear strapped to his right wrist, he withdrew a Mitchell's Derringer, a two-shot gun only five inches in length. The Mitchell's used .38-caliber ammunition. He also grabbed a handgun to strap to his left leg, about three inches above the ankle. This gun was a four-shot C.O.P. .357 Magnum, five and a half inches long, double-action, with four barrels constructed of stainless steel. This baby, he reflected, would blow away anything at close range. It made for a dandy surprise package.

Blade eyed the section of the north wall containing the edged weapons, the swords, knives, stilettos, shivs, and others. He would take the two Bowies, and for a backup he chose two daggers, a matched pair, with razor-sharp blades and silver handles. One would be sheathed on his left forearm, the other to his right calf. A folding Buck knife, placed in his right pants pocket, completed his personal arsenal.

Geronimo was standing in front of a rack marked "Miscellaneous," filled with an incredible array of unusual and varied weaponry. Most of it was Oriental: an ancient naginata and the later yari, both spears, the former with a curved blade, the latter employing a straight cutting edge; a pair of ton-fa; a bo, or hardwood staff; six pair of nunchaku, each consisting of two lengths of wood connected by chain or cord; and several sai. The rack also contained a section labeled "Early North American," and it was this part that arrested Geronimo's attention. Several Indian spears were secured in slotted grooves in the wood supporting the rack. Under the spears, positioned with the blades facing one another, patterned after an original Apache design but actually made in the 1900s, hung a pair of matching tomahawks, the versatile light axe used by many of the North American Indians. They were the only tomahawks the Family owned, although they did possess dozens of axes and hatchets. Ordinarily, Geronimo employed a hatchet in his daily activities, but this expedition to the Twin Cities was a special occasion, calling for a suspension of his reluctance to use the tomahawks. They were special, one of the few physical ties to a culture long gone, a way of life and a people Geronimo admired and revered and a time in which he fervently wished he had lived.

Geronimo was the only Family member with

any vestige of Indian heritage in his blood, and even that was minimal. His parents had died when he was quite young, before they could give him a brother or a sister. Geronimo, so far as he knew, was the last of the Indians, a condition he seldom talked about but acutely felt. He considered himself something of an outcast, the last of a noble breed, and different from the rest of the Family. He harbored a profound sense of obligation to his unknown Indian ancestors, a duty he feared would remain unfulfilled. If he was the last Indian, and he was unable to find a suitable mate, then the line of the exalted red man would perish with his death. The prospect terrified him.

But if I am to die on this mission, he thought, then I will greet the Great Spirit bearing the trademark of my forefathers.

Geronimo removed the tomahawks and hefted the handles in his hands. A perfect balance! He slipped the handles through his belt, one on each hip. He would carry the Arminius in a shoulder holster under his right arm.

"I'm ready," Hickok announced from the doorway to the Cell Block.

Geronimo moved to join him, passing Blade. "Problems?" he asked.

Blade was staring at a case of knives, his chin resting on the knuckles of his left hand. "No, not really," he answered. "I thought I had made up my mind about what I'm taking, but now I think I'll add one more item."

Geronimo saw the contents of the case. "Throwing knives?"

"You never know," Blade observed. He opened the case and extracted a black sheath containing three quality Soligen throwing knives. "I can attach the sheath to my belt in the small of my back. Hickok says you can never have enough backup."

"Wouldn't it be ironic," Geronimo realized, "if we take all this hardware, and we do encounter some people, and they turn out to be as friendly and spiritual as our brother Joshua?''

"Ironic, yes," Blade agreed. "Realistic, no. If anyone else has survived, they're existing on an animal level of existence. Thank the Founder for the Home! Where would we be without the security the walls provide, and how long would the Family have lasted without the provisions the Founder stored? We'd be living in caves and fighting the mutates with clubs."

They were slowly walking towards Hickok.

"I wonder how they will react to us," Geronimo mused, and Blade knew he was referring to any survivors of the Big Blast, living and foraging in a world devoid of luxury and scantily supplied with the basic necessities.

Hickok suddenly made a show of clearing his throat. "Why don't Geronimo and I mosey on over to F Block and stock up on our victuals? You can catch up with us later, pard."

Blade wondered what on earth he was talking about, and then Jenny appeared in the doorway.

"Howdy, ma'am," Hickok said. "Nice day if it don't rain."

Jenny ignored him, her eyes locked on Blade.

"I'll see you in a bit," Blade said to his friends.

"If you can't find us," Hickok cracked, "check the south forty. We might be roundin' up some critters for brandin'."

Geronimo took Hickok by the right arm and forcefully propelled him from the Block. He smiled and nodded at Jenny, then followed the gunman, wondering where Hickok's own girlfriend was.

"We're finally alone," Jenny said, stating the obvious.

Blade nodded. There was a large oak table in his immediate left. He pivoted and placed the weapons he would take on top of the table.

"We need to talk," Jenny said.

"I know."

"If all goes well, I expect you'll be leaving sometime tomorrow," Jenny mentioned.

"I know," he replied.

"And there is a good chance I might never see you again." Her lovely green eyes were watering.

Blade couldn't bring himself to respond.

"Oh, Blade!" She ran to him and threw her arms around his neck. "I can't stand the thought of losing you! I'll die if something happens to you!"

"Nothing will happen," he said confidently.

"You can't be certain of that," she said softly, beginning to sob.

A warm, moist tear streaked a path down Blade's neck, followed by several more.

"It will be all right," he assured her, hugging her to him, stroking her blonde hair with his right hand.

Jenny released her pent-up emotions, the tears flowing freely, crying on his broad shoulder.

Blade patiently waited for her outburst to pass. There wasn't a thing he could say to ease her hurt. Worse, he felt the same way. He forced himself to remain calm, to conceal the grief. If he broke down, it would only compound her misery.

There was a commotion outside, voices raised excitedly, from the direction of the digging.

Jenny cried until her tear glands were dry, her eyes red and puffy, her nose running. Finally, her weeping ceased. "I'm sorry," she whispered into his ear.

"For what?" he asked. Blade glanced around the chamber for any material she could use. Nothing appropriate. He gently pushed back until he was clear of her encircling arms and removed his shirt. "Use this." He handed it to her.

Jenny didn't argue. She wiped around her swollen eyes, and dried her cheeks and nose. "Thanks. I needed that."

Blade tossed the shirt onto the table. He embraced her again, savoring the closeness of her pliant body, the warmth she generated.

"I can't help myself," she explained. "I don't want you to go."

"I don't want to go, either," he admitted.

"Then why . . .?" She stood back, puzzled.

Blade clasped her to him. He couldn't bear to look into her eyes, afraid he would lose control. "You heard Plato. Someone must go, and Alpha Triad has as good a chance as any of the others. I don't want to leave you, honey, but the Family's welfare must come first. You know that."

Jenny silently nodded her understanding. She took a deep breath. "Take me with you, Blade. Please."

"I can't."

"Please!" she pleaded.

Blade drew her to the table and she leaned against the edge, staring up into his face, her expression appealing. Give me strength, he prayed to the Spirit.

"I can't take you with me," he stressed, his deep voice turning husky with sentiment. "Much as I want to." He placed a finger over her red lips to prevent her from interrupting when she started to speak. He had to finish, to get it all out in the open before he weakened and she saw how affected he really was. "If I took you along, I'd be constantly concerned for your safety. I'd worry about you first whenever danger threatened. It wouldn't matter if only my safety was involved, but we must think of Hickok and Geronimo and Joshua. I have an obligation to them, a duty, a responsibility to perform at my peak, to mesh with them as one member of a well-trained team. If I permit myself to become distracted, my attention to waver during crucial moments, I could endanger all of them and cause their deaths. We can't allow that to happen.

You can understand, can't you?"

Jenny looked down at the floor, and Blade wondered if she would cry again. He couldn't blame her.

"Can't you?" he repeated.

Jenny nodded. She wiped another tear from her left eye.

Blade placed his hands on her shoulder. "Dearest, if there was any way possible to take you along, I would. You'll be safer in the Home with the Family. I'll be able to completely concentrate on the matters at hand. It won't be easy, being separated. Who knows for how long it will be? But be assured, I will return. We'll all come back. It will be harder on you, I think. The waiting, with little to occupy you. The bottom line is, we have no other choice. Try and look at the bright side."

"The bright side! What bright side?" she demanded skeptically, brushing her blonde bangs from her eyes with her left hand.

"When I return," Blade said, smiling, his eyes conveying the warmth of his tender affection, "I intend to ask a certain lovely lady to bind to me, to become my eternal mate. If she'll have me," he amended hastily.

Jenny's eyes widened and brightened. She gripped his arms. "Do you mean it, really and truly?" she asked excitedly.

"Really and truly," he affirmed. "Truly and really."

"Oh, Blade!" She laughed and clung to him, trembling.

"Are you okay?" he asked, overjoyed he had managed to cheer her up.

"Couldn't be better!" Jenny grinned and kissed him, hard, on the lips. "To marry, to be man and wife! I can hardly wait!"

"You mean you still want me, after learning about all of my quirks?"

"Silly. Your quirks are your more loveable aspects. Oh, darling!"

They embraced in a long, lingering kiss. Blade felt the pressure of her full breasts against his chest, and his manhood, aroused, strained against her.

"Mmmm. Nice. I hope you know that tonight you are all mine," Jenny stated.

"I wouldn't have it any other way," he agreed. "But right now I'd better join Geronimo and Hickok and assist them in stocking our supplies for the trip."

"I'll walk with you to F Block," she remarked.

Blade picked up his weapons, one at a time, strapping the knives to his body as he'd planned. The Commando was equipped with a brown leather shoulder strap, and he slung the automatic over his right shoulder.

Jenny watched him, apprehensively.

Blade took her proffered hand and they walked from A Block and headed in a northeasterly direction, toward F Block.

"You're armed to the teeth, aren't you?" she casually asked.

"Eleven weapons, in all," he answered. "If they get me, it won't be without a fight." Instantly, he noted her eyes watering, and he regretted making the stupid statement.

"What all are you taking?" she kept the conversation going, her voice level.

"The Commando." He touched the carbine. "Two Vega automatics, one under each arm. My Bowies, of course. The three throwing knives on my back, a dagger on my right leg and another on my left arm, and a Buck knife in one of my pockets."

"You sure that's enough?"

He looked at her, thinking she was joking, but she was quite serious. "I think it's enough."

Jenny became silent, thoughtful, and they continued walking, covering half the distance to F

Block, nearing a small stand of oak trees to their right. Blade glanced at the growth and was surprised to note someone sitting at the base of one of the trees, leaning with his back against the trunk.

"Isn't that Joshua?" Jenny saw him too.

Blade realized it was. Joshua was sitting in the lotus position, his eyes closed, apparently meditating.

"I don't think we should disturb him," Jenny said.

"I agree."

They were abreast of the trees now, and Blade's attention was arrested by movement in the tree above Joshua.

"Did you see that?" he asked.

"What?"

Something small, with reddish brown fur, was moving along a limb directly over Joshua's head.

"I see it," Jenny declared. "Looks like a squirrel."

Blade thought so too, but he was bothered by the movement. If it was a squirrel, the motions it was making were erratic, different from normal. Was his imagination playing tricks on him, or was there some unusual element about this animal? Squirrels and other small game were not uncommon in the Home. They couldn't pose any threat unless they became rabid or . . .

The squirrel paused on the end of one branch, exposed, the sun revealing the reason it was moving oddly.

Blade heard Jenny's sudden intake of breath as he reached for the Vegas in a cross draw, thanking the Spirit he had left his shirt in A Block, that there was no chance the guns could snag on any fabric.

"Joshua!" Jenny screamed in warning, and Joshua's eyes opened.

Blade was running, closing the range. He wasn't Hickok. He needed to be sure. "Move!" he shouted.

"Roll to your right, now!"

Joshua obeyed immediately, the roll saving his life.

The squirrel chattered and launched itself from the limb, narrowly missing Joshua's leg. It landed agilely on the grass and whirled, facing Joshua.

Joshua saw the menace and he braced for the next attack.

Blade couldn't wait any longer. He raised the right Vega and fired three times, trying to aim as he ran.

The shots missed.

The squirrel, distracted by a spray of dirt from one of the bullets, spun, spotted Blade, and charged.

Blade tried three shots from the left Vega. The small red squirrel, a male only eleven inches in length, could cover the ground at tremendous speed. One of the shots nicked it on the right side and it twisted, but didn't slow, pus spraying into the air.

"Blade!" Jenny yelled.

Frustrated by his lack of marksmanship, Blade tossed the Vegas to one side and drew his right-hand Bowie.

The red came in low and fast, fearless, intenton biting and rending.

Blade crouched, knowing he had one chance, realizing the rodent would be on him if he missed.

The red was four feet from Blade when it sprang, launching its body at his midsection.

Blade swung, the Bowie arcing, the blade connecting, catching the red at the neck, slicing off the deformed head.

"You got it!" Jenny exclaimed.

Blade watched the headless body flop on the grass, blood and pus forming a pool around it. He repressed an urge to continue hacking the body, to chop it into tiny little pices. How he hated the mutates!!! Every damn one of them had to be exterminated! After all, one of them had killed his father.

"What's going on, pard?"

Hickok and Geronimo ran up, guns at the ready. Joshua joined the group.

"Blade got a mutate," Jenny explained proudly.

They saw it. Geronimo knelt and carefully, visually, inspected the body and the head.

"A squirrel!" Hickok stated in sheer disgust. "There's no telling what shape and size these things come in. Remember that time a mutated frog hopped up from the moat and attacked some of the Family? A frog! Mutates can be anything."

"I've never seen a mutated insect or bird," Geronimo observed. "Only animals and reptiles and amphibians."

"That must be important," Jenny stressed.

Joshua placed his right hand on Blade's shoulder. "Thank you, my brother, for the rescue. I am not yet ready for the trip to the other side."

Blade was glaring at the remains of the mutate.

"Are you all right?" Joshua asked.

Blade grimly nodded.

"I see you bagged the critter with your Bowie." Hickok grinned. "Didn't you hear shots? Ten or twenty?"

"Blade fired six times," Jenny detailed.

"And missed?" Hickok asked, feigning amazement. "Maybe, instead of the Vegas, you should take a flame thrower." He paused, snapped his finger, and playfully poked Blade in the side. "Too bad the Family doesn't own a flame thrower, isn't it? Then you'd really be cookin'!"

Despite his revulsion and resentment at the mutate, Blade allowed himself to relax.

"Better yet," Hickok quipped, "a tank! That way, if you missed with the cannon, you could still run it over and crush it to a pulp."

"Will you lay off him?" Geronimo stood. "He creased the thing once. A squirrel isn't the easiest of targets, not even for you."

"I'll lay off when he gives me some sign he's still the same adorable hombre we've come to know and appreciate as loco."

"One more crack from you," Blade said, smiling, "and this loco is going to see if you'd like having pearl handles for your supper."

Hickok laughed. "Now that that's settled, shouldn't someone go tell the Family everything is fine? They had to hear the shots."

"I'll go," Joshua volunteered, and jogged towards the digging site.

"I should bury the remains," Geronimo said. "I'll get a shovel and be right back." He departed.

"We've got most of the food packed," Hickok informed Blade. "Come and check it when you want." He strolled off.

"I can't get over the way he constantly picks on you," Jenny said, critizing Hickok. "Why in the world does he do it?"

"Because he cares," Blade answered.

"You call that caring?"

"Yes."

"Well, Nathan has a funny way of showing he cares for someone. He's always riding you." Jenny wouldn't let the matter rest.

Blade retrieved the Vega automatics. "Jenny, he doesn't ride me any worse than he rides himself. You've got to understand that Hickok has trouble relating to people. He likes to get his guns do his talking, and you can only do that with your enemies. He's uncomfortable around his friends because he has difficulty showing he cares, and he tries to mask his genuine feelings behind a flippant attitude and wisecracks. Believe me, Hickok would give his life, gladly, for any member of the Family. That's one of the reasons he makes such an outstanding Warrior."

"If you say so," Jenny said, her tone implying she had her doubts. "I just can't understand what

Joan sees in him."

"Ask her," Blade advised, scouring the trees,
searching for any sign of life, wondering if other
mutates were lurking in the foliage. Highly unlikely.
Mutates never stopped hunting, never ceased
seeking flesh to consume. If any were still in the
trees, they would be coming after the humans as
precipitously as the red squirrel had done.

"Hickok mentioned the frog that attacked us."
Jenny was staring at the dead squirrel. "If memory
serves, that was about eighteen months ago.
Right?"

"Right," Blade agreed.

"We know the frog clambered out of the moat,"
Jenny continued her line of reasoning. "How do you
suppose this squirrel got in here?"

"I wish I knew."

Jenny gazed at the distant walls. "Do you think
it could get over the walls? Could there be enough
for its claws to grip?"

"I don't know." Blade had seen squirrels perform remarkable climbing feats, including running
straight up the trunk of tall trees. The walls
protecting the Home were constructed of brick, the
joints even and the mortar smooth. How could a
squirrel get inside the Home?

"I don't believe the mutate came over the
walls." Geronimo was back, bearing a shovel, and he
had overheard the last part of their conversation.

"You don't?" Jenny asked.

"Look at the mutate," Geronimo directed.
"Very closely."

Blade crouched and studied the squirrel, and
only then did he notice that this mutate was unique,
different from any other mutate he had ever seen.
"It's half and half," he observed.

"I saw the difference earlier," Geronimo said.

The red squirrel was a mutate, but not a complete mutate. Only the right side, the paws, the

spine, and the left side of the rodent were deformed,
oozing pus, covered with sores and dry brown skin.
The rest of the red was your typical squirrel, covered
with normal reddish brown fur.

"I've never heard of one like that," Jenny
remarked.

"Neither have I." Blade stood. "We should
inform Plato about this."

Joshua came jogging up to them. "Plato wants
everyone at the digging site. They are ready to open
a chamber they've uncovered," he announced.

"We can't leave this lying here in the open,"
Blade said, pointing out the obvious.

"Some of the children might stumble across it."
Jenny underlined his meaning.

"I'll bury the mutate," Geronimo offered. "We
can advise Plato about it after this mystery
chamber is opened."

"Want us to wait for you?" Blade asked him.

Geronimo shook his head. "It won't take long.
You'd better be on hand when Plato unveils his
secret."

Jenny took Blade's hand. "First, we'll stop and
grab you a shirt."

Joshua was already returning to the pit.

Jenny was eager to reach the uncovered
chamber, and she hurried, pulling Blade along.

Blade smiled back at Geronimo.

Geronimo grinned and bent to the task of
burying the mutate.

Blade put the red squirrel from his mind for the
time being, speculating on the chamber they were
about to open. Was he right? Was it some kind of
vehicle the Founder had buried for a special purpose? If so, and if Plato was aware of it, why hadn't
he informed any other Family members? Possibly,
Blade reflected, Plato was afraid some of the Family
might be tempted to use whatever it was before it
was really needed.

Jenny cast a backward glance at Geronimo and the squirrel. "I just hope there aren't any more mutates in the Home," she said.

Blade gritted his teeth at the idea. You and me both, he thought to himself, then repeated it out loud for her benefit. "You and me both."

How he hated the damn things!

6

The Family had completely uncovered the opening to the underground chamber, and tied lengths of stout rope to the three iron rings imbedded in the concrete. Ten men were assigned to each rope, and they now held the rope in their hands, their legs braced, awaiting the command to pull.

Plato gave it. He raised his left hand over his head. "On the count of three," he shouted for all to hear. "One." The men tensed and tightened their respective grips. "Two." He saw Blade and Jenny press their way to the front of those surrouding the pit. Hickok stood off to one side, his hands looped under his belt buckle. Joshua was standing quietly in the center of the crowd. "Three!" Plato called.

The men dug their heels into the ground and pulled, their muscles straining, a determined set to their features.

Nothing happened.

"Pull!" someone shouted. "Pull!"

The men grunted and heaved, exerting all of their strength.

Plato knew the door was designed to swivel outward when the rings were pulled on. Had the mechanism rusted or broken, preventing the door from operating properly? To be so close!

"It's working!" a Family member yelled.

Everyone heard a loud, grating, grinding metallic noise as the massive recessed hinges, unused and unlubricated for a century, protested a slight movement. The entranceway jerked open several feet and stopped, resisting further tugging on the ropes. A sibilant hissing, similar to the sound of steam escaping from a boiling pot of water, could be clearly heard.

"Keep at it!" another person goaded the men on the ropes.

The hissing, still audible, was decreasing in intensity.

The rope pullers were striving with all their might.

The hissing had stopped. Plato speculated it had been the sound of air being drawn into the chamber, or expelled from it, probably the former.

The hinges squeaked as the door began swinging out and down. It was designed to pivot completely outward and rest on the ground.

A dozen excited voices were urging the men on.

The entranceway was now open a good six feet, and the more it opened, the less the hinges scraped, and the easier it become to pull on the ropes.

"It's going!" a woman enthused.

It did. With a resounding thud, the entranceway swung fully open and landed on the rough ground. The men nearest the door had to scramble backwards to get out of the way in time.

A huge, dark, gaping hole was revealed.

The Family members broke into spontaneous applause, evincing their appreciation for the effort exerted by the men on the ropes.

Plato's hands were shaking from nervous anticipation.

"What now?" Blade, wearing a faded, patched fatigue shirt, was standing at Plato's side.

"We'll need torches," Plato directed.

Blade faced the Family. "Would some of you get some torches?"

Eight of the Family hastened to comply,

entering F Block. Each Block was well supplied with torches constructed by wrapping layers of birchbark around the top, or broader, end of a length of oak or maple. The Family's supply of candles, sparingly used over the years, was dwindling despite efforts to conserve them. Carpenter had stocked an enormous reserve of candles and matches; the Family still had cases of candles and matches stacked in the underground chambers below the Blocks, secure from the elements and the nullifying effects of moisture. While most of the original supplies were depleted, a few stockpiled items, such as the weapons, candles, and several other items, if stringently preserved, would last for years to come. The Family's population was not a factor in consumption. Carpenter had started his Family with fifteen couples, and over the decades the population had grown to only seventy-three. The harsh lifestyle, a high mortality rate, and the creeping senility had all combined to limit Family growth and expansion.

The torches were brought. Plato took one and indicated another should be given to Blade. "You and I will venture down first," he said as a woman lit his torch. "The rest of you will wait until we come back up."

"Need a back-up?" Hickok as at their side.

"Thank you," Plato answered. "I don't believe we'll encounter any danger your guns could dispatch. Still . . ." He eyed a pile of coiled rope on the ground near his feet. "We will tie this rope about our waists before we enter the chamber, and several of you will play out the rope as we advance. When we stop on our own, we will yank on the rope twice. If the rope should go completely slack, and we haven't given the signal, haul us up as quickly as you can."

"What's this for?" Blade asked as he tied one end of the rope around his middle.

"There is the slightest possibility of encountering toxic fumes," Plato replied. "We must take every precaution."

The Family was now crowded around the entranceway.

Jenny peered into the hole. The waning sunlight illuminated a ramp leading down into whatever lay below. "You be careful," she said to Blade.

Blade smiled, then led the way, holding his torch aloft with his right hand.

Plato paused before entering and looked at the faces surrounding him. "If the Spirit is willing," he announced, "our expedition can proceed as planned tomorrow."

Blade and Plato descended the ramp, their flickering torches enabling the Family to follow their progress.

"There is a musty, dusty scent down here," Plato remarked. "Not surprising, when you consider the last time this chamber saw the light of day."

The ramp angled lower, the torchlight reflecting from polished walls ten feet away on either side, and from the ceiling twelve feet above their heads.

"This ramp shouldn't be very long," Plato commented.

Blade was peering into the darkness ahead. His feet suddenly touched a flat surface, evidently the floor of the underground chamber.

"See what I meant?" Plato grinned.

They stopped, pulled on their ropes twice, and raised the torches as high as they could.

"Will you look at that!" Blade exclaimed.

"Absolutely incredible!" Plato agreed.

The chamber was relatively small, only twenty feet by twenty feet. Along the walls were stacked various containers. Their fascination was prompted by the object resting in the center of the chamber, undisturbed since parked there a century ago.

"What is it?" Blade asked.

"Your father told me it's called a SEAL."

"A seal? You mean like that aquatic animal we

have pictures of in the library?"

"Something similar," Plato smiled. "The word of mouth, passed down from Leader to Leader, was that this transport vehicle was called a General Motors Prototype Solar-Energized Amphibious or Land Recreational Vehicle, otherwise known by the acronym of SEAL."

"Did they give all their vehicles such long names before the Big Blast?"

"Some, apparently. I saw a picture of a large white truck called a Sanitation Retrieval and Disposal Conveyance Unit, a vehicle manifestly disliked by some people."

"Why do you say that?" Blade wanted to know.

"Because someone had scrawled the word 'garbage' across the face of this photograph. Quite puzzling."

They fell silent, gawking at the SEAL, the first motorized vehicle they had ever seen. Carpenter had provided two trucks and a jeep for the Family, all three vehicles maintained for nearly twenty years after the Third World War. Eventually, parts had worn out that couldn't be replaced, and the vehicles had been hauled into the woods and abandoned. The rusted hulks were only five hundred yards from the Home, and it was a special treat for the small children to be permitted, under guard, to trek to the junkers and stand in the presence of this reminder of prewar industry and mechanization.

The SEAL had been Carpenter's pride and joy. He had known his trucks and jeep would last only so long as fuel was obtainable and the parts could be replaced. The beauty of the SEAL was its power source, the very sun. The sunlight was collected by two solar panels attached to the roof of the SEAL, the energy converted and stored in a bank of six revolutionary new batteries stored in a lead-lined case under the SEAL. The experts had told him that, if the solar panels were not broken and the battery casings weren't inadvertently cracked, the SEAL should never want for power, unlike the fossil-fueled cars, wagons, and trucks. Additionally, the solar collectors on the SEAL were prototypes, designed to function at a more efficient rate than any previous collector. Carpenter had personally financed the research for the SEAL. The financially strapped automotive executives had welcomed his support, confidently predicting that they were developing the recreational vehicle "of the future." Carpenter had never revealed his ulterior motive for insuring the SEAL was constructed according to his specifications, incorporating unique capabilities and unusual functions. The automakers had assumed he was another strange eccentric with enough money to purchase whatever he wanted and indulge in flamboyant toys. Little did they realize the SEAL was not intended to be a plaything, but a salvation.

Carpenter had projected several assumptions, and derived conclusions from the thorough consideration of all possible and probable contingencies. *If* the Home was spared from damage or destruction in the world-wide conflagration, and *if* the Family could survive and persist to subsequent generations, and *if* it become necessary for it to venture from the Home, a typical conventional vehicle would be out of the question, lacking an adequate fuel source and being hardly rugged enough to endure the structural strain of the undoubtedly altered terrain. The idea of regularly tended asphalt highways being maintained after World War Three was ludicrous.

The SEAL, Carpenter had hoped, would enable his latter-day followers to overcome such obstacles.

Carpenter had been aware of the temptation the SEAL would pose. If it were left above ground, with ready access, someone might be enticed to take it for a spin, as it were, and thereby jeopardize the Family's one shot at a successful extended trip.

Carpenter had appreciated the risk he took in directing the information concerning the SEAL's existence to be passed on by word of mouth from one Leader to the next, but he had believed it was a gamble worth taking. He wanted the SEAL intact and fully functional when the Family would need it.

That time had come.

Blade was mesmerized by the SEAL. He had seen the junkers, the trashed trucks and the jeep, and had studied photographs of various vehicles in the Family library, but this was the first operational transport anyone had laid eyes on in eighty years. He searched his memory, trying to recall if this SEAL resembled any of the pictures he had seen in the books he'd studied. There was one photo, of a vehicle called a van, the SEAL bore a likeness to, but not in every respect. The general contours were similar, but that van was constructed of metal with windows built into the center of each wall panel. This SEAL appeared to be made entirely from some sort of glass. Blade reached out and touched the front section.

"Is this glass?" he asked Plato.

Plato touched the substance. "No, it isn't," Plato answered. "This is a special plastic. I was told it is heat-resistant and shatterproof. You could shoot a Magnum at it at point-blank range and the bullet would not penetrate the substance."

Blade held his torch closer to the SEAL. "Why can't I see inside?"

"The plastic is tinted, enabling those within to see out. Anyone outside, however, can not see in. A sensible security precaution."

"Is the whole thing made of this plastic?" Blade inquired.

"Only the shell." Plato began circling the SEAL. "The front, sides, back, and roof. The floor is a metallic alloy. The engine is air-cooled and self-lubricating. If everything I was told about the

SEAL is true, and I have no reason to doubt it is, then I know you'll be astonished and delighted by the numerous distinctive features built into it. I envy you."

Blade followed Plato. "You envy me?"

"As Hickok correctly noted," Plato said, running his left hand along the SEAL, "just think of the adventure! Yes, I envy you a great deal."

"I must admit, despite my concern for Jenny, that I'm excited at the thought of what we may find out in the world."

They stood at the rear of the SEAL. Rungs of a ladder, imbedded in the plastic, led to the roof of the SEAL.

"You can climb up to inspect the solar collectors," Plato commented.

"Solar collectors?" Blade was puzzled.

"I can see I have a lot of explaining to do," Plato said. "Let's check the interior."

They continued their circuit of the SEAL. Plato stopped next to a door on the driver's side. He slowly reached for the handle, hesitated, then pulled. The door swung quietly open.

"Wow," was all Blade could say.

"Wow indeed." Plato leaned into the SEAL. "Ahh. What's this?" There were several items lying on the driver's seat.

"What's what?"

"These." Plato removed two folders and a set of keys.

"What have you got there?"

Plato studied the folders. "One is labelled 'Operations manual for the Solar-Energized Amphibious or Land Recreational Vehicle' "

"Couldn't they have just said 'Instructions'?" Blade asked.

Plato grinned. "This second folder is from the Founder! I'll need to read it first."

Blade gazed over the outline of the SEAL. "I

still can't believe it."

"Believe it." Plato knelt and scrutinized the undercarriage. "Everything appears to be intact. Now if it's only functional. . . ."

"Don't you think it will work?"

Plato was examing one of the four huge tires, the one nearest the driver's door. "If the Spirit smiles on us, it will operate as designed. Hmmm."

"What is it?"

"I wonder what this tire is made of? I had read that rubber was a prime component, but this is not rubber-based."

"I bet the others are getting antsy," Blade announced.

Plato attempted to rise, but his knees pained him, his right leg lanced with an excruitiating spasm. He started to fall.

Blade silently grabbed Plato by the arm and lifted his mentor to his feet.

"My gratitude," Plato thanked him.

Blade nodded and led the way toward the ramp. "The Family will go crazy when they hear what we've uncovered," he predicted.

They stopped shy of the hole, removed the ropes, then exited. Plato briefly informed the Family of their find, and pandemonium erupted. Everyone began talking at once, asking questions, pressing towards the ramp, wanting to see for themselves. Plato was crowded to the edge of the ramp before Blade intervened, stepping forward and placing himself between Plato and the rest of the Family. He raised his arms over his head, glaring, and they stopped.

"Calm down!" he ordered. "Calm down! You'll all see it soon enough."

Hickok positioned himself beside Blade, his hands on his Colts. His presence, despite the fact they knew he wouldn't use his guns on a Family member, promptly sobered them.

Geronimo joined them.

"Please, loved ones!" Plato asserted control again. "We have a lot to do before the Alpha Triad can leave tomorrow. We must remove the SEAL from the chamber and bring it up here."

"What do you want us to do?" a man called Sinatra, the best vocalist in the Family, asked.

"As many men as possible should go below," Plato directed. "We will push the SEAL up the ramp."

"I'll pick the men," Blade offered.

"Fine. While you're engaged, I'll peruse this manual."

Blade selected a score of the strongest men. He led them below, half bearing torches.

Plato walked to a mound of dirt and sat down, resting his sore joints and tired muscles. He opened the Operations Manual and began reading.

Time passed. The setting sun was touching the western horizon.

Blade emerged from the passageway, his face a study in consternation.

Plato looked up from his reading, anticipating what was coming. "Problems?"

Blade sighed. "I'm afraid I have bad news."

"Such as?"

"Don't take this too hard." Blade was frowning. "I know how much you were counting on the SEAL, but it's broken."

"Broken?" Plato suppressed an urge to laugh.

"I'm sorry. We've tried our best. We pushed and pushed and couldn't budge the thing one inch. The SEAL just won't work," he said sadly.

Plato laughed.

"What's so funny?" Blade was confused.

"I just read a portion of the instructions pertaining to your difficulty." Plato handed Blade the keys. "Before the SEAL can be moved, you must insert one of the keys into something called an ignition, located on something else called a steering column attached to the steering wheel. Turn the key towards you until it clicks. This won't turn the engine over, but it will permit you to engage the transmission by slipping a lever into a position marked with a large N for neutral. Once accomplished, you should be able to push the SEAL to the surface.''

Blade held the keys up. "These things certainly were complicated."

"It's my understanding that every aspect of prewar society was vastly more complicated and nerve-racking than any reasonable person would have a right to expect," Plato commented. "I thank the Spirit daily I was not born in those times."

"You're happy where you're at?" Blade had never broached this subject with Plato, and he was surprised Plato would make such a statement.

"Quite content actually," Plato said.

"With all the hardships? The clouds? The mutates? Wouldn't life have been easier before the Big Blast?"

"Easier?" Plato mused a minute. "Who ever said life should be easy? Hardships might intimidate the average and cower the fearful, but they rightfully should inspire you to greater heights of spiritual awareness. Ever remember, Blade, life is a study in contrasts. How can any person claim to aspire to unselfishness if he or she isn't constantly engaged in conflict with an ego clamoring for attention? How can anyone develop loyalty if he or she never faces temptation? How could we develop a love for truth if, by contrast, error and evil weren't waiting to ensnare us? How could you appreciate the exquisite bliss of love if you hadn't known the tormenting pain of loneliness?" Plato stared off at the sun, half hidden from view. "Yes, life was easier before the Third World War. I could argue that this very ease was responsible for an atrophy of the human potential for growth. Ease promotes complacency, and complacency is deadly for society and the individual. I readily admit our lifestyle leaves something to be desired, but I prefer living in the here and now."

"Never thought of it that way," Blade said.

"You'd better hasten below," Plato advised. "We want the SEAL up here before nightfall."

"Right."

Plato watched Blade descend the ramp. The poor youth had so much to learn before he could assume the mantle of leadership. Experience was the best teacher. If the Alpha Triad and Joshua survied the trip to the Twin Cities, they would return wiser and no worse off for the wear and tear.

The tip of the sun protruded above the horizon. Not much light left. Plato resumed his reading of the manual.

The Family was still posted around the pit, waiting for the SEAL to emerge. Meals had been prepared and distributed among those waiting. No one wanted to miss the greatest event in recent Family history. The entire Family was on hand, except for the Warriors guarding the perimeter of the Home.

Plato suddenly remembered the folder from the Founder. He had completely forgotten it in his haste to understand the functional operation of the SEAL. He placed the Operations Manual on the ground and picked up the other folder. On the cover, written in Carpenter's own hand, were the words "To The Leader."

Plato opened the manila folder and began reading:

"I feel peculiar writing a message to someone who will live decades after I am gone. To you, and to the rest of those left, I extend my love and my prayer for your continued safety and survival. This letter will be buried with the SEAL. I've hired a construction crew to bury the SEAL before any of those I've selected will arrive at the Home. I don't want anyone to know about the SEAL. They might want to see if loved ones in New York or California survived, and I can't allow that to happen. We must stay isolated if we're to have any chance at all. It's coming, and coming soon. You can almost feel the fear in the air. All the talking in the world hasn't helped. Mankind is about to commit the ultimate folly, self-obliteration. If it weren't so pitiful, it would be humorous. Whoever you are, I want you to know I've done my best. Eventually, those left will need to find out what has happened, will have a need for reliable transportation. The SEAL is my gift to you. I've spared no expense in having it made, and if any vehicle can stand up to what's coming, the SEAL can. Read the Operations Manual before you try to activate the SEAL. My scientists are confidently optimistic the SEAL will work when you need it. They don't know my real reason for having it made, and they'd probably laugh if they did. I've insisted on a nearly indestructible vehicle, one that could still run ten years or one hundred years from now. They think I'm a harmless crank. Maybe I am. I don't know if this compound I've built, this Home for my loved ones, will still be standing after the missiles are launched and the bombs dropped. I might have wasted countless hours and millions of dollars for nothing, but deep inside something keeps telling me that it won't be in vain. I don't mind telling you, though, I'm tired. Weary in my soul. It's taken a lot out of me, building the Home, stocking it, and, the worst part, deciding which of my family and friends would be invited here before the world goes mad. How do you pick thirty from all the people you know, all those you've met and loved and liked during a lifetime? It isn't easy. I don't know what else to say. I pray the SEAL will work for you. There are so many questions, aspects I wonder about. How many men and women are alive? Have we grown and prospered? Did the Home provide the protection I hoped it would? Are you any more loving and considerate toward one another than my contemporaries are, or have you succumbed to this mass paranoia? Have I wasted my life? I wonder if I'll ever know. Whoever you are, relay my love. Remember me as one who gave it his best shot. I hope I wasn't firing blanks. Kurt Carpenter.''

Plato straightened, his back sore. He realized he had bent over the yellowed paper to see better as the light decreased.

The sun was gone. Fires were being built around the entranceway. The air was cool, a strong breeze blowing in from the west.

Jenny approached him, carrying a blanket. ''Here.'' She handed it to him. ''It's starting to get nippy.''

Plato wrapped the blanket around his shoulders. ''Thank you.''

''Anything important?'' She pointed at the folders.

Plato nodded. ''One contains the instructions for the SEAL. The other is a letter from the Founder.''

''Oh? What does it say?'' she asked, her curiosity aroused.

''It tells me that, despite our reverence whenever we think of Kurt Carpenter, he was a human being with sentiments and shortcomings similar to our own. I suspect he went to his grave a torn man.''

''What makes you say that?''

''Look!'' someone cried, and the Family was quickly clustered around the opening.

''It's the SEAL!'' Jenny clapped her hands together.

The front of the vehicle was slowly emerging from the entranceway, the firelight glinting off the tinted windows and body.

"Oh! It's beautiful!" Jenny was hopping up and down to get a bitter glimpse over the heads of those nearest the pit.

Plato stood, with difficulty.

The SEAL was almost out, the men still pushing.

Plato heard a young child, perched on his father's shoulders, squeal in alarm. "Will it eat me, daddy?" the boy inquired.

The SEAL stopped moving, the men, many of them, sprawling on the ground.

Blade came through the crowd and gave the keys to Plato. "It was incredibly heavy, even in Neutral," he said. "took us a while to grasp we had to keep one hand on the steering wheel if we wanted it to go in a straight line. If that ramp were any longer, the SEAL would still be in hibernation."

"You've done well."

"What's next?"

"A good rest," Plato advised. "I'm going to sit by a fire and finish this manual. Tomorrow, hopefully, you can start. If it won't function, we may have no recourse but to use some of the horses."

Jenny put an arm around Blade's waist. "Let's find a quiet spot where we can snuggle."

Blade and Jenny, arm and arm, walked away from the Family and the fires in an easterly direction. They reached the edge of a tilled field, the corn waist-high. A quarter moon was overhead, the stars points of bright light.

Jenny leaned against Blade. "It's so beautiful out here tonight," she sighed.

Blade nodded.

"I don't want you to leave tomorrow," she said.

"Are we going to go through all that again?" he demanded.

"No." Jenny kissed him on his left cheek. "We

settled that this afternoon. I'm resigned to it, I guess."

Blade ran the fingers of his right hand through her hair. "I will miss you more than words can ever say," he acknowledged.

"I wish I were carrying your child," she announced unexpectedly.

"What?"

"You heard me. I want to have your child," she repeated. "Our child," she corrected. "A little Blade to remind me of his daddy."

"You make it sound like I won't be coming back."

"There is that possibility," she pointed out.

Blade stared up at the stars.

"Well, what about it?" she asked him.

"What about what?"

"About me having our child."

"Be serious," he admonished her.

"I've never been more serious."

"You know it's impossible," he reminded her.

Matrimony and child-rearing were taken as the supreme social responsibility by the Family. Carpenter had attributed part of Western civilization's decline to the breakup of the family and the instability of the home. He considered the home fundamental to the preservation and maintenance of society. In his diary he discouraged his followers from engaging in promiscuous sex. Instead, he staunchly advocated monogamy, promoting marriage and the creation of children as one of the prime duties of any daughter and son of the Spirit. Carpenter viewed marriage as an eternal binding, and this description resulted in the Family applying strict guidelines to the relations between the sexes. Children before marriage—or binding, as it become generally known—were firmly discouraged. The Family's tight-knit structure, the genuine love of the parents for their offspring, tended to perpetuate the traditional Family values.

Violations were rare. The situation was further compounded by the constant fight for survival. Children required constant protection and supervision. Every Family member wanted children, but no one wanted more than he or she could handle. Children were a necessity for the continuation of the Family, not an idle luxury indulged in on a passing whim. Nurseries, day schools, grade schools, and the like were all things of the past. Parenthood could not be studiously avoided, nor could the responsibilities be shirked and passed to someone else. From infancy, the Family members faced the often grim realities of existence.

"You know it's impossible," Blade reiterated when Jenny didn't respond.

Jenny squeezed him as hard as she could. "I know," she admitted. "I'm just dreaming."

"One day your dream will become a reality," he predicted.

"I want you to know I'm holding you to your promise," she said.

"I was serious," Blade stressed. "When I return, if you're willing, you and I will bind. We'll get a cabin and start a family and thank the Spirit daily for our blessings."

Jenny smiled broadly. "It sounds almost too good to be true, doesn't it?"

"Plato has said that your life is only enjoyable if you work at making it what you want," he philosophized. "If you really want something, go for it."

"I can't think of anything I want more than to be your mate," Jenny said. "I'll be counting the days until you return."

Blade leaned down and gave Jenny a warm, protracted kiss. She reached up and wrapped her arms around his neck.

"Think you can find us a soft patch of grass somewhere, big guy?" she whispered.

"Do you have something in mind?" he teased

her.

"I want to remember this night forever."

Blade turned serious. "Just remember what I said about not having children. I won't have you carrying a child and bearing the responsibility of rearing it without me by your side. Don't try and make me lose control."

"Why, honey," she said softly into his right ear, her hands stroking his neck, her legs pressing against his, "I don't have the slightest idea what you mean by that. How could little old dainty, defenseless me ever make a strong, strapping hunk like you do something against his will?"

Jenny kissed him again, entwining her tongue with his.

I could be in serious trouble here, Blade reflected.

The breeze picked up.

They were standing fifty yards east of the row of cabins used by the married couples. Tilled fields and clusters of trees, preserved natural areas, continued eastward until encountering the protective moat and the outer wall. At night, Warriors were posted on the western wall, at positions nearest the Blocks. Periodically, a Warrior would patrol the compound, making a circuit of the Blocks and the cabins, but not bothering to check the eastern half of the Home, the portion devoted to agriculture. Only lovers and those enjoying a solitary stroll used the eastern section at night. They believed they were secure behind the wall, the barbed wire, and the moat. No one would attack the Home at night; there were too many mutates and other monsters abroad in the woods. But from a tactical standpoint, the Home was most vulnerable in the eastern sector, and after dark.

Blade mentally noted that fact when he heard the twig snap.

Jenny broke their embrace. "What's wrong?" She

glanced at the rows of corn and several nearby trees.

"Why do you ask?" Blade scanned the corn. The noise had been loud, distinct.

"You suddenly tensed up." She grinned. "Hope it wasn't my kisses! Are they that bad?" Jenny giggled.

"Shhh," Blade whispered. His Warrior instincts were warning him that something was amiss, some element in the night was out of place. But what?

Jenny sensed his concern and stepped back a step, freeing his arms.

Blade faced the cornfield and drew his right Vega. Were his nerves playing tricks on him? What could possibly be wrong? The odds against someone invading the Home at night were astronomical. Could it be another mutate?

"Blade . . ." Jenny gripped his left arm.

"What is it?"

"I thought I saw something move."

"Where?"

She pointed to a clump of trees ten yards away, situated at the edge of the cornfield.

Blade turned, studying the trees. He wished he had Geronimo's exceptional night vision. What should he do? Investigate? And expose Jenny to possible danger? No way. He would get her out of there, find Hickok and Geronimo, and come back.

"Let's head back," he said casually.

Jenny took several steps, then froze, inhaling deeply.

Blade spun, following the direction of her frightened gaze.

Something was blocking their path, standing about twelve feet in front of them, something big and bulky, the features indistinguishable in the dimness of the night.

Blade drew his other Vega and aimed both at the thing.

From behind them came the sound of rustling in the corn.

"There are more of them behind us!" Jenny stated the obvious.

"You are surrounded," said the form in front of them in a deep, growling voice. "Drop your guns or we will kill the woman."

Blade risked a quick glance over his right shoulder. More of them were advancing on them through the rows of corn. He counted at least six, maybe more. Who were they? What did they want?

The giant in front of them answered his second question. "We want the woman. We won't harm you unless you interfere. don't make the Trolls angry," he added in a threatening tone.

Trolls? What in the world were Trolls?

"Blade . . ." Jenny said softly.

"Stay close to me," Blade whispered. He had to get her to the row of cabins between the fields and the blocks. Many of the married couples would be in their cabins, and he would find help. First things first.

"You Trolls want this woman?" Blade asked grimly.

"Trolls always want women," the Troll in front of them replied.

"Well, just try and take her, bastard!" Blade whirled, the Vegas extended, and fired four times at the shapes in the corn. They dived for cover.

Blade twisted for a shot at the one ahead of them.

It was gone.

"What the. . ." Blade gave Jenny a shove. "Run! Head for the cabins! I'll be right behind you."

Jenny tore off, making good speed, Blade on her heels, searching for any sign of the Trolls.

Forty yards to go and they'd reach the cabins.

Blade spotted a shadow slithering along the base of a row of bushes to their north and snapped off a shot. The shadow disappeared from view.

Thirty-five yards to safety.

Blade could hear shouting from the direction of

the cabins. His shots had been heard; help would be on its way.

"Blade!" Jenny abruptly screamed, terrified.

Several black shapes had jumped up and engulfed her.

"Jenny! No!"

The Trolls were swarming on her, overpowering her.

Blade couldn't risk a shot. The bullet might accidentally strike Jenny. He didn't even break his stride as he dropped the automatics and drew his Bowies, making for the nearest looming shadow.

The Troll had turned to face Blade, the feeble moonlight gleaming on a metallic substance as it made a sweeping arc at Blade's head.

Blade ducked and lunged, burying his right Bowie to the hilt in the Troll's abdomen.

The Troll grunted and collapsed.

Blade surged upward, leaping at the second form.

"Blade!" Jenny was still fighting for her life.

A hard object unexpectedly crashed into Blade's head from behind and he toppled to the turf, his senses swimming.

"Blade!" Jenny screamed, kicking one of the Trolls in the groin.

"Finish him off!" someone ordered.

Blade tried to concentrate, but his consciousness was jumbled. He realized he had dropped his Bowies.

Someone gruffly yanked his head back, pulling on his hair, nearly bending his neck to the snapping point, exposing his jugular.

At the same time there was the sound of a solid blow landing and a body fell to the ground.

"Finally!" said the voice of the first Troll. "Get her and let's get out of here."

Blade was struggling, trying to break free. His vision cleared and he saw a Troll towering over him, one arm upraised, a knife in hand, ready to strike.

7

Hickok and Geronimo were standing next to the SEAL, admiring the vehicle and discussing their impending departure, when all hell broke loose.

Although ordinarily most Family members would retire shortly after the onset of night, many of them were still awake, too excited over the recent developments to turn in. Plato was seated by a fire, immersed in the Operations Manual to the SEAL. The Omega Triad was on guard, the three Warriors on the west wall, alert for any danger. All was peaceful and quiet.

Until the four shots shattered the darkness.

Hickok and Geronimo spun, facing east.

"What was that?" Plato called to them.

"Came from near the cabins," Hickok ventured.

"A bit past it, I'd say," Geronimo said, assessing the distance.

A smallish figure darted up to them, a lean, wiry man with angular facial features and uncanny speed.

"Any orders?" asked his newcomer. He was carrying a katana, a long sword, at the ready.

Hickok glanced at him, wondering for the umpteenth time how any person could choose the name of a mongoose at their Naming. Rikki-Tikki-Tavi was the leader of the Beta Triad. Each Triad had its respective head, but each of the three other Triads, the Beta, the Gamma, and the Omega, were in turn led by the Alpha Triad in times of concerted action.

"Guard Plato," Hickok directed. "We'll investigate." He ran off, Geronimo keeping pace at his side. They had placed the Henry and the Browning in the SEAL earlier, but they still had their other weapons.

A woman suddenly shrieked, the sound coming from their right, from the direction of F Block.

They stopped, mentally debating which way to go, when they heard Jenny yell Blade's name somewhere directly ahead.

The two Warriors covered the ground at full speed, heedless of the risk of tripping and breaking a leg. They reached the cabins. A man and a woman were standing outside the front door of one cabin, the man with a rifle, the woman with a candle.

"What's going on?" the man asked as Hickok and Geronimo passed him.

"If you find out," Hickok shouted over his left shoulder, "let us know!" There was another gunshot up ahead.

They heard Jenny scream again, closer this time.

Hickok was scanning the terrain, searching for any indication of movement. Where the blazes were they? What *was* going down?

Jenny, sounding scared, cried Blade's name for the third time.

"Where are they?" Hickok snapped in frustration.

"There!" Geronimo tapped Hickok's right shoulder and pointed.

Hickok spotted them. There was enough moonlight to reveal both Blade and Jenny was were down. Dark forms flitted around them.

Geronimo slowed a bit, drawing his cherished tomahawks.

Jenny was being lifted and carried by a pair of the fitures. There were six or seven milling about.

Hickok saw one of them standing over Blade, a knife in one hand. Blade suddenly thrust his right hand into the neck of his foe, his thick fingers rigid and extended. He surged to his feet and was immediately struck on the head again by another of the forms.

Time to even the odds a mite. Hickok stopped, crouched, and drew his right Python, the motion a blur, the Colt an extension of his body, firing two shots into one of the things looming above Blade. His friend was prone on the ground.

One of their attackers whirled and there was the crack of a revolver. His hurried shot went wild.

So! They had guns too! Whoever *they* were! Hickok returned the shot, his aim better. The thing clutched at its head and dropped.

Geronimo had borne a little to the right, and now he closed in, bearing down on one of the figures. They appeared to be men dressed in baggy robes of some sort.

There was the sound of commotion, gunshots and yells coming from the area of the Blocks. Were there more of them? What were they after?

Geronimo gave his war whoop and launched himself into the air, slamming into one of them, sending the figure sprawling to the ground. Before it could regain its footing, Geronimo swung his left tomahawk, imbedding the edge in the skull of his foe.

The others were slinking off into cover. Jenny had disappeared.

Blade groaned and attempted to rise, getting to his knees, still unsteady.

Hickok was at his side, supporting him. "Whoa there, pard! Take it easy!"

"Jenny . . ." Blade mumbled. "Where's Jenny?"

Hickok caught Geronimo's eye and nodded due east.

Geronimo understood, heading after the ones who abducted Jenny.

"Jenny," Blade said softly, struggling to stand.

"It's okay," Hickok tried to assure him. "Geronimo is going after her. Those things don't stand a chance against that red man."

"Got to help her," Blade stated weakly. His head throbbed and blood matted his hair.

"You've got to rest a minute," Hickok said. "You won't do her no good trying to catch up in this condition. Leave it to Geronimo."

Geronimo was making his way through the cornfield, listening for the slightest noise, hoping his deductions were correct and the attackers were making for the east wall. But why had they taken Jenny? An answer occurred to him and he felt inexplicably cold. Great Spirit! It couldn't be!

There was motion ahead. Someone was running through the corn, bearing east.

Geronimo increased his speed. Slowly he began to overtake his quarry, a solitary running form. Where were the others and Jenny? What if he didn't catch up with them? Where were they from? How would the Family locate their lair? He needed one of them alive.

The one ahead of him became aware of pursuit and turned. Too slow.

Geronimo hit him low, at the knees, toppling him to the turf. He jumped up and struck, the flat side of his right tomahawk smashing against his opponent's exposed chin. Again. And again.

The attacker groaned and slumped against the corn stalks.

Good! The Family had a prisoner.

But where was Jenny?

Geronimo made for the east wall. He could track at night, but the task was time-consuming and time was one precious commodity he did not possess at this moment. Apparently, the attackers had entered the Home from the east. It only made sense they would exit the same way. He passed field after field. Stands of trees whisked by. No sign of anyone else, though.

Even in the subdued light the wall was clearly visible. In credibly, as he neared the moat, Geronimo spotted several flowing phantoms clambering up the inner wall. How were they doing it?

The attackers reached the top of the wall and vanished over the side, all save one.

Geronimo reached the edge of the moat, the water lapping against the bank. He knew it would be useless to swim the moat and attempt to follow them. There was no way he could scale the smooth surface of the inner wall. He gave vent to a rare outburst of anger.

"Damn!"

The last of the figures was at the top. It paused, and an eerie, cackling laughter floated down from above. Then the last attacker disappeared over the top.

"Damn!" Geronimo repeated, wondering how Hickok and Blade were faring.

Hickok was supporting Blade and moving as rapidly as he could toward the Blocks. Gunfire and shouts punctuated the night. Obviously there had been more than one group of assailants.

"Jenny . . ." Blade was saying, over and over.

"She'll be okay," Hickok tried to assure him, grunting at the effort required to carry Blade's bigger body. "You know, pard," Hickok added, "far be it for me to criticize a friend in a time of crisis, but you sure as blazes are falling down on the job a lot lately. I think you're losing your edge."

Blade jumped in his arms.

"Just great!" Hickok muttered. "What next?"

There was the blast of a shotgun and a woman shrieked from the area of the cabins, some of which were now in view.

"This is getting awful repetitious," Hickok said to himself, gently lowering Blade to the ground.

A rifle cracked to his left.

"Don't go anywhere," Hickok said to Blade, drawing his Pythons. He jogged to the cabins and rounded the rear of the nearest one.

And ran into bedlam.

A dozen or more Family members were engaged in frantic, hand-to-hand combat with their mysterious enemies.

Hickok spotted a dark form on top of one of the Family, beating him on the head with a club. His left Colt bucked and the adversary jerked backwards onto the grass. To his right, twenty feet away, two attackers were trying to subdue a woman, one holding each arm as they endeavored to pull her into the night. Hickok recognized her, Juliet, kicking and twisting in a frightened frenzy.

"That's no way to treat a lady," Hickok announced, gratified when the two antagonists turned his way, even happier when his two shots caught them in the head. "Piece of cake." He grinned.

A bullet slammed into Hickok from behind, catching him in the fleshy part of his left shoulder, spinning him around, shocking him.

I can't believe it! Hickok thought. I've been shot! He glanced down at his shoulder, aware of a vague numbness, surprised at the lack of pain. Guess he never really expected it to happen to him!

"So long, sucker!" stated a gruff voice. "You've wasted your last Troll!"

Troll?"

A fist hammered into Hickok's stomach, doubling him over. The next blow, on the right cheek, knocked him to his knees.

Got to concentrate, Hickok realized, his stomach sore and his cheek throbbing. This is getting serious!

There was the click of a hammer being drawn back.

Hickok gazed up, into the barrel of a Marlin 45-70, the rifle only inches from his head. He was still holding the Pythons and he tried to bring them into play, amazed when his arms refused to respond.

The Troll laughed. "Any last request, asshole?" he taunted the gunman.

"Just a comment," Hickok replied. "You talk too much!" He rolled, sweeping his legs under the Troll. The Marlin blasted close to his left ear as the bulky form fell. Hickok's left arm was still numb, but he forced his other arm to steady the Python as he planted a slug between the Troll's eyes.

Two other Trolls disappeared in the darkness.

His ears ringing, Hickok rose to his feet.

The fighting was winding down.

A tall Troll, armed with a double-edged axe, started to follow his retreating companions, but he inexplicably paused, hefting the axe in his hairy hands.

Hickok, about to shoot the Troll, hesitated, wondering why the man had stopped. He understood when he heard the piercing kiai, the focused cry of a martial-arts master, and saw Rikki-Tikki-Tavi dart into view.

The Troll with the axe charged, swinging.

Rikki danced to one side, his left foot flicking out, connecting, shattering his opponent's right knee, staggering the Troll. Rikki swung his katana, the razor-keen blade severing the Troll's head from his body. Blood gushed out, resembling a miniature geyser. The arms flopped twice and the body toppled over.

"You sure are messy, pard," Hickok observed wryly.

"Are you seriously hurt?" Rikki asked, noting Hickok's shoulder.

"Just my pride," Hickok replied. "But I have learned a very valuable lesson tonight."

"Oh?" Rikki-Tikki-Tavi scanned the area. Bodies were everywhere. There was no sign of the intruders. Family members were assisting injured companions. "What's that?"

"I'll never, ever make fun of a certain mongoose again."

Rikki-Tikki-Tavi laughed.

8

Plato, standing near the SEAL in front of E Block, gazed over the assembled Family and felt tears moistening his tired eyes. The early morning sun was bright, glaring, causing him to squint as he addressed them.

"Last night was the worst night in Family history! And do you know whose fault it was? Ours!" There were murmurs among the Family members, many shifting uncomfortably. Plato averted his eyes. He could scarcely stand to see the injured, to look at his maimed loved ones, to observe their saddened expressions. It wouldn't do, though, to permit them to perceive his sorrow. He must be strong, befitting a Leader.

"It was our fault because we became complacent," Plato said, confronting them with the truth. "Over the years we've become sloppy, careless. In the early days, right after the Big Blast, the Family posted Warriors on every wall at night, not just the west wall." He sighed, weary to his core. "We began believing we were secure in the Home, safe from attack. Who could scale our tall walls? Who would dare assault us? Well, we have our answer, and a terrible price has been paid for our folly. I know you must have many questions about last night, and here is the man with the answers."

Plato beckoned and Hickok stepped alongside him. Geronimo was leaning against the SEAL.

Blade was still in C Block, being tended to by the Healers.

"We know how they got in," Hickok began, holding aloft a long rope with a grappling hook attached to one end. He used his right arm. His left was pressed against his side. The Healers had informed him the wound was not serious. They had applied therapeutic herbs and a compress and argued when he stubbornly refused to accept a sling. "We found this still attached to the top of the east wall. They apparently used these to scale the outer wall. Once on top, they used wire cutters to get past the barbed wire. From there it was easy to climb down the inner wall, swim the moat, and do what they came here to do. We think there were two groups. One came over the east wall, the other over the south. Our initial estimates place their strength at about two dozen."

"How many did we get?" someone asked.

"We killed eleven and took one alive," Hickok answered. "But what's of more concern to us is the damage they inflicted. Four of our Family were killed, nine injured, and . . ." He paused, reluctant to continue. "And eight of the women were taken captive."

A young woman of seventeen started crying. "Where's my mom?" she asked Hickok. "Where's Lea?"

The gunman experienced a lump in his throat. "We'll find her, Cleopatra. Don't worry."

"Is that a promise?" she inquired, tears streaking her face.

"That's a promise," Hickok responded, a harsh edge to his voice. "The women," he said, speaking louder so those in the back of the group could hear him, "were the primary target."

"Why?" a man wanted to know.

"Your guess is as good as mine," Hickok retorted.

"Do we know where the women were taken?" a woman demanded.

"We'll know shortly," Hickok assured her. "Any more questions?"

There were none.

Plato stepped forward. "Take time to rest and eat. We will hold another Family conclave when the sun is directly overhead. Plans must be made to add new members to our Warrior ranks and revise our defense strategies. Don't fear for our female friends and loved ones! We will be sending Warriors to retrieve them." Plato faced Hickok. "Where is our prisoner being restrained?"

"The one Geronimo caught is in there," Hickok replied, jerking his right thumb at E Block.

"Let's question him." Plato led the way into the building. Hickok and Geromino followed.

Just inside the doorway, bound hand and feet, propped on his knees, was the captured Troll. E Block was the Family library, the main source of diversion and entertainment. Kurt Carpenter had personally selected the thousands upon thousands of volumes lining the cramped shelves.

Standing immediately behind the Troll, katana in hand, was Rikki.

"Has he spoken?" Plato asked Rikki.

The head of Beta Triad simply shook his head.

Plato studied their captive. The man was young, maybe in his twenties, with brown hair worn long, falling to the center of his back, and an unkempt beard. His brown eyes glared defiantly up at them. His attire was unusual, even by Family standards, consisting of a loose-fitting tunic, covering him from his neck to his knees, and a large cloak or robe and sandals. Both the tunic and the cloak were constructed from bear hide. He was filthy and his body reeked.

"I understand you are called a Troll," Plato stated, hoping to elicit a response.

He was successful.

The Troll spat on him.

Before Plato could intervene, Hickok back-handed the Troll on the mouth, knocking him to the concrete floor.

"Please." Plato grabbed Hickok's right hand. "We mustn't descend to his level."

"It's the only level he'll understand," Hickok snapped.

The Troll giggled, rising to his knees again.

"Where are your fellows taking our women?" Plato asked him.

"Wouldn't you like to know?" the Troll answered, leering at them.

"If you tell us," Plato told him, "we'll release you."

"A Troll never rats, you old bag of bones!"

"We must know," Plato insisted.

"I'll never say a word," the Troll confidently stated.

"Yes, you will," said a new voice.

Blade was standing in the doorway, naked from the waist up, his skin caked with patches of blood. The Healers had tended to a gaping gash in his head, caused by the edge of a hatchet. Just a shade lower, and he would not have recovered.

"I ain't tellin' you nothing, asshole!" the Troll declared, grinning at Blade.

Blade slowly entered E Block. He drew his right Bowie.

"Blade, don't!" Plato exclaimed.

This time it was Hickok who clamped his good hand around Plato's narrow left wrist and held fast. "Sorry, Plato. Can't let you interfer with my pard," he apologized.

Blade reached the Troll. His lips were compressed, a thin line of restrained rage, his features hard, his grey eyes glaring.

"If I were you," Hickok advised the Troll, "I'd

speak up real quick like.''

"You don't scare me," the Troll arrogantly countered.

Blade used his left hand to grip a handful of the Troll's hair above his right ear. He began cutting the hair close to the scalp. The Troll bucked and attempted to pull loose, but Rikki seized him by the shoulders and pinned him in place.

"What are you doing?" the Troll demanded, his tone tremoring.

Blade finished cutting the hair. "I am going to ask you this only once," he said quietly. "Where are the Trolls based?"

"Blade, don't!" Plato reiterated, sensing what was coming.

"Kiss off, bastard!" the Troll roared at Blade.

Calmly, precisely, Blade slashed the Troll's right ear off.

The Troll screeched at the top of his lungs, pain staggering his senses, heaving against his bounds and striving to rise. Rikki maintained his iron grip. Jagged folds of flesh hung where the ear had been. Blood seeped down his side.

"You prick!" the Troll bellowed at Blade. "Prick! Prick! Prick!"

"You have to admire his vocabulary," Geronimo commented.

Blade crouched and pressed the bloody point of his Bowie against the Troll's crotch.

The Troll froze, his eyes widening in abject fear.

"Now that I have your undivided attention," Blade said softly, "I'm going to ask you some questions. If you don't answer them, if you pause to so much as sneeze, I'm going to push my knife clear through your balls. Do you understand?"

The Troll nodded, his body quaking uncontrollably.

"Good." Blade applied slight pressure to the Bowie. "Where are the Trolls based?"

The Troll tried to speak, his lips twitching, his throat bobbing.

"I can't hear you," Blade goaded him.

"F . . . F . . . Fox," the Troll blurted.

"Fox?" Blade repeated. "Where or what is Fox?"

"There is, or was, a town called Fox on the map of Minnesota," Plato recalled. "East of here a ways."

The Troll quickly nodded his head, his hair flying. "That's it! That's the place!"

"How did you get here?" Blade inquired.

"What do you mean?" The Troll required an elaboration.

"On horses, some mechanical means, or foot, what?"

"On foot. What's a mechanical means?" The Troll appeared confused.

"Why did you attack us?"

The Troll almost grinned, but caught himself in time. His eyes rested on the gleaming Bowie and he gulped. "We wanted to get as many of your women as we could."

"Why?"

"We're always running out of them."

"Running out of women?" Now Blade was the one who was puzzled. "Why?"

"They're always dying on us. Can't hack it, I guess."

"But why come here? It took a lot of effort to scale our walls. You must have had some idea of how many of us there were, and you must have known we were well armed. Why risk it? Aren't there any other women left out there?"

"Not in our area," the Troll answered. "We've already raided everywhere else we knew of."

"How did you know about us?" Blade wanted to know.

"Oh, a long, long time ago one of us got hold of

one of your women."

Blade eased the Bowie a fraction into his groin. "You're lying. None of our women were ever taken by Trolls. I would know."

"I'm telling the truth, man! I'm telling the truth!"

"When was this woman allegedly taken?" Plato questioned the Troll, his interest aroused.

"Let me think. . . ." The Troll bit his lower lip, nervously watching the Bowie. "It was some time back. Six? No! It was seven seasons ago."

"Seasons? Do you mean years?" Blade asked.

"Yeah. Seasons. Years. They're the same thing to us."

Hickok noticed Plato blanch and his knees sagged. Then he recovered.

"This woman . . ." Plato seemed to have difficulty speaking. "Did she have a name?"

"Yeah. her name is Nadine."

Hickok quickly placed his good arm around Plato's waist to prevent the Leader from collapsing. Plato lowered his face and groaned.

"What's the matter with him?" Rikki-Tikki-Tavi solicitously inquired.

"Don't you remember?" asked a newcomer. "Nadine is his wife." Joshua entered the Block. He walked to Plato's side and took him from Hickok. "I'll tend to him." Joshua's gaze rested on the Bowie Blade held. "Is that necessary?"

"Don't interfere," Blade admonished him.

"He may be our enemy," Joshua persisted, "but he is still a child of the Creator, just as we all are."

"Joshua." Plato surprised everyone present by standing tall and stepping free of Joshua's embrace. "Shut up."

"If I hadn't heard that with my own ears," Hickok wryly interjected, "I wouldn't believe it."

"Is Nadine still alive?" Plato asked, a pleading quality to his voice. "You must tell me!"

The Troll nodded. "Yup. Sure is. Amazing too, when you come to think about it.

"Why is that?" Blade probed.

"Like I told you before," the Troll reminded him. "They don't usually last long once we get them."

"Why . . . not?" Plato's hands were trembling.

The Troll went to reply, but apparently thought better of it.

"Answer him," Blade said, applying additional pressure to the Bowie.

"Go ahead. Do it!" The Troll stared at Blade. "But I won't say a thing about the women. You'd kill me for sure then!"

Blade slowly stood and placed his Bowie in its sheath. "Rikki, take our guest to C Block and let the Healers bandage his ear. . . ."

"Or what's left of it," Hickok said, smirking.

Rikki jerked the Troll to his feet. "You heard the man." With a deft flick of his wrists he cut the rope tying the Troll's feet. "Move it. One false move and you won't be thinking about the ear you've lost. You won't have a head to think with." Rikki shoved the Troll towards the doorway.

"Go easy on him," Joshua urged.

Rikki stopped for a moment next to Hickok. "I almost forget. Wanted you to know I wasn't defying your order to protect Plato last night. Two other Warriors showed up and I left them with him while I went after you. Plato was not in danger, and I knew I would be of more assistance where the combat was heaviest."

"Do you hear me complaining?" Hickok smiled. "If you hadn't shown up when you did, I'd have wasted a bullet on the creep."

"That creep," Joshua interjected, "was a son of God, like us."

Rikki and the Troll left.

"I'd like to go with them," Joshua said to

Blade. "Maybe I can persuade this Troll to open up.
I might learn some valuable information for you."

Blade nodded and Joshua departed.

"So what's our next move?" Hickok queried.

Blade was stroking his chin. "Those eight
women are in great danger. I don't know what the
Trolls do with them, but whatever it is, it can't be
anything pleasant. It is imperative we leave as soon
as possible and go in pursuit. We'll go all the way to
Fox if need be."

"You would experience difficulty attempting to
overtake them on foot," Plato said. "I recommend
you take some of our horses."

"No."

"No?"

"We'll take the SEAL," Blade stated.

Plato shook his head. "I would vigorously
oppose any such action. The vehicle is too
important. It is our only way of getting to the Twin
Cities."

"Granted," Blade conceded. "But you just
admitted we'd never catch them on foot, not with
the head start they have. If we use the horses, how
many of them do you think will make it back? What
with the damn mutates and everything else out
there, we'd be lucky if even one of them survived."

"I still fail to comprehend any sound argument
for utilizing the SEAL," Plato stated.

"How about this for an argument," Blade
continued. "You said it was, what, hundreds of
miles to the Twin Cities? Quite a trip when you
consider we have no experience whatsoever with the
transport. How far is it to this Fox?"

"I'd need to check the map," Plato replied,
perceiving the direction this reasoning was taking
them, "but if memory serves, about forty or fifty
miles."

"There you have it." Blade smiled. "Consider
this run to Fox as our test run. It will prepare us for

the longer journey to the Twin Cities. We'd have a better chance of getting to Fox and back. And if that isn't enough," Blade said, getting personal, "then think of Jenny and Nadine and the others. Every minute we waste debating is another minute they're closer to death. I say we get the SEAL ready and leave as soon as possible."

Plato's brow furrowed as he considered their predicament. Finally he nodded agreement. "It's against my better judgment, but we'll do it. I can have the transport prepared shortly."

"Let's get to it." Blade placed his left arm around Plato's slim shoulders and they walked outside.

Hickok was grinning from ear to ear.

"What's so funny?" Geronimo asked.

"Did you see the look on that Troll's face when Blade shoved his Bowie into his nuts?"

"Abject terror," Geronimo said, chuckling.

Hickok sighed happily. "I just love it when the big guy gets forceful!"

9

"If you fall behind," the huge, bearded Troll angrily announced, "you die!" He motioned for the women who had stumbled to stand.

Jenny assisted Mary in rising. "You've got to be more careful," Jenny warned her. "These fiends will kill us without any hestiation at the slightest provocation."

"I'm sorry," Mary nodded. "I'm just so tired."

"Aren't we all," Jenny agreed.

"Cut the chatter!" one of the Trolls commanded. "Move!"

The women silently obeyed, Jenny in the lead. The Trolls had tied the women together using one long rope, looping it around each woman's neck. The biggest Troll, the one with the beard, the evident leader of this foray, held one end of the rope in his brawny left hand. In his right he held a machete; around his waist he wore a cartridge belt and a revolver. Eight other Trolls flanked him, four on each side, covering the string of captured women. Behind the row of women, constantly scanning the rear for any indication of pursuit, walked seven more Trolls.

Jenny's feet were killing her. How long had they been walking? She estimated it was well into the afternoon of the day following their abduction, and all eight Family women were extremely fatigued. They had been on the move all night and all day. The

Trolls were wary, expecting the Family to swiftly retaliate. The leader, in particular, seemed disappointed when pursuit failed to materialize. Jenny had to admit her own disappointment. Where were their rescuers? Why hadn't anyone shown up yet? If the Warriors had started on the trail immediately after the attack on the Home, they certainly would have caught up to the Trolls by now. Where were they?

"Can't we stop?" Mary whispered. "I don't think I can go much further."

Jenny glanced over her shoulder. Mary, a young Tiller, was behind her. In order came Daffodil, Saphire, Angela, Lea, Ursa, and Joan. All of the women, Jenny noticed, were relatively young, in their twenties or thirties. The Trolls hadn't bothered with the older women. What was the reason? As if she couldn't guess.

Joan, the blonde at the end of the tether, tripped and sprawled on her hands and knees. All of the women stopped.

"Get up, bitch!" one of the Trolls grabbed her by her long hair and yanked her erect.

Jenny was worried. Joan was their secret weapon, their knight in disguise. The Family was guarded by four Warrior Triads, each Triad containing three Warriors. Out of the twelve Warriors, only one was a woman. Only one woman in recent years had expressed an interest in becoming a Warrior. That woman, a decade ago at her Naming, had selected the name of the heroine she had read so much about in the history books in the Family library. Joan of Arc, the fabled warrior woman.

The Troll was still gripping Joan by the hair. She was sporting a large cut on her forehead and her left eyebrow was swollen, the eye puffy. Despite her injuries, ignoring the pain, she suddenly swept her right elbow back and up, catching the Troll on the nose, breaking it, blood spraying from his nostrils.

The Troll released Joan, bawling in commingled discomfort and fury. "You bitch! You damn bitch!" He was carrying a metal club, a section of steel several feet long. "I'll kill you for this!" He raised the club over his head.

There was the sound of a gun being cocked.

All eyes turned to the mountainous Troll, the leader. He was pointing his revolver at the one with the busted nose. "You won't kill her, will you, Buck? Not if you know what's good for you."

Buck wavered, wanting to crush Joan's face in, but afraid of the consequences. "You saw what she did! She broke my nose, Saxon. Can't I kill her? Please?"

The giant Saxon shook his head. "I have other plans for her. For all of them."

"But the bitch broke my nose!" Buck vehemently protested.

"That she did!" Saxon agreed, and started laughing.

The other Trolls took up the merriment.

"Bested by a woman!" one of them said, grinning.

"Maybe next time he'll pick on someone his own size!" another sarcastically commented.

Buck, stung, lowered his club and glared at Joan.

"Saxon," Jenny faced the colossus, "we need a rest. Can't you spare just a little time?"

Saxon thoughtfully stroked his bushy beard. "I guess we can at that. Doesn't seem to be anyone after us. That surprises me."

Me too, Jenny mentally agreed.

They were moving across a field choked with bushes and rife with weeds. Ahead, a mile off, was the edge of a forest. The sun was beating down, the heat oppressive, almost unbearably so for the month of June. The sky was tinged with a touch of gray.

The global nuclear blasts had propelled massive

quantities of dust and pulverized rubble into the atmosphere, turning the sky dark, reducing the amount of sunlight reaching the surface. The planet had experienced a marked increase in volcanic activity after the war, many of the volcanoes still active. The records revealed that for over five years this cloud had literally clogged the sky, before it had begun to settle and disperse. Gradually, the color of the sky had changed from a dark gray to a light gray and, finally, to a shade of blue in certain areas. Within a decade, much of the cloud was gone. The dramatic rise in volcanic eruptions, however, continued to spew ash and dust into the atmosphere, and at least twice a year the sky over the Home would change to a darker gray as the air became filled with volcanic residue. This effect seldom lasted longer than six hours, borne away by the winds. Plato predicted the eruptions would terminate within fifty years.

The cutting off of sunlight had cooled the temperature over the entire world. Growing seasons had been eradicated or drastically curtailed. Only the hardiest crops and vegetation had survived. A century later, in many areas, growing seasons were approximately the length they were before the war, although climatic extremes were heightened. The summers were infernally hotter, the winters were chillingly colder.

"Sit down right where you are," Saxon ordered. "Take a break."

About two yards of rope separated each woman, allowing ample room for them to sit without cramping one another. They formed a small circle, shoulder to shoulder, so they could whisper without being overheard.

"How are you feeling?" Jenny asked Joan as soon as they sat down in the grass.

"Not too hot," Joan admitted, frowning. "I was sleeping in B Block, heard the commotion, and ran outside. Somebody let me have it before I even knew what was going on. My head is killing me." She brushed some dust off of her faded brown pants and green blouse, patched in over a dozen spots.

"Anyone else hurt?" Jenny inquired.

The rest shook their heads.

"Where are the Warriors?" Lea, one of the Family Weavers, ran her fingers through her disheveled black hair.

"That's what I'd like to know," commented Saphire, a brunette.

"I thought they would have caught up with us by now," Jenny mentioned.

"What's with you dummies?" Joan demanded, peeved.

"What do you mean?" Daffodil asked.

"You think the Warriors dropped everything and took off after these clowns two seconds after the Home was hit? Be serious. The perimeter had to be secured, the injured tended to, and plans made." Joan stared at the Trolls, clustered together, talking and laughing. "These bastards are going to pay for what they've done!"

"What do you think the Warriors will do?" Lea questioned.

"They'll send one of the Triads after us," Joan reasoned.

"Just one?" Ursa wondered.

"You think they'd send all of the Warriors and leave the Family defenseless? No, just one Triad. Probably Alpha."

"It could be any Triad," Jenny disagreed.

Joan grinned. "Be serious. Blade won't want anything to happen to his sweetie."

"Now who would that be?" Daffodil giggled.

"Doesn't mean a thing," Jenny stubbornly retorted.

"If you believe that," Joan said, smirking, "then you don't know Blade like I know Blade. He'd follow you to the ends of the earth. Take my word for it. Blade, Hickok, and Geronimo will be on our trail, if they're not already.''

"Aren't you and Hickok an item?" Lea asked Joan.

"We're just good friends," Joan answered defensively.

"Then why are you blushing?" Lea pressed her point.

"How soon before Alpha catches up with us?" Ursa wanted to know.

Joan shrugged. "No way of telling. Doubt they'd use the horses. On foot, could take them a day or two.''

"What if they use the SEAL thing?" Angela, a mousy woman with wide eyes, interjected.

"Then I wouldn't have any idea," Joan acknowledged.

"Why do you think they're all wearing those bear robes?" Lea asked, gazing at their captors.

"Beats me," Joan said. "Only an idiot would wear those robes in this heat.''

"What are they going to do with us?" Daffodil inquired in a frightened tone.

"Don't worry about it," Joan advised.

"Aren't you scared?" Daffodil asked.

Joan gave Daffodil's right shoulder a reassuring squeeze. "This reminds me of a story I heard once about several of the Family who decided to go climb this big cliff. . . .''

"Where was this cliff?" Daffodil, a lean brunette, one of the Family artists, interrupted.

"Let me finish," Joan said. "They were climbing this big cliff when one of the men slipped and fell. As he passed his friends on the way down they heard him talking to himself.''

"What was he saying?" Lea bit.

"Well, every time he passed someone they heard him say . . .'' Joan paused for effect. "So far, so good!"

Jenny noticed Saxon as looking at them. "I think our rest is almost up. Joan, you should be in charge. We must try to stick together. Stay hopeful. Help will come."

"Here comes the big one," Daffodil stated.

Saxon strolled over to them. "On your feet. We're moving out." He stepped close to Jenny. "I like blondes. Behave yourself, and I'll claim you after the testing."

"Testing?" Jenny wanted him to explain.

"You'll see." Saxon walked back to the other Trolls.

"You know," Lea said optimistically, "it doesn't seem like they intend to hurt us."

"Oh no, they won't kill us," Joan snapped. "It isn't too much fun raping a dead body."

The women slowly stood.

"My aching muscles," Lea complained.

The Trolls assumed their original positions. Saxon picked up the end of their tether.

"Can't we have some water?" Jenny requested.

"There's a stream up ahead a ways," Saxon informed her. "We all get a drink when we reach it."

Joan had overheard. "If there's a stream up ahead," she said, "then why don't you you Trolls jump in it? Bathing more than once a year wouldn't hurt, you know!"

Saxon's eyes narrowed. "Everybody knows bathing is bad for you. Weakens you." He raised his voice so all the Trolls could hear. "This one sure likes to use her mouth, doesn't she?"

"So what if I do?" Joan wouldn't be cowered.

"So if you like using it so much," Saxon told her, "you'll get your chance. In the pen."

"The pen? What's that?"

"It's a place where you'll be able to flap your gums all you want, bitch."

The Trolls cackled.

"Now move your asses!" Saxon yelled. "Or else!"

So much for Mr. Nice Guy, Jenny reflected. She sadly gazed over her left shoulder.

Where was Blade?

10

Plato was tired.

With the assistance of some of the Family members, he had loaded all of the Alpha Triad's provisions, food and ammunition and medical supplies, into the SEAL. There were two bucket seats in the front of the vehicle, one for the driver and the other for a passenger. Between the bucket seats was a control console for several of the SEAL's special features. Behind the bucket seats was another seat, running the width of the transport. Behind this rear seat was a large area for storage. Two spare tires and tools were kept in a recessed compartment under the storage area.

Plato walked to the SEAL, the vehicle gleaming in the afternoon sun, and opened the driver's door. Under the dashboard, in the center, hung a red lever. Plato gripped the lever and pushed it to the right. The Operations Manual explained that this lever would activate the solar collector system, if it was still properly functional.

"Any word on this mechanical critter, old-timer?" asked someone behind him.

Plato turned.

Hickok, Blade, and Geronimo were fully armed, ready to go. Blade was giving Hickok a dirty look.

"I will know more in an hour." Plato grinned. "The Operations Manual states that the solar energization process takes sixty minutes to achieve optimum performance levels. Every morning of your journey, one hour before you intend to drive, place the red lever under the dashboard in the right-hand position."

"Fine by me," Hickok said. "But I've got one question."

"Which is?" Plato rolled down the driver's window.

"What the blazes is a dashboard?"

"Haven't you studied the books in the library dealing with modes of transportation?" Plao inquired.

"Sure." Hickok shrugged. "But mainly I just looked at the pictures of the cars and the trucks, specially some of those race cars. Imagine being able to travel at over one hundred miles an hour! I never got into the mechanical aspect, though."

"Suffice it to say, you have a lot to learn. All of you. Take the Operations Manual with you and read it as you travel. Earlier I placed the additives in the engine. They were stacked in cartons in the chamber housing the SEAL all these years."

"Additives?" Blade repeated.

"Yes. The engine in the SEAL is unique, unlike any in the world at the time of World War Three. It's described as self-lubricating when in truth a small amount of lubricant must be added before it can operate."

"Do you really think the SEAL will work?" Geronimo queried. "After all this time?"

"I honestly can't say." Plato sighed and leaned against the transport. "The Founder had confidence it would. He spent a sizable portion of his fortune devising it."

"What's this?" Hickok bent over and picked up a yellow can from the ground near Plato's feet.

"It's one of the additives," Plato explained.

Hickok sniffed at the opening Plato had made in the top of the metal can. "Smells awful," he commented, scrunching up his nose. "Glad we don't drink this stuff."

"The SEAL drinks that stuff," Plato stated, smiling. "One can every fifty thousand miles. We'll need to retain a record of the odometer mileage."

"What the blazes is an odometer?" Hickok asked.

Plato sighed.

"Blade!" a woman abruptly yelled, urgency conveyed in her strident tone.

The men whirled.

Nightingale was running their way, her brown hair flying.

"What is it?" Blade demanded as they moved to meet her.

Nightingale bent oer, almost out of breath. "The Troll..." she managed to say before she began wheezing.

Plato placed his left hand on her shoulder. "Take your time. Breathe slowly."

Nightingale was gulping air. She had covered the two hundred yards from C Block as fast as her legs would carry her.

"What is it?" Blade asked her again.

"The Troll got away!" she finally exclaimed.

"What?" Blade gripped her arms. "How? Where did he go?"

"We were tending him," she explained, "fixing his wound, when Rikki asked Joshua to watch the Troll while he went outside and undo his ropes, said his circulation was being cut off. I objected, but it didn't do any good. Joshua untied the Troll's hands, and before we could prevent it, too fast for us to do anything, the Troll picked up a chair and hit Joshua, knocking him down. One of the other Healers screamed. Rikki came running in, and the Troll got him as he came through the door. The Troll took Rikki's sword. He was coming this way. Didn't you see him?" She was out of breath again.

"He ran behind E Block," Hickok deduced, "keeping the building between him and us."

"He's making for the east wall," Geronimo speculated.

"Get him," Blade ordered, looking at Geronimo. "You're the fastest. Besides, Hickok and I aren't in any shape for a foot race."

Without another word, Geronimo wheeled and ran in pursuit of the Troll. He carried his Browning in his right hand as he concentrated on maintaining a steady pace. No sense in tiring himself out too soon. There were acres to go and the Troll had a head start. How far ahead was he?

A scream shattered the heat of the day, coming from the area of the cabins.

Now he knew. Geronimo hastened his pace, dreading the worst. If only the lookout on the wall had spotted the escaping Troll! He would have sounded the alarm, blown the horn, and alerted the entire Family to the threat.

Someone was sobbing.

Geronimo reached the first row of cabins. A woman was on her knees next to a fallen man, blood covering his chest. She glanced up as Geronimo approached and pointed due east.

"He went that way!" she shouted, tears filling her eyes. "He cut Jefferson! Cut him bad!"

Several others were gathering.

"Get the Healers!" Geronimo told them as he passed. There was little he could do for Jefferson; insuring the Troll did not escape was his first priority. If the Troll got away, you could bet he would flee to Fox and warn the other Trolls that a rescue party was definitely on the way. Geronimo frowned. He couldn't allow that to happen.

Birds were singing in nearby trees. Butterflies wafted on the wind.

Geronimo ignored the scenic beauty as he plowed into the cornfield, the sharp leaves lashing at his arms. He disregarded the stinging sensation and focused his attention on his body, pushing it as far as he could. Hig leg muscles were beginning to tighten.

Field after field passed.

Geronimo marveled at the ease with which he could navigate the terrain, compared to his slow pace of the night before when he wasn't sure of what was what.

The moat was closer.

If he remembered correctly, there was one last field, a stand of trees, a cleared space and the moat.

Still no sign of the Troll. How was he expecting to scale the wall? Had the Trolls hidden ropes and grappling hooks along the moat?

Geronimo reached the trees, limbs pulling at him as he dodged between two trunks and stopped, searching the moat for any sign of the Troll.

The movement of his head saved his life.

As Geronimo looked right his peripheral vision detected the flashing gleam of the katana blade as it sliced at his neck. He twisted, automatically bringing up the Browning, holding the stock in his left hand and the barrel in his right, blocking the katana. The clang of metal striking metal was loud, reflecting from the wall and seeming to fill the cleared space.

The Troll kept coming, swinging the sword again and again, bearing down, keeping the pressure on, preventing Geronimo from using the Browning.

Geronimo back-pedaled, waiting for an opening, thankful the Troll wasn't skilled in Tegner.

Kurt Carpenter had stocked almost five hundred thousand books in E Block, the books he envisioned the Family would require to overcome the obstacles it would face. Survival books. Hunting and fishing. Metalsmithing. Natural Healing. How-to books proliferated. He had provided two dozen books on hand-to-hand combat written by a man named Bruce Tegner. Each of the books contained concise, step-by-step diagrams and instructions, complete with detailed photographs of every movement and position. The library contained Tegner's books on judo, jujitsu, karate, aikido, jukado, kung fu, savate, and numerous other styles of martial combat. Tegner's books were the Family's source of tutelage in the martial arts, and the training sessions eventually became known as Tegner sessions, or simply Tegner. The Family Elders shared the responsibility of training the younger Family members during their schooling years. One of the Elders, a former Warrior, conducted classes in the art of Tegner. Rikki-Tikki-Tavi was his star pupil.

Geronimo silently thanked the Great Spirit that this Troll was no Rikki-Tikki-Tavi.

The Troll was clumsily striving to force the katana past the Browning, to pierce Geronimo's guard and disembowel him.

Geronimo was holding his own. He detected a trace of fatigue in the Troll's swings, and he knew it was only a matter of time before he could bring the Browning to bear. What should he do? Blow the reeking weirdo in half, or take him back to Blade alive?

The matter was taken from his hands.

He tripped.

Geronimo's right foot caught on a large rock and he fell backwards, hard, his right hand loosing its grip on the Browning and the gun fell to one side.

The Troll spotted his opening and vented a cry of triumph as he closed in, raising the katana for the coup de grace.

Geronimo twisted, avoiding the shimmering blade.

The Troll misjudged the force of his lunge and stumbled.

Geronimo sprang to his feet, his tomahawks in

his hands.

"I'm going to cut you to pieces!" the Troll boasted.

"Drop the katana," Geronimo warned, "and you'll live."

"Screw you!" the Troll bellowed, aiming the blade at Geronimo's head.

Geronimo ducked, and as he came up under the blow he buried his right tomahawk in the Troll's forehead.

The Troll stiffened, blinked once, gurgled, and fell.

"There it is!" someone said, and Rikki-Tikki-Tavi emerged from the trees and retrieved his prized katana.

"Glad you could make it," Geronimo casually commented. "I'm just fine, thank you. I appreciate your concern."

Rikki held the gleaming sword upright in his hands, his eyes carefully checking it for damage.

"I hope your sword is okay," Geronimo sarcastically quipped.

Rikki slowly ran his left hand the length of the shining blade. "Nobody, but nobody," he matter-of-factly stated, "takes my katana from me. Ever."

Geronimo watched the blood oozing from the Troll's head. "It's too late to tell *him*." He paused, then added an afterthought. "I know a fellow who feels the same way about his Colts, and another who goes to bed at night with Bowie knives at his side."

"And you?" Rikki quizzed him. "What about you?"

Geronimo stared at the tomahawk in his hand. "I see what you mean," he confessed.

Rikki-Tikki-Tavi smiled. "It is the nature of the Warrior."

11

Plato stood back, appraising the SEAL. He had rechecked the engine, secured the hood, climbed on the roof to examine the solar collectors and underneath to check the special batteries, and verified the dash indicator displayed a full charge.

Blade, Hickok, and Geronimo were standing beside him. The rest of the Family was gathered around the SEAL, knowing the momentous event was about to occur. The starting of the SEAL.

"I should warn you," Plato said to the Alpha Triad. "I've done the best I can, but it may not be good enough."

"How do you mean?" Blade asked.

"Despite hours in the library studying various modes of transportation, this is the first motorized transport I've encountered. I've studied the manual, and in preparation for this day I've also perused the entire collection of automotive literature. It's just that . . ." He paused, thoughtfully biting his lower lip.

"What is it, Plato?" Geronimo politely goaded him.

"It's just that I can't guarantee you the SEAL will work as it's supposed to." Plato slapped his right hand against his thigh in frustration. "Despite all of my studying, basically the vehicle is alien to me. Reading about something is only a fair substitute for experiencing the reality of whatever you are reading about. Absolutely nothing can take the place of actual experience. Even then, my reading has basically been in vain because the SEAL is unlike any other motorized vehicle in use before the Big Blast.''

"So what you're saying," Hickok said, pondering Plato's words, "is that this thing could break down in the middle of nowhere and we could find ourselves stranded, surrounded by mutates and only the Spirit knows what else?"

"I believe you've gleaned the gist of my meaning," Plato admitted.

"Wish I hadn't," Hickok mumbled. "So much for the wonderful world of technology."

Joshua, his left shoulder heavily bandaged, joined them. "Are we ready?" he inquired.

Plato noticed the Warriors ignored Joshua. "We appear to be all prepared," he proclaimed. He held the keys out. "Who wants to attempt to drive it first?"

Hickok grabbed the keys before the others could move.

"Are you certain you're up to it?" Plato questioned. "You must exercise caution. We can't afford to damage this vehicle."

"I've still got one good wing," Hickok said, grinning.

"But are you positive?" Plato pressed him.

"A piece of cake," Hickok assured them. He opened the door, climbed into the driver's seat, then closed the door.

"Our moment of truth," Joshua stated solemnly. "I never expected to see the day when we would be riding in a solar-powered vehicle."

"We hope," Blade added. "Well, whenever you're ready," he said to Hickok.

Hickok was staring at the dashboard, his brow furrowed.

"I thought you said this was a piece of cake,"

Plato reminded him.

"It is," Hickok replied defensively.

"Then what's the problem?" asked Geronimo.

"How do you start this critter?" Hickok reached out and touched a small vent, his movements, for once, hesitant, uncertain.

"You place that key in the ignition," Plato directed, "then turn the key."

"That's nice to know," Hickok snapped, frustrated. "What the heck is an ignition?"

Plato restrained an impulse to laugh. He showed Hickok the ignition, Hickok placed the key in the slot and paused, and all of them tensed expectantly.

"Here goes nothing, pards," Hickok stated, and twisted the key.

They were braced, anticipating a loud noise, having read that engines produced a considerable sound, and they were still startled and amazed when the engine kicked over, caught briefly, sputtered, and stopped.

"I've killed it!" Hickok moaned. "I did something wrong!"

"I don't believe so," Plato assured him. "Try again."

"You sure?" Hickok asked doubtfully.

"Trust me. One more time."

Hickok took a deep breath, closed his eyes, and turned the key again.

The SEAL roared to life and the engine idled for a minute, then it abruptly died.

"Damn!" Blade cursed.

"Once again," Plato directed.

Hickok tried it one more time.

The SEAL shook as the engine turned over and achieved performance level. The longer it ran, the quieter it became. Within a very short time the metallic rumble was reduced to a muted whine.

"We did it!" Blade shouted.

"Yahoo!" came from Hickok.

The Family cheered wildly.

"Thank the Spirit," Joshua said, touching the Latin cross he wore around his neck.

"It functions," Plato said to himself. "It actually functions." He could scarcely accept the evidence of his own eyes. The Founder's vision had actualized, had borne fruit! The SEAL, the unique and exclusive prototype for a generation of vehicles the world would never know, was operative!

"How do I make this thing move?" Hickok wanted to know.

"Push down and back on that lever." Plato pointed at the shift. "Watch that small gauge in front of you, above the steering column. A small arrow should stop on the letter D."

Hickok gingerly shifted as instructed.

"What next?"

"Do you see those two pedals on the floor by your right foot?" Plato asked.

Hickok glanced down at the floor. "Yep. I see 'em."

"Well, to initiate motion, the Manual says we should press down on the right pedal," Plato stated.

Hickok nodded his understanding, raised his right foot, and forcefully tramped down on the accelerator.

Pandemonium erupted.

The SEAL lunged forward, and only fleet feet and quick reflexes enabled those Family members standing directly in front of the transport to leap aside before they were run over. Several women screamed, children bawled, and a few of them shouted an unflattering term or two in Hickok's direction.

The SEAL was racing across the compound.

Hickok's petrified face appeared, protruding through the open driver's-side window. "Help! How do I stop this blasted critter?" he shouted. The SEAL hit a deep rut, the motion lifting Hickok and cracking his head against the roof. He winced and concentrated on steering the SEAL in a straight line.

Blade ran to Plato's side. "How does he stop it?"

"If he'd only remove his foot from the right pedal, it would slow down," Plato answered.

"He's probably too shocked to think of that," Blade pointed out. "What else?"

"The left pedal," Plato said urgently. "He must depress the left pedal and the SEAL will cease all motion."

"Blade, look!" Geronimo cried in warning.

Blade whirled.

The SEAL was fast approaching a huge tree.

"Hickok!" Blade broke into a run, Geronimo at his side, Joshua trailing behind.

In the SEAL, Hickok's eyes widened at the sight of the tree. "Who the hell put that there?" he shouted to no one in particular. What the blazes was he supposed to do? He'd never ridden in a motorized vehicle before. How would you stop the thing? Let up on the right pedal? For all he knew, that might damage the SEAL. Why were these things so complicated? The drivers in prewar society must have all been certified genuises.

The tree was dangerously close.

Hickok fumed. He angrily jerked on the steering wheel with his good arm and the transport lurched to the right, narrowly missing the tree. He maintained the pressure on the steering wheel, executing a wide circle, then released it, straightening the SEAL, proud of his feat. That was when he noticed he was now heading directly back at the grouped Family members. "Get out of the way, you idiots!" he shouted. "Get out of the way!"

Blade and Geronimo appeared next to the open window.

"Press on the left pedal!" Blade yelled, his hands cupped, encircling his mouth.

"The left pedal!" Geronimo chimed in.

The SEAL surged ahead and they fell behind.

"The left pedal," Hickok repeated for his own benefit. "Got it, pard." He shifted his right foot and slammed it on top of the left pedal.

The SEAL reacted as if it had smashed into a brick wall, coming to an immediate stop.

During the hectic ride, Hickok had kept his right hand glued to the steering wheel, gripping it with all his strength, his muscles straining. Only his grip aided him now, the force of the sharp halt propelling him forward, his momentum elevating him from his seat and smacking his body against the windshield. His hand never relinquished its grasp on the steering wheel, and his battered body swung back down, crashing in a twisted heap on the bucket seat.

Blade and Geronimo were nearest to the SEAL. They saw Hickok's moccasins protruding above window level.

"Do you think he's..." Geronimo left the thought unfinished as they reached the SEAL.

Blade yanked the door open.

Hickok's head was resting on the seat, his body doubled over on top of him, his ankles and feet resting on the back of the seat, his right hand still holding the steering wheel. He was breathing rapidly, deeply.

"Are you okay?" Blade asked, concern chiseled in his features.

"Fine," Hickok mumbled. "Piece of cake."

"Just one thing, pard," Hickok said, interrupting their levity.

"What?" Blade leaned over his friend.

"When we make the Fox run..." Hickok released the steering wheel. His fingers and wrist ached like the dickens!

"What about when we leave?" Blade inquired.

Hickok stared pleadingly into Blade's eyes. "You figure you could do the driving?"

12

"I'm going to make a break for it as soon as it's dark," Joan whispered to the others as they sat in a circle.

The Trolls had permitted another break. Saxon was upset because the stream was still nearly three miles ahead of them. Their march was delayed when a mutate, a former raccoon, crossed their path. Fortunately, they spotted it before it saw them and hid until the foraging creature left the area. The mutate had dallied, searching under logs and in bushes, hunting grubs and rodents.

Now the mutate was gone, and Saxon called a break while he dispensed instructions to the other Trolls.

"You can't be serious!" Lea objected.

"You'd be alone out there." Angela's eyes widened as she gazed at the surrounding forest.

"You wouldn't stand a chance," Ursa opined. "Don't do it."

"I can't allow the opportunity to go by," Joan countered.

"How do you figure?" Jenny asked her.

"Simple." Joan kept her gaze surreptitiously on the Trolls. "My head has cleared up. When they get us to their base, wherever it is, I bet they keep us under lock and key. It would be a lot harder to escape then. For some reason, these dummies haven't even bothered to frisk me. I have a pocketknife in my back pocket. It will be easy to cut this rope and make a break for it. I'll get to the Home and bring help.''

"I don't know. . . ." Jenny felt uneasy at the proposal.

"You really think you can do it?" Daffodil interjected.

Joan smiled. "Piece of cake."

"Now where have we heard that expression before?" Lea asked.

"And she says he's just a friend." Saphire stressed the last three words and the women laughed.

"What the hell is so funny?" Saxon walked over and glared at them.

No one responded.

"I don't understand you," Saxon said.

"Why?" Jenny inquired.

"Most women would be going to pieces about now," Saxon stated. "The Trolls are known far and wide. Our name strikes fear into the hearts of men and women. When we raid a town or camp, the people roll over and give us what we want. They know better than to cross the Trolls."

"The Family didn't roll over," Joan proudly reminded him.

"No," Saxon said, glowering at her, "they sure didn't. Can't understand it either."

"It's not difficult to understand," Jenny stated.

"Oh?"

"We never heard of you before," Jenny explained.

"Everyone's heard of the Trolls," Saxon boasted.

"Not us," Jenny affirmed.

Saxon seemed puzzled. "You might be right," he reluctantly agreed. "I told one of your men who we were. Surprised me when he tried to blow us away." A thought struck him. "Your Family has a lot of guns, don't they?''

Joan cast a warning glance at the other women and tapped her lips with her left index finger.

"Answer me," Saxon ordered.

The women remained silent.

Saxon stepped up to Angela and clamped his muscular right hand around her thin neck. "Answer me or I'll snap it like a twig!"

"We have guns, sure," Joan hastily admitted. "Don't know if you could call it a lot or not."

"How many?" Saxon grinned maliciously as Angela feebly endeavored to extricate herself.

"I've never counted them," Joan angrily snapped.

"That many?" Saxon released Angela, the germ of an idea growing in his mind. He reached under the folds of his bearskin cloak and withdrew his machete.

Where does he keep that hidden? Jenny wondered.

Saxon retrieved the tether from where he had dropped it earlier. "Let's move!"

Jenny noticed two of the Trolls were leaving the group, walking west, back the way they had come. "Checking our trail?" she asked Saxon.

Saxon stared at the departing Trolls. "It's just plain strange."

"What is?"

"No one after us yet. It's not right."

"You nervous?"

Saxon looked at her. "Nope. Careful." He turned and led the way as they moved through a dense portion of the forest.

"Mind if we talk?" Jenny questioned him.

Saxon shrugged. "Makes no nevermind to me. Just keep your voice down."

"Why are you called Trolls?" Jenny pushed a protruding limb from her path.

"We've always been called the Trolls."

"Where did you get your name?"

"How should I know?"

Jenny frowned. This was getting her nowhere. "Where are you taking us?"

"Fox."

"What's Fox?"

"You'll see."

She decided to be blunt, hoping her next question would not provoke him. "Why do you Trolls steal women?"

Saxon laughed lightly. "What a stupid question. How else would we get our women?"

"In our Family," she elaborated for his benefit, "the men ask the women to be their mates. The women go willingly."

"And what if the woman doesn't want the man?" Saxon probed.

"Then she doesn't have to become his mate."

Saxon laughed again. "Sounds like a dumb way of doing things. Our way is easier."

"You just take your women against their will," Jenny said, irritated. "You bully them, frighten them, and intimidate them. Is that any way to conduct a relationship?"

"Works for us."

Jenny fell silent for a while, pondering the futility of trying to reason with him.

The sun was heading toward the western horizon, the gleaming orb visible whenever they crossed small clearings.

"What do you Trolls do with your women?" Jenny interrogated the giant.

"The usual," was his gruff reply.

Calm yourself, Jenny mentally constrained her rising anger. "What is the usual?" she pumped him.

"Our women wash and sew and tend the children. They cook for us and service us at night. Or whenever."

"Service you?" Jenny repeated.

Saxon chuckled. "A big girl like you must now what I mean."

"What if the woman doesn't want to service you?"

"We chop her into little pieces and feed her to Wolvie."

"Wolvie?"

"You might get to meet him. Better hope you don't, though."

"Why?"

"Because," Saxon twisted and grinned at her, "if you meet up with Wolvie, it will be the last meeting you ever have."

Jenny involuntarily shivered as goose bumps broke out all over her body. Was there a cold breeze picking up? Or was she reacting to the malevolent gleam in Saxon's eyes and his leering expression?

Blade, where are you? She gazed over her right shoulder, suppressing an impulse to panic and attempt to flee. You better come soon. Real soon. Or you'll be having your children with someone else.

"Pick up speed!" Saxon bellowed. "I want to reach that stream by dark."

They reached a particularly compact tract of brush, compelling them to crouch and weave and contort their bodies to gain passage through the undergrowth.

Jenny flinched as a thorn bit into her left leg. She pulled the offending limb from her calf and concentrated on following the path Saxon was making. She could see him clearly and the two women behind her, but the others were hidden by the vegetation. She wondered how her sisters were holding up. Especially Angela. She was the weakest of the lot.

The brush ended and they found themselves at the edge of a clover-covered field.

Saxon studied the position of the sun. "We should make that stream by night, no problem. We'll build some fires and start again at first light."

"Saxon!" one of the Trolls shouted. "Saxon!"

Saxon whirled as Buck ran up to him.

Jenny glanced at the other women and immediately knew the reason for the alarm.

"What is it?" Saxon asked Buck, annoyed at the outburst. "It better be important."

"The women!" Buck was so excited he had difficulty forming the words. "It's the women!"

"What about the women?" Saxon still hadn't seen.

"One of them is gone!" Buck screamed.

Saxon's face clouded in uncontrolled fury. "It's the bitch with the mouth," he said after he counted the captives.

"How did she do it? How?" Buck was unable to prevent his neck muscles from twitching.

Jenny recognized a nervous condition when she saw one. The Trolls all appeared to be markedly deficient in the intelligence department. Some of them, she had noted, would not speak unless they were spoken to. They were unnaturally reserved, almost withdrawn. A pattern was taking shape, but the implications of it all eluded her.

Saxon grabbed Buck by the front of his tunic. "It's your fault, isn't it? You were supposed to keep watch, make sure none of them slipped away. What happened?"

Buck was trembling in wretched terror. "I don't know, Saxon! I don't know! Please don't hurt me! Please! Please!"

"Hurt you, Buck?" Saxon said. "Why hurt you?"

"You mean you won't hurt me?" Buck asked, amazed at his good fortune.

"No," Saxon grinned. "And don't you want to know why?"

Buck was afraid to ask.

"Don't you want to know why?" Saxon repeated.

"Why?" Buck finally, timidly, inquired.

Saxon jerked Buck off his feet, suspending him in midair. "The reason I won't hurt you is because you are the one who is going to go after the bitch. You will take two others with you. You will find her trail and track her until you catch up with her. You will not come back until you do. Is that understood?"

Buck nodded his understanding.

Saxon dropped him to the ground. "Then get going before I decide to cut your fingers off and make you eat them!"

Buck scrambled to his feet, still nodding. "On my way, Saxon."

"If you catch up with Galen and Trent," Saxon stated, referring to the two Trolls he had sent to check for pursuit from the Family, "have them help you. You must stop her from reaching their Home. We'll cover our tracks once we cross the stream, but she can still help them find us. You must find her first."

Buck motioned for two other Trolls to follow him. He ran to the brush and stopped. "What do we do with her when we find her?" he asked.

"You can have some fun, if you want." Saxon grinned.

"And after?" Buck licked his thin lips. He liked the idea of having fun with her. It would pay her back for what she had done to his nose. Damn, how it hurt!

"After?" Saxon stared at Jenny. "Kill the bitch!"

"Right." Buck stooped to enter the brush.

"Buck!" Saxon called.

Buck froze, fearful Saxon had decided to chop his fingers off after all. "Yes?"

"Bring me her head."

"Her head?"

"Her head," Saxon ordered.

"You got it."

13

"We've wasted enough time as it is," Blade said, peeved. "We are leaving, now."

All the Family members were gathered for their departure, except for the Warriors on the walls. Plato had checked and rechecked the SEAL and wanted to go over it one more time.

"I agree," Hickok chimed in. "Enough delays, already! Let's get this critter rolling."

"After what you went through," Geronimo said, kidding him, "I'm surprised you're in such a hurry for your second ride."

"Something tells me," Hickok remarked, sighing, "I'll never hear the end of this."

"Count on it." Geronimo beamed.

"We should study this map," Plato said, holding up a map of Minnesota. "We need to determine the fastest route to Fox."

Blade took the map. "We'll read it as we go along."

Joshua walked up to them. "I'm ready to go," he announced.

"You're not going along," Blade informed him.

"But . . ." Joshua started to protest, looking at Plato for support.

"But nothing," Blade interrupted. "If Plato wants us to take you with us when we go to the Twin Cities, we will. Not now."

"Why not?" Joshua asked.

"Because we aren't on a peaceful mission," Blade patiently explained. "We're going to rescue the women. There will probably be fighting and killing. It's no place for someone like you, someone who won't kill under any circumstances."

"Maybe I could reason with them," Joshua objected. "I could talk to them and prevent any bloodshed."

"Like you did with the one earlier?" Blade reminded him.

Joshua frowned, downcast. He tried one last appeal. "What do *you* say?" he asked Plato.

"Reluctantly," Plato said, "I must agree with Blade. This time. You can go with them to the Twin Cities. By then your shoulder will be healed."

"It's not my shoulder that hurts the most." Dejected, Joshua strolled off through the massed Family.

"I didn't mean to hurt his feelings," Blade said, apologizing to Plato.

"I know," Plato replied.

"Have you seen my violin?" Hickok asked Geronimo.

Blade grinned. "Hickok has a point. We're leaving." He opened the driver's door and climbed up into the bucket seat.

Hickok winked at Plato. "Don't worry, old man. I'll take real good care of your protege." He walked around the transport and clambered into the front on the passenger side.

Geronimo silently climbed into the back seat.

"Rikki!" Blade called to the diminutive Warrior.

Rikki-Tikki-Tavi, katana in hand, stepped up to the window.

"You're in charge of the Warriors until we return," Blade directed.

"Put your mind at ease," Rikki responded. "The Home will be secure while you are away."

"Don't forget to post guards on all the walls from now on," Blade fretted.

"It will be done," Rikki stated.

"And begin selecting candidates," Blade said. "We must pick three new Warriors and add another Triad after I return."

"I understand," Rikki replied.

"He knows what to do, pard," Hickok interjected. "Maybe you want to stay here and babysit and Geronimo and I will go after the Trolls?"

"See you when we return," Blade said to Rikki.

"Be well." Rikki moved aside, and Plato moved next to the window.

"Take care of yourselves." The Leader gripped Blade's shoulder. "Bring our sisters back to us."

"We will," Blade predicted.

"I can't emphasize enough how crucial it is that you avoid damaging the transport," Plato stressed.

"Darn!" Hickok threw in. "Does this mean I can't enter the SEAL in the Indy 500?"

"What's the Indy 500?" Geronimo asked.

"It was an annual auto race before the Big Blast," Plato answered. "It's mentioned in several books in the library."

"Time to go," Blade announced. "Get everyone away from the SEAL."

"Stand back!" Plato shouted so everyone could hear. "Step away from the vehicle!"

The Family promptly obeyed, giving the SEAL a wide berth, many remembering Hickok's earlier attempt at navigation and hoping Blade could perform better. The path in front of the transport was completely cleared.

"The Spirit be with you!" Plato spoke on behalf of the Family.

Blade nodded and reached for the key. "Here we go."

"Say, Blade . . ." Geronimo spoke up.

"What is it?" Blade paused, ready to turn the

engine over.

"You aren't, by any chance," Geronimo asked, grinning from ear to ear, "a graduate of the Hickok School of Driving, are you? If so, I think I'll change my mind and stay here."

"Ouch." Hickok slumped in his seat and folded his arms across his chest. "Knew I wouldn't hear the end of it."

Blade turned the key, relieved when the SEAL started. "Hold on," he said to the others, just in case. He shifted into Drive and gently pressed on the proper pedal. The transport slowly moved forward.

The Family cheered.

Blade waved as the SEAL crossed the compound. The drawbridge was already open, Brian and several men at the control mechanism.

"Aren't you doing something wrong?" Geronimo leaned over the bucket seat.

"What?" Blade nervously asked.

"Well, you seem to be avoiding the trees," Geronimo pointed out. "As I recall, that's not the way Hickok did it."

Hickok made a show of closing his eyes and groaning.

Brian and the others waved as the vehicle drove over the drawbridge.

"We're on our way," Blade said, stating the obvious. He gingerly turned the steering wheel, directing the SEAL on a southerly course. Once they were past the brick wall, he would turn the SEAL due east. Blade realized his palms were sweating. He couldn't help himself, fearful the vehicle would break down at any moment.

Plato had told him everything appeared to be in working order, that the passage of time had not caused the deterioration of any vital part. The Founder had planned for this contingency, expecting many years might elapse before the

Family required the transport. His engineers had incorporated the latest, state-of-the-art, sometimes purely theoretical, knowledge and scientific developments into the vehicle's design and construction. As Plato had pointed out earlier, the use of fluids was confined to an absolute minimum. The chemical composition of various parts of the SEAL, such as the body, the tires, the seals, and gaskets, was a radical departure from the methods used in constructing conventional products. The chemist who had devised the formula for the tires had told Carpenter he had perfected a process the tire manufacturers would gladly kill to suppress: a process for producing an indestructible synthetic tire.

Blade drove the SEAL at a sedate speed, still unsure of his ability and the SEAL's capability.

"You certainly do drive slower than Hickok," Geronimo pretended to complain. "Although, I will admit, we do have a better chance of reaching our destination this way."

Hickok glanced at Geronimo. "Are you enjoying yourself?"

"Immensely." Geronimo beamed.

"You ever notice, pard," Hickok said, facing Blade, "how them Injuns have such a pitiful sense of humor?"

Geronimo laughed. "Yeah. And have you ever noticed how the white man has such a long history of making a fool of himself?"

Blade was focused on the field ahead, on dodging holes and ruts and boulders and trees.

"Hey, Blade?" Hickok nudged his right shoulder. "You still with us, or what? I'd hate to think we were wasting all this grand entertainment."

"What?" Blade looked over at Hickok. "Sorry. I wasn't paying attention."

"We noticed," Hickok said.

"What did you say?"

"Nothing important." Hickok noticed the Operations Manual lying on the console and picked it up. "So what's on the agenda, big guy?"

"We head east, following the map," Blade stated. "When we get tired, we rest inside the SEAL for safety's sake. . . ."

"Gee, I hope you'll let us out to tinkle," Hickok commented.

"We make the run to Fox, rescue the women, and return to the Home," Blade finished.

"It certainly sounds easy enough," Geronimo mentioned.

"Easier said than done," Blade admitted.

"Aren't we in an optimistic mood?" Hickok quipped.

Blade felt his neck and arm muscles beginning to relax as the time passed. He was gaining valuable confidence, both in himself and the transport. The needle on the speedometer wavered between ten and fifteen. They reached the end of the wall and bore east.

"You know," Hickok observed, reading the Manual, "they take an awful lot for granted in this book. They talk about things like you should already know what a lot of them are. Listen to this." He quoted from the contents: " 'When the SEAL is driven over sixty for five minutes, overdrive automatically engages, reducing the strain on the transmission and assuring even engine performance at crusing speed.' " Hickok glanced up at Blade, annoyed. "What's that supposed to mean? What's an overdrive? What's a transmission? This entire Operation Manual appears to be like that! I can't make hide nor hair out of some of these instructions."

"We'll just have to do the best we can," Blade said.

"Hope it's good enough," Hickok griped.

They lapsed into silence, Geronimo lost in

thought, Hickok immersed in the Manual, and Blade driving.

This isn't so difficult, Blade reflected, relaxed, thankful Plato had taken the time to give him a crash course in the transport's basics. His mind drifted, recalling the events leading up to Jenny's abduction. Was she still alive? She better be! The Trolls would rue the day they attacked the Family!

"Blade!" Geronimo suddenly yelled. "Look out!"

A huge boulder loomed directly in their path.

"Damn!" Blade cursed and jerked on the steering wheel. The SEAL swerved to the left, narrowly missing the boulder.

"Do you mind?" Hickok casually chided Blade. "I'm trying to read."

"Oh no!" Geronimo slapped his right palm against his forehead.

"What's wrong?" Blade asked. Geronimo appeared to be in genuine torment.

"It's what I've always feared!" Geronimo wailed.

"What?" Blade urgently demanded.

"That whatever Hickok has," Geronimo said, smiling, "is contagious."

14

What was that noise?

Joan dropped to her hands and knees behind a large log, listening. What had she heard?

Birds sang, and the leaves of the trees rustled in the breeze.

Nothing else.

She sighed, feeling the fatigue in her limbs and an intense pain in her head, the lingering result of the blow she had suffered when the Trolls assaulted the Home. Her exertion had agitated her wound.

How far had she come?

Four miles maybe.

Joan knew there would be pursuit. She was doing her best to disguise and cover her tracks, exactly as Geronimo had instructed her. But she couldn't spend too much time on erasing her trail; her first priority was reaching the Home. A competent tracker would be able to follow her—slowly, to be sure, but he wouldn't be fooled.

A branch snapped to her left.

She *had* to reach the Home. The Warriors would have no idea which direction the Trolls were taking. They would find the spoor, all right, but it would require time, a precious commodity, one they couldn't afford to waste.

Up ahead, a squirrel began chattering in alarm.

Joan regretted leaving her sisters. What choice did she have? That thicket had provided the perfect opportunity for her escape, preferable to waiting for dark. Now, at least, she had some daylight on her side.

The squirrel was having a veritable temper tantrum.

Why?

Joan eased through the undergrowth, wishing she had her gun. Anything would be of more help than a three-inch pocketknife. Her faded brown pants and green blouse were torn and dirty.

Voices.

She froze, getting her bearings.

The voices were right ahead of her. Sounded like two men. Three guesses who.

Joan eased onto her belly and crawled forward, carefully avoiding twigs and limbs that could break and give her away.

"I'll be glad when we get back to Fox," someone was saying.

"I can't wait to pork the new flesh," said the second.

Joan stopped behind a tall, leafy bush and gently parted one branch.

The two Trolls were busily engaged in wiping out any trace of the path their group had made, wiping the ground with clumps of long grass, carefully obliterating every track they found.

"Which woman will you screw first?" asked the younger of the two Trolls. He was armed with an axe.

The older Troll grinned, exposing a gap where three of his top three teeth had once been. "It's hard to pick one of 'em," he admitted. "They're all so healthy. Not like the usual scrawny flesh we get."

"Yeah." The younger Troll beamed. "You know, Galen, we should get some real good years out of this bunch."

Galen nodded. "A lot of years before we'll have to feed 'em," he agreed. "Maybe, Trent, we'll have to raid this Family again."

"I don't know." Trent frowned.

"What's the matter?" Galen asked.

Joan couldn't see any weapon on the older Troll, on Galen. That concerned her. It meant he had it hidden under that bulky cloak all the Trolls wore. She didn't like surprises in matters of life and death.

"Did you see all the guns they had?" Trent was saying.

Galen nodded.

"I didn't think there were that many guns left," Trent continued. "Guns are so scarce. Where do you suppose they got so many?"

"Beats me." Galen shrugged. "Maybe the next time we hit 'em, we should steal guns and forget the women."

"There's an idea." Trent smiled. "Tell Saxon about it when we get back."

"You want to get me killed?" Galen stopped his wiping and stared at the younger Troll.

"Killed?"

"You know damn well," Galen growled, "Saxon don't like no ideas unless they're his. He'd bust my head for sure."

"Sorry," Trent apologized sheepishly. "Didn't think."

"Well, you better use your head around Saxon," Galen warned. "I've seen him kill people who looked at him the wrong way. He gets in these strange killing moods, and you'd better watch him when he's in one of 'em. Mark my words."

"I will," Trent said earnestly.

Joan silently removed her pocketknife from her back pocket and opened the small blade. It was now or never. The Trolls were abreast of her position, still unaware of her proximity. If she could strike swiftly, the element of surprise would work in her favor. Maybe she could get them both before they could react. She paused, recalling instruction

Hickok had imparted when she was training to become a Warrior. "If you're feeling tense," the gunman had stated, "and you have the time, take just a second to relax. Take a deep breath and clear your head. Nervousness never helped anyone in a death fight. I learned an important point studying books on the gunfighters of the old West. The best gunfighter, the one who survived the most gunfights, wasn't always the fastest. It was the calmest, the one with the steadiest nerves. Remember that." She had.

Now it was time to put her training to use.

Trent was nearest, stooped over, obscuring tracks. His axe was in his left hand; he was dusting the trail with his right.

Joan leaped to her feet, crashed through the bush, and lunged.

Someone had trained the Trolls well.

Trent saw her coming out of the corner of his right eye. He dropped the grass, straightening, his hands bringing up the axe. He never made it.

Joan swept her right hand up, the three-inch blade shining in the sunlight, and buried the knife to the hilt in Trent's left eye.

Trent screeched, grabbing for his punctured eyeball, falling backwards.

Joan spun, facing Galen.

The older Troll was already armed, braced for her. He was holding not one, but two gleaming long knives in his hands. Each blade was over six inches long. He gave the impression of someone familiar with their use.

"Well, if this ain't a surprise," Galen said to her. "The bitch herself! How'd you get away?"

Joan ignored him, searching for anything she could utilize to defend herself.

"Look what you did to poor Trent!" Galen stared at his hapless companion; Trent had yanked the blade from his eye and was flopping on the ground, screaming and hollering, blood all over his face and chest.

There was nothing Joan could use. Where was the axe?

"Now you're going to get yours," Galen assured her, glaring. "Bitch!" He charged, the knives extended, his arms outspread.

Joan remembered her Tegner.

As Galen closed in, intent on a cross slash, Joan dropped to the earth, landing on her right side, her legs clamped together and already in motion, sweeping in a half-circle, catching the Troll behind his knees and toppling him forward.

"Damn!" Galen exclaimed as he landed on his clenched fists and his knees, retaining his grip on his knives. He glanced at the woman next to him.

In that instant, Joan brought her right elbow back and out, slamming the bony edge into Galen's mouth. She immediately rolled away, beyond the range of his knives, and jumped to her feet.

Galen heaved erect, spitting blood and two teeth from his lower gum. His eyes glared his rage.

Joan waited for his next move, hoping his fury would get the better of him.

It did.

Galen came in recklessly, swinging his knives, neglecting skill and technique, only wanting her dead.

Joan dodged to her left, but not quick enough. The tip of one of the knives tore into her right shoulder, not deep, but she felt a burning sensation and her blouse darkened with her blood.

Galen laughed and bore in again, the knife in his right hand now crimson.

Joan's feet hit a fallen branch and, before she could recover her balance, she found herself flat on her back with Galen standing over her, prepared for the kill.

She kicked him in the balls.

Galen gasped, but he stayed on his feet, the tunic absorbing most of the shock of the blow. He dived, sweeping the knives down, aiming for her chest.

Joan grabbed for his wrists as he landed on her body. She knew she couldn't hold him for long; the Troll was wiry and strong, the result of years of hard living. His fetid breath assailed her nostrils as he leered at her, his eyes inches from hers. Blood fell from his mouth onto her face.

The knives were getting closer to her straining bosom.

Funny how the mind could work sometimes. Her thoughts flashed on Rikki-Tikki-Tavi. "When you're in a fight," he had told her, "there are no rules. It's you or the enemy. Do whatever you must to come out on top." She vividly recollected the lesson and instantaneously obeyed.

Galen sensed success; he was laughing, loudly.

Despite her revulsion, Joan opened her mouth and bit down as hard as she could on Galen's nose, her teeth penetrating the soft skin, tearing into it and rippng it off, the cartilage crunching.

Galen howled, pulled free, and stood.

Joan scrambled to one side, her fingers contacting something long and hard. She glanced down.

The axe.

Galen was backing away, blood pulsing from his ruined nose, pain making him careless. He took his eyes from the woman.

The axe arced down and embedded itself in his skull, the keen blade splitting his cranium like a sword through a melon, the blood and cranial fluid splashing outward. The Troll blinked twice, dead on his feet. He fell slowly, the axe still in his head.

Joan stared at her fallen opponent, catching her breath. He had come so close!

Trent was lying still, unconscious but alive, his chest rising and falling.

Joan knew she would need to finish him off. She moved toward him, then stopped, bothered by a peculiar feeling in her mouth.

What?

Joan spat, and watched horrified as Galen's nose dropped to the ground. She felt her stomach toss and doubled over, retching.

Maybe, she reflected in her misery, this Warrior business wasn't all she had cracked it up to be.

She finished vomiting and actually smiled.

Hickok would be proud of her.

Where the hell was he?

15

"Where the heck are we?" Hickok asked. One moment he was reading the Operations Manual, the next the motion of the transport affected him and lulled him to sleep. He was angry at himself for dozing off.

"About ten miles east of the Home," Geronimo informed him.

"Have a nice nap?" Blade grinned.

"I can't believe I fell asleep!" Hickok said.

"We all had a long night," Blade reminded him. "If I wasn't slightly nervous driving this thing, I might be tempted to catch forty winks too."

"As for me," Geronimo chimed in from the back seat, "Indians are famous for their iron will and superb endurance. I may need a catnap in five or ten days."

Hickok fondly gazed over his shoulder. "I'll tell you one thing about Injuns, pard. They are the best tellers of tall tales you'll find anywhere."

"I do believe," Blade glanced into the small mirror dangling above the dashboard, observing Geronimo's smiling face, "that Hickok just said you're full of it."

"He should know," Geronimo rejoined.

Blade was glad their sense of humor was still intact. Humor served as a release mechanism, as a means of harmlessly venting the tension they invariably felt in critical situations. All of them were extremely worried about the women, but they could not afford to allow their concern to eat at them, to dull their fighting edge. Humor helped relax them, and at the same time it kept them sharp and prepared for the unexpected.

"How far ahead of us do you think the Trolls are?" Hickok asked.

"Depends on whether or not they've stopped for rest," Blade replied.

"If they kept to a brisk pace," Geronimo speculated, "and really pushed the women all day today, then they could be halfway to Fox by now, maybe further."

"That's what I figured too," Hickok agreed. "Can't you push this thing any faster?"

Blade was reluctant to increase their speed, apprehensive his ability to steer and negotiate the obstacles in their path might not be adequate. But Hickok had a point. Speed was essential. The speedometer, as Plato had called it, was usually indicating between fifteen and twenty. He was keeping the transport to the open spaces as much as possible, bearing on an easterly course.

"If we damage the SEAL," Geronimo said, as if he could read Blade's thoughts, "we damage the SEAL. Nothing we can do about it. What's more important anyway? This vehicle, or our sisters and loved ones?"

Blade increased the pressure on the accelerator, watching the needle climb to twenty-five, thirty, thirty-five, and forty. The ride was still smooth, the bumps absorbed by the four mammoth tires and the heavy-duty shock absorbers.

"Now we're cooking," Hickok stated, delighted.

"I've been studying this map," Geronimo announced.

"And?" Blade swerved to bypass a stand of tall pine trees.

"I think I've found a way to make better time,"

Geronimo stated.

"How?"

Geronimo had examined the map while Hickok was napping. It was beside him on the seat, open. He picked it up and spoke while he confirmed his calculations. "I'm not positive about the mileage involved," he began, "but eventually we'll encounter a stream. When we do, I advise heading south."

"Why south?" Blade inquired.

"Because if we follow the stream south," Geronimo responded, "we run into a major highway. Listed as number eleven on this map. Highway 11. It takes us right to Fox."

"Think this highway will still be there?" Hickok doubtfully asked.

"Beats me," Geronimo admitted. "It's been a century, after all. But you never know."

"Sounds good to me," Blade decided. "Are there any other towns between us and Fox?"

"Let me see," Geronimo ran his left hand along the red line marking Highway 11. "Yep. We'll pass through two small towns. The first is called Greenbush. The second, a bit bigger, is called Badger."

"How far apart are they?" Blade wanted to know.

"I make it as nine or ten miles from the stream to Greenbush," Geronimo answered. "Nine more miles from Greenbush to Badger. And another seven miles or so to Fox."

"They sure put their towns close together before the Big Blast," Hickok commented. "Hard to accept the fact there once were so many people in the world."

"I remember reading they even had a population problem," Blade mentioned. "Too many people in some portions of the globe."

"Well," Hickok said, grinning, "they sure found a quick solution to that thorn in their side, didn't they?"

"That they did." Blade sighed. His mind couldn't quite grasp the horrible reality of the Big Blast, the devastating consequences for the human race. After all, he'd never known what it was like before the missiles were launched. He could not relate to the world as it had been, only as it was now. His lack of remorse never bothered him, though. How could he feel any emotion for people he'd never known? Anger was another story. He deeply resented what the moronic assholes had done to the planet, to the environment and the ecology.

"Think we'll find anyone in these towns we'll pass through?" Hickok thoughtfully asked.

"Don't know," Blade replied. "The Family records say the Government evacuated most of the population during the Third World War. Some folks might have stayed put."

"I've always been convinced," Geronimo confidently stated, "the Family isn't alone. If we survived, then others did. The Trolls have proven that point."

Hickok made a snorting noise. "I sure hope, pard, that anyone else we meet up with is more hospitable than the blasted Trolls."

"You and me both," Geronimo agreed.

They drove on in reflective silence.

Blade thought about Jenny, dreading her welfare. There was a reason to be hopeful. He doubted the Trolls would kill any of the women outright. Why go to all that trouble, assault an armed fort, just to kill the women you take prisoner? Made no sense. The Trolls needed their women alive. But why take women by force? What had that captured Troll meant, earlier, when he said they were always running out of women? How do you run out of women? There were so many unanswered questions!

The sun was at the western horizon, night almost upon them.

"Are we stopping when it gets dark?" Hickok asked.

"We better," Blade said, annoyed at the pending delay. "It would be too easy to wreck this thing at night. We'll sleep inside and begin again at the first crack of dawn."

"You mean," Geronimo corrected him, "we'll start an hour after you've thrown that red lever under the dash. Remember?"

"How will we know when an hour has passed?" Hickok questioned. "We left our sundials back at the Home."

"We just keep watch on this." Blade reached out and tapped a gauge in the center of the dash. "When this needle is all the way to the right, it means we have a full charge and can take off."

"Don't worry," Geronimo assured them. "We'll begin as soon as we can. I know how anxious you both are to catch up to the Trolls."

"Aren't you?" Hickok demanded.

"Oh, sure." Geronimo smiled. "But you guys have a certain, shall we say, vested interest in this mission."

"Meaning what?"

"Oh, come on!" Geronimo laughed. "Jenny and Joan."

"Joan and I are just good friends," Hickok said testily.

"Why," Geronimo asked, looking at Blade, "are you two always so touchy about your personal relationships?"

"Get yourself a 'personal relationship,'" Hickok said, mimicking Geronimo, "and you'll understand."

"I pray to the Spirit," Blade said, his grip on the steering wheel involuntarily tightening, "the women are all right."

"If anything happens to them," Hickok vowed, "I won't leave a Troll alive!"

16

Joan was being followed.

The sun was high in the morning sky, a bright yellow island in a sea of azure blue.

She paused, listening. Her muscles ached and her right shoulder pained her if she made any quick movements. The lack of sleep was the worst part of her ordeal. She had decided to walk through the night, aware of the great personal risk, but motivated by her keen appreciation of the responsibility she had to her captured sisters. Twice during the night she had been compelled to climb nearby trees when ominous growls sounded from the surrounding vegetation. She was armed with the axe and the two long knives, but they would be useless against a large mutate or any other big carnivore.

What was on her trail?

Joan resumed her determined march, her pace unflagging. If a mutate was after her, it would simply charge, heedless of the clamor it might make. Wild dogs would be howling with glee as they closed in. The big cats would be completely silent; you wouldn't know a cat was after you until too late. Every so often she would hear a twig break or a branch rustle. Something was attempting to close in on her undetected, biding its time, waiting. For what?

It had to be the Trolls. Saxon would not permit

her to escape. He would send some of his men after her. How many?

Joan concentrated, resisting the gnawing influence of her almost overpowering fatigue. She had hoped, by moving all night, to get a big lead on her pursuers. Apparently they had not stopped to rest either. Whoever was on her heels wanted her real bad.

A small field opened up ahead, waist-high grass wavering in a stiff northerly breeze.

She found her mind wandering, her thoughts straying to her childhood. She recalled her schooling years, her tutoring by the Family Elders, and her subsequent Warrior training. Her mother had attempted to dissuade her from becoming the first female Warrior in many years. "Be a Healer," her mother had urged her, "or a Weaver or Tiller. Anything but a Warrior!" Her mother had feared for her life. The Warrior mortality rate was four times higher than that for the rest of the Family, and with ample justification. The Warriors were usually the first ones to encounter danger; they were pledged to give their lives in the protection of the Family and the Home.

The wind was increasing.

Joan reached the field and started to cross. The grass was thick, tugging at her moccasins and tangling around her ankles. She hoped she wouldn't inadvertently step on a snake. The very idea made her skin crawl.

A bee buzzed by her head.

She held the axe aloft, over her head, preventing the handle from catching in the growth. The knives were securely tucked under her leather belt.

If she pushed herself, she reasoned, she might make it back to the Home by nightfall. Back to the Family. To Hickok. She was becoming especially fond of the flashy gunman, and she knew he was strongly attracted to her. His lips had told her as much several nights before the attack, when they were lying in a secluded grove. He was the first man she had ever wanted. During her youth, her tomboy years, the opposite sex had been a source of competition to best any way she could. In her teens, to her surprise and dismay, none of the men had seemed particularly interested in her. Then, to her astonishment, there was Hickok, shocking her one day at target practice. "You shoot well," he had said, coming up behind her on the range. "You have a good eye." He had awkwardly fidgeted with his gunbelt. "Goes with your great body."

Her heart had nearly stopped.

Joan smiled with the pleasant memories. The long walks, the star-filled nights. Others had noticed. Her sisters had teased her. He had brought out emotions in her she never imagined existed. Many of the women had envied her. Hickok was considered quite a catch.

Involved with her reflections, she failed to notice the sudden stirring of the grass to her left.

When Plato had announced the Alpha Triad would be leaving for the Twin Cities, that Hickok would be gone for a lengthy spell, she had run off and cried, angry and hurt. Why hadn't he told her? Why did he shy away from her after the announcement was made?

A wall of trees loomed in front of her.

Joan stopped and glanced over her right shoulder. Still no sign of the Trolls.

That was when Buck hit her. He jumped up, his club swinging, clipping her on the jaw as she whirled to confront him.

Joan fell, her vision spinning, onto her back.

Buck closed in, his metal rod raised. "We owe you, bitch! For my nose and for Galen and Trent. This is for them!" He brought the steel bar down.

Joan used the axe handle to block the blow, the impact jarring her shoulder and aggravating her knife wound. She rolled and rose to her feet, the axe poised.

Buck was gone.

She knew she was in trouble. The wind was whipping the grass, lashing the leaves of the trees, and drowning out any sound the Trolls might make. They were toying with her, drawing out their fun, engaging in a little game. She was too exposed in the field, a virtual sitting duck.

Joan bolted, covering the intervening space to the trees and darting into the woods.

Behind her, someone laughed.

She ran, limbs tearing at her body, her eyes never still, dreading the next attack.

"Run, bitch! Run!" Buck was somewhere to her left.

Joan reached the trunk of an old tree, its girth wide, many of its limbs dead. She stopped for an instant, getting her bearings.

An arrow thudded into the trunk inches from her head.

Someone laughed.

Joan ducked around the tree and churned up a steep hill, an ache growing in her side, the exertion taking its toll.

"Run, bitch!" Buck was enjoying this immensely.

The hill crested, the other side a steep drop of thirty feet. She slowed, took a deep breath, and jumped.

"Run! Run!"

Joan winced as she landed, her legs buckling under the strain. She fell forward, onto her face, dirt filling her mouth.

The laughter wouldn't stop.

Move! Get up and move! She tried to will her legs to function, to obey her, but they refused. There was a bank in front of her. If she could only get to the other side, maybe she could hide.

"The hunt is over," Buck announced.

Joan shifted onto her back and looked up.

Buck and two other bearded Trolls were standing on the drop-off.

"Want her dead?" asked a brawny Troll with a bow. A quiver of arrows was perched on his back.

"Not yet," Buck answered, grinning. "I've got plans for the bitch! Cover her."

"Saxon did say we could have fun with her," stated the third Troll, a sword in his left hand. "But he also said he wants her head. Should we cut it off before or after we have our fun?"

Buck pondered the question. "After," he finally replied. "I may want to use her mouth."

The other Trolls nodded their understanding.

"Cover her," Buck repeated. He sat and slowly slid down the steep incline.

Joan knew what he intended to do. She grabbed one of her knives and pulled it free from her belt.

"Drop it!" ordered the Troll with the bow. An arrow was notched, the string drawn, his bead on her chest. "Now!"

Joan reluctantly complied.

Buck reached the bottom and stood, leering at her, swinging his club back and forth. "I told you, bitch," he bragged, "I told you I'd get you for what you did to me." His busted nose was still swollen and discolored.

"Anytime," Joan said sweetly. One of the knives was hidden from their view, under her left arm. The Troll with the bow would probably nail her, but she would make sure she gutted Buck first.

Buck dropped the steel bar and began hiking his tunic above his thighs. "This is going to be fun," he told her.

"If you don't mind my saying so, pard," interjected another voice, "I reckon the lady would rather slurp horse piss than oblige the likes of you."

Joan twisted, craning her neck, her eyes

widening in disbelief, her pulse racing in relief. It
couldn't be!

It was.

He stood on the bank, smiling, his right arm
casually draped in front of his body, his left pressed
against his side.

The Trolls seemed flabbergasted.

"Kill him!" Buck found his voice, dropping his
tunic.

The Troll with the bow elevated the point of his
arrow, compensating for the distance, knowing
there was no way this stranger could draw his guns
before he loosed the shaft. He saw a blur and felt
something slam into his torso and he fell, the bow
and arrow tumbling from his limp fingers. The
string released, the shaft driving into the ground.

The Troll with the sword turned to run.

"Leaving our shindig so soon?" asked the gunman. He shot the second Troll in the back of the
head. "That leaves you." He swiveled, pointing the
Python in his right hand at the Troll with the broken
nose. His left Colt was still in its holster.

Buck backed away. "No, mister! Please! I don't
want to die!" he pleaded.

Joan struggled to her knees, her gaze fastened
on his face. "Hickok." She whispered the name, her
eyes brimming with love and tears.

"Please! Don't!" Buck held his hands in front of
his body, as if they could offer some protection from
the inevitable.

"You sure are a wimp, pard," Hickok stated.
The Python roared and Buck was slammed into the
drop-off, a red hole gaping in the center of his
forehead. "Never could abide wimps," Hickok commented, twirling the Colt into its holster. He
jumped from the bank and landed beside Joan.

"Howdy, ma'am," he said. "Can you use a lift?"

Joan sobbed and clutched at his legs.

Hickok dropped to one knee and held her. "Hey,

it's okay! I didn't realize. I'm here. You can let it all out."

The silence of the forest engulfed them as she quietly cried in his arms. Gradually, the birds and other wildlife resumed their daily activities, their patterns of living disrupted by the intruding humans and the shattering gunfire.

Blade and Geronimo appeared on the bank.

"So here you are," Geronimo said, the Browning in his hands.

"We heard the shots," Blade explained, the Commando at the ready.

"Thought maybe a wasp attacked you while you were relieving yourself," Gernonimo added. He moved to inspect the dead Trolls.

Blade walked over to Hickok and Joan. "Is she all right?"

Joan raised her tear-streaked countenance and nodded. "Just very tired and sore," she told him.

"Is Jenny with you?" Blade asked hopefully.

Joan shook her head. "Just me. I escaped to tell you the Trolls are heading east, to a place called Fox."

"We know," Hickok informed her.

"You know?"

"We caught one of the Trolls," Blade elaborated. "We prevailed upon him to tell us where you were being taken."

"Remind me sometime," Hickok said, squeezing her left shoulder, "to tell you how we did it. You might want to employ the technique yourself some day."

Geronimo joined them. "The Trolls are dead."

"Was there any doubt?" Hickok asked.

Blade stood, debating their next move. "We'll collect any weapons and toss them in the back of the SEAL. Joan, if you're not up to it, Hickok can take you to the Home and Geronimo and I will go to Fox to rescue the other women."

"I feel up to it," Joan declared.

"Are you sure?" Blade pressed her. "It looks like your right shoulder has been cut. You're completely bushed. We can manage without you."

Joan gritted her teeth and rose to her feet, Hickok by her side, supporting her. "I'm going with you, Blade. I'll have some time to rest up before we reach Fox. Did I hear you right? You're using that vehicle we dug up?"

Blade nodded.

"Even better. You won't really need me until we reach Fox." She paused. "I've got to go, Blade. I owe it to my sisters I deserted. . . ."

"You didn't desert them," Hickok quickly objected. "You did what you had to do."

"I still feel like a deserter," Joan said softly. "You must let me come with you."

Blade found three pairs of eyes focused on him, awaiting his decision. Instinctively, he wanted to send her back to the Home out of harm's way. But she was a Warrior; she knew the consequences. In addition, he did not know how many Trolls there were. Another good gun might come in handy. "Okay," he told them. "You come along. We'll need you."

Hickok hugged Joan. "Let's get you to the SEAL. I'll tend to your wound."

They trekked toward the transport, parked forty yards away to the west.

"How did you find me?" Joan asked Hickok as they walked arm in arm.

"By accident," Hickok explained. "It's like Geronimo said. I needed to relieve myself. Blade stopped, and I was watering this tree when I heard someone shouting and laughter. Naturally I came to investigate and found you."

"I'm glad you did." She stretched and pecked him on the cheek.

"These Trolls are going to pay for what they've

done," Hickok promised, his lips a compressed line. "I owe them."

Up ahead, Blade was fighting waves of sadness. Finding and rescuing Joan was great, but she reminded him so much of his beloved Jenny it hurt. Both were blondes; Jenny had green eyes, Joan blue; Jenny was inches shorter than Joan, but fuller of figure; Joan's facial features were broader, her frame more muscular; both women were attractive and intelligent. Every time he looked at Joan, he saw Jenny. Just what he needed to keep his mind on the matter at hand!

17

Morning on the third day after the assault on the Home.

Saxon raised his arm for the column to halt. They were on top of a sloping rise. Below them, a narrow valley meandered for a mile, ending in a cluster of buildings.

"Fox!" Saxon announced for the benefit of his wary captives.

Jenny peered at the distant town. They were almost there, and still no sign of any Warriors. Where were they? Had something happened to Blade? Was that the reason their rescue hadn't materialized?

The eleven Trolls and seven women tramped down the rise.

"At last!" one of the Trolls exclaimed. "Home at last!"

Saxon glanced at Jenny. "You women will get to rest tonight. You'll need it. Tomorrow is the testing for your services."

"What is this testing you go through?" Jenny asked, her curiosity piqued.

"Stupid woman!" Saxon guffawed. "It's you women who are tested, not us."

"What type of tests?"

"You'll see," was all Saxon would say.

The sun climbed as they crossed the verdant valley.

"I'm getting scared," Angela whispered.

Jenny smiled at her reassuringly. "We'll make it."

Shouts sounded in the town as they drew near. The Trolls had erected a wooden fence, encircling the northern half of Fox, with gates in the middle of each side. Faces, most of them bearded, appeared at the western gate and it was hastily flung open.

"Not as fancy as your big wall," Saxon said, indicating the fence as they approached, "but it and the fires keep the pus heads out."

"Pus heads?" Jenny repeated.

"You've got to know what the pus heads are," Saxon said. "They are all over the place. We saw one yesterday, remember?"

Jenny understood now. "We call them mutates."

"What?"

"Mutates."

"From now on," Saxon instructed her, "you will call them pus heads."

"If I don't?" Jenny defiantly countered.

"I'll feed you to Wolvie or Runt or Momma," he threatened her.

"Who are they?"

Saxon chuckled. "You'll see them soon enough."

Dozens of Trolls poured through the gate and surrounded the newcomers, many of them lecherously leering at the women.

"I think we're in big trouble," Mary stated.

The throng moved inside the fence and along several streets until they reached a paved square in the center of the town. A small platform was standing in the middle of the square. Saxon jumped onto the platform and held his arms aloft.

Silence descended.

"As promised," Saxon bellowed, "we have returned with more women!"

A great cheer went up among the assembled Trolls, mixed with clapping and whistling.

Saxon motioned and they quieted.

"I told you I would bring healthy females, and as always I have kept my word. Who leads you best?"

Slowly at first, with increasing frequency and volume, the massed Trolls chanted the name of their leader. "Sax-on! Sax-on! Sax-on!"

Saxon, Jenny saw, was eating up this adulation. She gazed at the buildings in their vicinity and noted their dilapidated condition. Cement was cracked, wood was warped, and trash and filth were everywhere. Didn't these people believe in sanitation?

"Tomorrow," Saxon shouted, "we will hold the tests to see how strong they are. Life to the strong and death to the weak!"

"Life to the strong and death to the weak!" most of the Trolls repeated.

Jenny abruptly realized only men were present. Where were the women? Surely the Trolls had more women!

"Many of our fellows did not come back." Saxon turned somber, pacing on the platform. "This Family is very strong. They have many guns! More guns than I ever saw! How would you like to get those guns?"

The Trolls went crazy at the prospect.

"I have a plan," Saxon told them. "When the time comes, we will attack their Home again, take their guns, and steal all of their women! Would you like that?"

A chorus of "Yes! Yes! Yes!" came from his cheering companions.

"I knew you would!" Saxon pointed at the women. "Lock them up until tomorrow morning. Then we will have our fun!"

The Trolls obeyed, three or four gripping each

woman, hauling them forcefully down another
avenue until they reached a three-story brick
building. Two Trolls, both armed with rifles, stood
guard outside a sturdy door.

Jenny, like the other women, found herself un-
ceremoniously shoved through the doorway. She
sprawled on her hands and knees on a rough
concrete floor, scraping her palms. The windows in
this putrid place were boarded over. Several candles,
placed in metal holders attached to the walls,
provided the sole illumination.

The door slammed shut behind them.

Angela was sniffling.

Jenny rose, removing the rope from around her
raw neck. She spotted other women, and children,
huddled along the walls.

"We're not alone," Ursa noted.

"Hello," Jenny addressed them. "My name is
Jenny."

No one responded. One child fearfully pressed
against her mom.

"We mean you no harm," Jenny assured them.
Her eyes were adjusting to the subdued lighting.
These women were a bedraggled and timid bunch,
attired in rags and animal skins, their hair unkempt,
their bodies slumped in an attitude of profound
despair. The children were the same. She counted
nineteen women and nine children.

"Did you say," spoke a squeaky, tiny voice,
"your name is Jenny?"

"I did." Jenny faced the direction the voice
came from, one of the darker corners of the room.

A shadow detached itself and came toward her.

"Who is it?" Angela asked fearfully.

"Quiet!" Lea shushed her.

"I knew a Jenny once," said the shadow, a
woman, as she limped across the floor. "It was in a
place I grew up, a wonderful, happy place called the
Home. . . ."

"The Home!" Jenny ran to the woman and gripped her by the shoulders, drawing her close to one of the candles.

The woman was old beyond her years, aged by hardship and wrinkled by torture. Her hair was gray, her eyes brown. She limped because her right foot was twisted at a right angle to her body.

"Who are you?" Jenny demanded. "We are from the Home too!"

Tears welled up in the older woman's eyes and she sagged.

"Help me!" Jenny directed, and Lea and Daffodil assisted her in gently lowering the older woman to the floor.

"I can't believe it. . . ." The older woman choked on her words. "I am so sorry!" She began crying, great racking sobs, her frail body trembling from the intensity of her emotion.

"It's all right," Jenny assured her.

"No," the older woman disagreed, "it isn't! You don't understand!"

"Understand what?"

"That you wouldn't be here if it weren't for me!" She rolled over, hiding her face, bawling.

"What does she mean?" Saphire asked.

"I don't know," Jenny replied. She raised the woman from the cold, dirty floor. "What did you mean by that?"

"I was the one who told them about the Home!"

"You did what?" Lea asked in an angry tone.

The gray-haired woman wept even louder.

Jenny, perplexed, held the woman's head in her lap and patiently waited for her to stop. There was something about this woman, a vague quality of familiarity.

"I have the feeling I know her," Ursa mentioned, confirming Jenny's intuition.

The poor woman cried and cried, but finally her tears subsided, her shaking stopped, and she grew quiet, wiping her forearms repeatedly across her nose.

The Family women surrounded her, while the other women in the dingy room kept their distance.

"Can you talk now?" Jenny inquired.

The woman nodded, sniffling.

"Good. Who are you?"

"Don't you recognize me?" her voice quavered.

"No." Jenny shook her head. "But I do feel like I should know who you are."

"I remember you," the woman stated proudly. "You're Jenny, the cute one who was always hanging around Blade."

"How did . . ." Jenny began to speak, but was cut short.

"And you," the weak woman said, looking at Lea, "are Lea. And Ursa. Saphire. Daffodil." She paused, smiling, pleased at her accomplishment. "But I don't know you two." She wagged a finger on her left hand at Mary and Angela.

The two youngest, Jenny mentally noted. "You still have not told us who you are," she reminded this stranger.

"My name," she hesitated, the words scarcely audible, "is Nadine."

Plato's wife! Jenny had known her, not intimately, but the two had conversed on occasion.

"You're Nadine?" Ursa asked skeptically. "Nadine disappeared about seven years ago."

"Yeah," Lea added. "Nadine had brown hair. She was a much younger woman than you appear to be."

"How do you know you're really Nadine?" Mary demanded.

Jenny glanced at the others, annoyed. "Give her a break! Who else would she be? Would another woman bawl her brains out like she just did? Who else would know our identities? A moment ago you said you thought you knew her," Jenny said to

Ursa.

"I'm sorry." Ursa frowned. "I didn't mean anything by doubting her. It's just that she looks so different."

Nadine smiled up at them. "That I do, child." She sighed, fussing with her hair, her bony fingers plucking at stray hairs and futilely endeavoring to shape them in some semblance of order. "You will look very different too, if the damn Trolls keep you for any length of time."

"Is that the reason you vanished?" Jenny probed. "The Trolls got you?"

Nadine sadly nodded. "It seems like ages ago. Plato and I were enjoying an outing, indulging his chronic curiosity. He went for firewood, and that's when two Trolls jumped me. They pinned my arms and one of them held his hand over my mouth. I struggled. . . ." She stopped, the memories almost too painful. "But they were too strong. They brought me here to Fox." Tears filled her eyes again. "And here I've languished for seven years. Seven years! You don't know how many times I've wished I had the courage to kill myself and end this terrible living nightmare!"

"You can't be serious," Ursa stated.

"Can't I?" Nadine said angrily.

"Why didn't you try to escape?" Mary, the Tiller, asked.

"Don't you think I haven't tried?" Nadine responded. "But the Trolls never leave the women alone, except in here when guards are posted outside. Women are too valuable to the Trolls. At least, until they reach a certain age."

"Where did these others come from?" Jenny glanced around the room.

"The same as you. They were kidnapped." Nadine struggled to a sitting posture. "The Trolls scour the countryside for females. The Home isn't the only inhabited center in this area."

"Why do the Trolls steal women?" Lea asked, leaning forward.

"It's a long story," Nadine replied.

"I think we've got the time," Jenny said. "Saxon told us we would be in here until our testing tomorrow, whatever that is."

Nadine unsuccessfully tried to suppress a groan.

"What's this testing business?" Saphire questioned.

"The Trolls put you through a series of tests designed to determine which of you is the fittest, which of you will make the best mates."

"I'll never mate with an ugly old Troll," Angela stated defiantly.

"If you don't, child," Nadine informed her, "then you will die a hideous death."

"I've noticed," Jenny observed, "all of the women in here are on the young side, with the exception of yourself."

Nadine nodded. "The Trolls only want young, healthy women. Once a woman reaches a certain age, in most cases, she's killed."

"What age is that?" Jenny asked.

"It's not a set age in years," Nadine answered. "The Trolls simply kill any woman when she becomes too old to handle servicing them any longer."

"Servicing?" Angela repeated.

"It's what they call it. I call it forced sexual bondage."

"But they haven't killed you," Jenny pointed out.

Nadine laughed. "It's certainly not because of my servicing skills! They keep me alive because I can read."

"Read?" Jenny repeated.

"Yes, read. Believe it or not, I am the only one in Fox who can read."

"They can't read?" Angela giggled.

"Where would they learn?" Nadine elaborated. "Where are the schools they attend? Organized education is virtually nonexistent. From what I have learned while here, the Family is a singular exception. Reading and writing are lost arts. When Saxon learned I could read, he was delighted. Incredibly, there is a brain in that hulking deviate. I'm alive today because Saxon decided I would instruct him. He's a pitiful student, but at least he doesn't molest me, and the other Trolls couldn't be bothered with an old hag like me."

"What about these women?" Jenny swept the room with her left hand.

"They're not as fortunate as I am," Nadine said softly. "Whenever a Troll wants them, any time of the day or night, they must . . . perform . . . or else."

"How disgusting!" Lea exclaimed.

"What else do they make you do?" Ursa, one of the Family Librarians, inquired. Kurt Carpenter had considered knowledge essential to the Family's survival; accordingly, selection as a Librarian was considered a high honor. Ursa was the heaviest of the Family women present. She wore her brown hair cropped close.

"We do," Nadine replied, "whatever the Trolls want us to do. We skin the game they kill and prepare their food. Every menial, servile job you can conceive of is entrusted to us." She pointed at one of the flickering candles. "We make their candles from animal fat, a messy, stinking operation if ever there was one."

"And if you refuse?" Jenny questioned her.

"What do you think?" Nadine responded.

"You said you're teaching Saxon to read," Ursa noted. "Read what? Do they have a library here?"

Nadine shook her head. "Just a few books and some old papers. Most flammable material has been utilized as fuel for their fires during the cold weather." She paused and glanced at the door. "A few of the papers I discovered were quite revealing. They provided a clue to the origin of the Trolls, if not their name."

"How do you mean?" Lea, the Weaver, asked.

"We know from the Family Library," Nadine explained, "a lot about the way of life before the Big Blast, about their social structure, their culture, or lack of it, their various institutions and general organization. For instance, we know they maintained facilities to contain the criminals, to restrain their insane, and to functionally integrate their mentally retarded. I've learned that shortly after the war, the state of Minnesota established a home for the retarded here in Fox, a very unique home. As part of a new program designed to convert criminals into productive members of the society through community indoctrination, the state set up this home for marginally retarded criminals. Its purpose, I've deduced, was to normalize these individuals by securing employment for them and allowing them to function in a quiet, rural setting."

"You think the Trolls came from this facility?" Daffodil deduced.

"Their descendents anyway," Nadine answered. "I don't know when they were first called the Trolls, or why. I did find one illuminating paper written by a man named Aaron, the head of the facility. Apparently the Government ordered an evacuation of the town and most people fled. A bus was to be sent from Minneapolis to pick up the criminals in his charge, but it never arrived. Aaron scribbled some notes on a piece of paper, steps he would take if help didn't eventually show up. One of the sentences could be the key to our current predicament."

"What was it?" Jenny asked.

"I have it memorized," Nadine said, quoting: " 'If we are left on our own, must find women. None left in town. *Must find women*!' "

Silence momentarily engulfed their little group. The door suddenly crashed open and a Troll stalked into the room.

"Are you all comfy?" He laughed.

No one else thought he was funny.

"Four of you will come with me," he barked, raising his right hand and pointing at four of the women standing near the right wall. "You and you and you and you. Move it!"

The women meekly complied, hastily departing.

The Troll looked at the Family members. "Get plenty of rest today and tonight, because you'll need your strength for the testing tomorrow." He grinned, pivoted, and walked to the door.

"I'm not looking forward to this testing business," Angela anxiously whispered.

"Oh, by the way." The Troll had stopped with his hand on the door. "I don't know if anyone has told you yet, but if you don't pass our tests tomorrow, you're in for a very nasty surprise. Sleep tight and don't let the bed bugs bite!" He cackled and exited, the door slamming behind him.

"Can't those bastards close a door quietly?" Ursa asked.

"What did he mean by that last comment?" Jenny glanced at Nadine.

"They haven't told you yet?" Nadine seemed surprised.

"No. Saxon mentioned feeding us to somebody called Wolvie, Runt, or Momma. Who are they?" Jenny noticed Nadine stiffen.

"They are not persons." Nadine gazed at each of them. "If you fail the tests, you will suffer the same fate as any woman who has outlived her usefulness to the Trolls." She paused, her face a pale, haunted visage.

"What will hapen to us if we fail?" Angela gripped Nadine's right shoulder.

Nadine stared into Angela's eyes. "You will be thrown, alive, into a pen of ravenous wolverines."

18

"This road makes our trip a lot easier," Geronimo commented. He was sitting in the front, in the passenger-side bucket seat. Blade was driving the SEAL. Hickok sat in the back seat, behind Blade, Joan's head cradled in his lap. She was stretched out on the seat, sound asleep.

"At least there aren't any trees," Blade admitted. They were cruising in a northeasterly direction on Highway 11, an artery the map referred to as a "principal paved route." Possibly, at one time, it was, but not now. The pavement was cracked and split, some sections completely buckled, grass and weeds growing in the fissures. A century of neglect had taken its toll. Blade carefully avoided a rut in the asphalt. Despite the damage nature had caused, the highway was still functional, probably because the road had not experienced any traffic for one hundred years. Traffic volume, Blade once read in the library, forced prewar societies to spend considerable portions of their budgets on highway repair each year.

"Badger should be just ahead," Geronimo stated while consulting the map.

Blade had to hand it to Geronimo. Their route had progressed exactly as he predicted. First, they had reached the stream and turned south. Within four miles the SEAL had burst through a thicket onto the highway and they had headed for the next town, a place called Greenbush. Joan had fallen asleep after Hickok had tended her wounds and bandaged her right shoulder. Seeing them so happy, so content to be together, had made Blade feel uncomfortable, reminding him of Jenny's absence and her dilemma.

Greenbush had been a monumental disappointment. Uninhabited, in utter disrepair, the buildings decayed, the vegetation reclaiming the land, it was an eerie reminder of life before the Big Blast.

"Sure is pitiful," Hickok had commented.

Blade had decided to head straight to Badger. He couldn't see any sound reason for stopping to explore Greenbush, and time was too crucial.

Nine miles had elapsed.

"There it is," Geronimo pointed.

Blade braked.

The buildings of Badger were visible, interspersed with numerous tall trees.

"From here," Geronimo observed, "it looks as run down as Greenbush."

"Let's find out." Blade gunned the engine. "Roll up your window," he advised Geronimo, a precautionary measure to prevent anyone from shooting them or hurling a projectile into the transport. Plato claimed the body of the SEAL could withstand a gunshot blast at close range.

"Somebody is home," Geronimo said.

Blade saw it too. Gray smoke was curling skyward.

"If they turn out to be Trolls," Hickok spoke up, "they're all mine."

Blade glanced in the mirror at Hickok's granite features. He was worried about the gunman, concerned for his friend. After Joan had drifted into slumber, while tenderly stroking her hair, Hickok had become uncharacteristically quiet and reflective. Blade would look back and see Hickok's lips compressed, his blue eyes hard. He could

imagine what the gunman was thinking, even understand and condone it, but the reprecussions could be
deadly for Hickok and those with him. Sheer blood
lust made a person reckless, heedless of his personal
safety, oblivious to everything but revenge.

Hickok wanted revenge.

The SEAL slowly entered the outskirts of
Badger. The structures here were similar to those in
Greenbush: gradually disintegrating, windows
shattered and doors off their hinges, the concrete
and brick buildings in better shape than the wooden-
frame houses.

"There!" Geronimo spotted the source of the
smoke.

Approximately fifty yards ahead, in the middle
of the highway, was a raging fire, the blaze con-
suming a neatly stacked pile of dry wood.

"This doesn't read right," Geronimo warned
Blade.

"I know." Blade braked the vehicle. It made no
sense. Who would build a fire in the center of the
road? More importantly, why? On a hot day like
today!

"Let's take the bait," Geronimo recommended,
twisting in his seat to retrieve the Browning. The
shotgun was leaning against the back of his bucket
seat.

"Should I wake Joan?" Hickok asked Blade.

"No need," Blade answered. "She's been through
an ordeal. You stay in the SEAL with her." He
shifted into Park and switched the motor off. "I'm
leaving the keys in the ignition," he said over his
shoulder. "If something should happen to us . . ."
He left the sentence unfinished.

"Understood," Hickok said.

Geronimo opened his door and slid out of the
transport. He glanced back at Hickok, grinning.
"You two try and behave yourselves while we're
away, okay?"

"Cute, pard," Hickok rejoined. "Real cute. You be careful, okay?"

Geronimo hefted the Browning. "They'll never know what hit them!"

"Don't forget!" Hickok advised. "Try for a head shot."

Geronimo was about to close the door. Instead, he opened it and leaned inside. "That reminds me," he mentioned. "When I was checking the Trolls you blew away, I found one shot through the heart. What happened? You suffer a memory lapse?"

Hickok smiled. "Nope. He was carrying a bow, and from where I stood it covered part of his face. So I went for a heart shot. I never said the head rule was chiseled in concrete."

Geronimo chuckled and closed the door.

Blade was waiting for him several yards in front of the transport, the Commando in his hands.

"How do we play this?" Geronimo inquired as he joined Blade.

"The direct approach," Blade ordered. He began slowly walking along the left side of the highway, while Geronimo did likewise on the right. Tumbled-down houses bordered Highway 11 at this point. Blade, analyzing the setup, spotted the probable ambush site. On his side of the road, directly across from the fire, was a crumbling brick wall. On Geronimo's side, again across from the blaze, was the rusted hulk of a large vehicle. Perfect positioning for a bushwhacking, as Hickok might say.

Blade pretended to concentrate on the fire, the Commando hanging slack in his arms, his senses alert, his nerves tingling.

Movement.

Blade wanted to smile. Whoever these people were, they lacked skill and training. He had seen someone move in the second-floor window of a house behind the brick wall.

Geronimo was keeping his eyes on the wrecked remains of what appeared to be a former bus.

What were they waiting for? Blade wondered. The fire was now only ten yards away.

A woman suddenly jumped up from behind the brick wall, a bow in her hands, the string already drawn, pivoting for a shot.

Blade was faster. He crouched, leveling the Commando, aiming for the top of the wall and not the woman. The Carbine bucked as he pulled the trigger, the bullets biting into the lip of the brick wall, spraying dust and chunks of brick in every direction.

The woman, startled, dropped from sight.

Geronimo's Browning boomed twice as a youth stepped into view, a spear in his right hand. The shots hit the bus near the youth's head, forcing him to leap to safety behind the bus again.

Blade saw a gray-haired man stand erect in the second floor window of the house behind the wall. The glass in the window had long since disappeared. The man held a rifle, but it was obvious he entertained little enthusiasm for using it. He was gaping at Blade and Geronimo, his mouth open, his brown eyes wide in surprise and disbelief.

Blade covered him with the Commando anyway.

"Don't shoot, mister!" yelled the woman behind the brick wall. "Don't shoot anymore!"

"Hold your fire!" the man in the window shouted. "We mean you no harm!"

"You've got a funny way of showing it," Blade countered. "Get down here on the double," he commanded. "Hold your rifle above your head when you come out the front door or I'll blow you away!"

The man nodded and vanished.

"And you!" Blade faced the wall. "Stand up with your hands in the air. Now!"

The woman, actually a girl in her late teens, did as he instructed. She had blue eyes and brown hair, worn cut off at the shoulders. The clothes she was wearing were tattered rags.

"You too!" Geronimo called to the boy behind the bus. "Leave the spear and step out. Now!"

The youth reluctantly emerged from hiding, his arms upraised. He wore torn jeans and a ragged brown shirt. His hair, like the girl's, was snipped at the shoulders, the brown strands oily. His brown eyes glared at Geronimo.

"You!" Blade gestured at the girl with the Commando barrel. "Get on this side of the wall."

She promptly obeyed, clambering through a gaping hole in the waist high wall.

"And you!" Blade looked at the boy. "Get over here."

The youth arrogantly shuffled across the highway.

"Move it!" Blade barked, swinging the Carbine to cover him.

The boy paled and increased his speed.

The elderly man stepped from the ramshackle house, the rifle held aloft.

Blade brought the Commando around and kept it trained on the man as he crossed a weed-choked yard and climbed through the hole in the wall.

"Lay the gun on the ground. Slowly," Blade ordered.

The man complied. All three were lined in a row: the scared girl, the haughty boy, and the bewildered man, their arms upraised.

"Looks like the posse collared some vicious outlaws," Hickok wryly commented behind Blade. "Might be the James Gang."

Blade glanced over his right shoulder. Hickok and Joan were just feet away, Joan carrying the Henry.

"I thought I told you to let her sleep," Blade said to Hickok.

"I was going to, pard," Hickok chuckled, "but

your Commando alarm clock woke her up."

Blade faced the amateur assassins. "Who wants to do the talking?"

"I have something I'd like to say," the boy with the oily hair said angrily.

"What?" Blade demanded.

The youth glanced at the man. "I told you, asshole, they were not Trolls, but *no*! The day you listen to me is the day I die of a heart attack!"

"You mind that tongue of yours," the old man retorted testily.

"Papa!" the girl chimed in. "Can't you two stop your fighting for a minute! At a time like this! These men may kill us!"

"No, I don't think so." The man shook his gray head, his eyes twinkling.

"And why wouldn't we kill you?" Blade asked him.

"You ain't natural killers like the damn Trolls." The man looked directly into Blade's eyes. "You could of killed my girl with that machinegun of yours, but you didn't. And your friend could of killed my son with that cannon of his, but he didn't. Nope. Somethin' tells me you won't kill us in cold blood." He paused, eyeing the Carbine with open appreciation. "What is that thing, mister? Never saw a gun like that in all my born days!"

"It's called a Commando Arms Carbine," Blade told him, amused.

"They were factory shipped as semi-auto," Hickok added, "but we converted it to full auto."

"What's that mean?" the man wanted to know.

"It means it can shoot a lot of bullets real fast, old-timer," Hickok responded.

"My name is Clyde, sir. This is my daughter, Cindy. And this contrary pup is my son, Tyson."

"Why did you attempt to kill us?" Blade queried.

"I thought you was Trolls," the old man replied,

and the boy made a loud snorting sound.

"You don't love the Trolls much, I take it," Hickok said.

"Sure as hell don't, mister!" Clyde exploded, his face reddening. "The damn Trolls should all be killed, and that's no lie! For years and years they've been after my family. Long time ago they took my dear Bess, the Lord bless her soul. We never know when some of them bastards might try and sneak up on us and take my Cindy. So far, though," Clyde said, laughing, "we been too smart for 'em! Even killed a few in our time. They're not too bright."

"You live here?" Blade gazed at the deteriorated buildings in their vicinity.

"We hole up where we can," Clyde said sadly. "Used to have a farm south of here a ways. My granddad owned it. But the Trolls discovered us. We've been runnin' and hidin' ever since."

"Why didn't you move away from here?" Geronimo chimed in. "Away from the Trolls?"

"Because he's too proud," Cindy answered.

"Too stupid," Tyson amended.

"Watch your mouth, boy!" Clyde fumed.

Hickok walked up to Blade and winked. "So what are we going to do with the James Gang here? Line them up against the wall and execute them?"

"Please! Don't!" the girl screeched, taking him seriously.

"Let me think." Blade studied the three, debating. What should they do with them? Leave them here, in effect banish them to a miserable life, a furtive existence of constant conflict with the Trolls? Clyde, apparently, wanted to retaliate against the Trolls for taking his wife. But what about the girl and the boy? Was this the type of life they should live? Never knowing a roof over their heads, never feeling safe and truly happy?

Cindy was staring at Joan. "You sure have pretty clothes, if you don't mind my saying so."

"You call these pretty?" Joan looked at her torn, dirty blouse and jeans. "You should see some of the clothes the women wear at the Home."

"The Home?" Cindy repeated.

"It's where we live," Joan informed her. "We make our own apparel or mend the garments still around from the time of the Big Blast."

"Big Blast?" Clyde reiterated.

"Clyde," Blade interrupted, "I have a deal for you."

"A deal?"

"You say you don't like the Trolls. . . ."

"You got that right!" Clyde confirmed.

"Neither do we. What do you know about Fox?"

"That's their filthy den. We've snuck up on 'em a couple of times and done in a few of 'em." Clyde cackled delightedly.

"So you're familiar with Fox?" Blade pressed him.

"I've seen it from the outside," Clyde said. "I've never been inside. No one goes inside and ever comes out again."

"At least you know the area. Here's my offer." Blade lowered the Carbine and stepped over to Clyde. "You help us rescue some friends from the Trolls, and after this is over you can come and live with us at our Home. What do you say?"

"I don't know. . . ." Clyde bit his lower lip, his brow furrowed.

"Oh please!" Cindy exclaimed, excited at the prospect. "Please! These are nice people, Papa. You said so, yourself. Please!"

"How do we know we can trust 'em?" Tyson asked suspiciously.

"You don't trust 'em?" Clyde asked his son.

"Nope."

"Then I know they can be trusted." Clyde beamed at his own wit and nodded twice. "You got a deal, mister."

"Good," Blade smiled.

"Say, pard." Hickok was grinning at Blade.

"What?"

"If these fine folks are coming with us," Hickok said casually, "don't you reckon they can lower their arms now?"

19

Their testing was about to commence.

The Trolls, approximately five dozen, most wearing the usual bearskin tunic and cloak, were assembled on a small field at the east edge of Fox. The area had been cleared of rocks and debris, and the grass and weeds were cut within six inches of the ground. The Trolls surrounded the center of the field, enthused over the imminent entertainment, talking loudly and making wagers, bartering over the projected outcome of the tests.

In the middle of the cleared tract, nervous and frightened, stood the Family women. Saxon and Nadine stood nearby.

"I'm so scared," Angela commented.

Jenny hated to admit it, but she was too. She studied the other women, gauging their state of mind, assessing their stability. Angela, the youngest and the smallest, was obviously petrified and would require watching. Daffodil, the Artist, seemed unconcerned. Lea, the Weaver, was absently fussing with her long black tresses, scowling at the Trolls. Ursa, the Librarian, was thoughtfully preoccupied. Mary, the tanned young Tiller, was in the best physical condition, the result of her long hours in the field. Saphire was glancing this way and that, her brunette hair bobbing, dismay plainly etched on her features.

Nadine joined the clustered women, limping painfully.

"Be brave," she encouraged them. "I survived this. You can too."

"I meant to ask you," Jenny said, hoping to divert their attention from the impending tests. "What happened to your right leg?"

Nadine grimaced and jerked her right thumb in Saxon's direction. "He did it, the slime!"

"What?"

"He wanted information about the Home," Nadine said wistfully. "I refused, so he tortured me."

"The prick!" Lea voiced her opinion.

"Indeed," Nadine agreed. "He broke the bone and it reset improperly. I've had this limp ever since."

"Oh, you poor dear!" Ursa said.

"He wasn't so smart." Nadine grinned. "I didn't tell him everything about the Home. Was he surprised to find so many guns?"

"He mentioned that, yes." Jenny laughed.

"Good." Nadine giggled. "I just wish our Warriors had killed all of them."

"They may yet," Mary reminded her.

"Do you think Joan reached them?" Nadine asked. Jenny had told her about Joan's escape the night before.

"If anyone could do it, Joan could," Jenny assured her.

"It's so far, though." Nadine squinted at the morning sun. "The only reason the Trolls waited so long to attack the Home was the distance involved. Too many mutates and other creatures. They usually confine their forays to a twenty- or thirty-mile radius, although sometimes they do make longer trips. Once, years ago, they went north, deep into Canada."

"Canada?" Jenny wanted to ask further questions, but she was prevented by Saxon's approach.

"Hope you all had a good rest." Saxon, in a cheerful mood, laid his expansive right hand on Jenny's left shoulder. She moved away. "Did you like your morning meal?"

"That slop?" Lea sarcastically cracked. "You've got to be kidding!"

"Sorry to hear that. I told them to make an extra effort, to make something you'd like. I'll need to punish the women who made your meal."

"No need for that," Jenny told him. "The meal was fine. We all like rabbit."

"You lied to me?" Saxon frowned at Lea. "It's not nice to lie to Saxon."

"The tests!" one of the Trolls yelled. "The tests!"

Saxon swiveled, scanning the encircling Trolls. "My brothers, it is time! Life to the strong and death to the weak!"

The Trolls responded in chorus: "Life to the strong and death to the weak!" Over and over and over.

Jenny remembered a conversation with Nadine in the early morning hours concerning the origin of the Trolls. Apparently, after Aaron was killed by a mutate, the criminals were left to their own devices. All of them were men. Naturally they wanted women. One of the brightest apparently found a paper Aaron wrote, detailing the wisest course to pursue with respect to mating between the retarded criminals in his charge and possible wives. Aaron knew his charges were genetically inferior. He realized their only hope of sustained existence as a viable community depended on finding women of normal or superior capacity. Aaron never advocated abducting women; he fully expected the criminals to die out in due course.

"You will stand over there," Saxon told Nadine, pointing to the sidelines. "I only let you come to show you that Saxon is not all bad. I want another lesson later," he added as Nadine dutifully shuffled away.

The Trolls were quiet now.

"We begin!" Saxon declared. "Line up here." He pointed at a wooden stake in the ground near his sandaled feet. All of the Trolls wore sandals constructed from deer hide. The exposed skin was caked with grime, blistered and gouged.

The seven women did as they were ordered.

"See the stake over there?" Saxon indicated another stake imbedded in the dirt twenty-five yards distant. "When I say go, you will run to that stake, around it, and come back to this one. Any questions?"

"What do we win if we're first?" Lea quipped.

"You stay alive," Saxon said somberly.

The assembled Trolls were waiting.

"Get set," Saxon prepared them. "Go!" he shouted.

The women ran, swiftly covering the distance, Mary in the lead, Jenny, Lea, Saphire, and Daffodil in a pack behind her, followed by Ursa and Angela.

As they rounded the far stake, Jenny glanced over her soulder and saw Angela trip and fall, smashing her elbows as she came down. The Trolls were cheering and boosting their favorites. Jenny ignored them and wheeled, running to Angela and assisting her to stand.

Some of the Trolls began booing.

Saxon advanced across the field.

The other women slowed, apprehensively watching Saxon.

"Are you all right?" Jenny asked Angela.

"I think so," Angela answered. "My elbows hurt."

"Just what the hell do you think you're doing?" Saxon queried as he reached them.

"I was only helping. . . ." Jenny turned to explain, completely unprepared for the fist Saxon buried in her stomach. She doubled over, wheezing.

"You don't help the others!" Saxon leaned over her, glowering. "That's not the way it works! We only want the best. You let the others worry about how they do, and worry about yourself. Understand?"

Jenny nodded, struggling to control her quaking body.

"Good!" Saxon straightened. "When you're better, we run the race again. And this time . . ." He paused to stare at each of the women. "No one helps anyone else."

After Jenny recovered, Saxon lined them up again. "Remember what I told you," he growled before starting the race. "Go!"

Angela lost.

Next, the Trolls produced a ten-foot length of stout rope. A woman would grab an end, Saxon would stand in the center of the rope, and the two women would heave and pull until one of them was hauled past Saxon. By elimination, the Trolls determined the relative physical strengths of each woman, from the strongest to the weakest.

Angela was the weakest.

The third test was a series of calisthenics, Saxon simply goading them until they dropped.

Angela dropped first.

"Stay here!" Saxon directed the weary, sweating women.

Jenny, sitting on the ground like the rest, watched him cross the field and consult with a trio of Trolls. She was bothered by her intuition; she felt something dreadful was about to take place.

Saxon returned, smiling, the benevolent despot. "On your feet, now! We're going for a little walk. We have a surprise for you."

The Trolls closed in on the women, forming a human barrier, the stench of their collective odor almost overpowering.

"I think I might puke," Lea announced.

"If you do," Jenny recommended, "puke on the Trolls."

Saxon led the crowd across the field, into Fox, past ruined buildings, houses trashed by Trolls seeking plunder or wood for their winter fires, and along remarkably preserved streets. In the decade prior to the Third World War, Fox, like many other rural towns, had experienced an upswelling in population as thousands of city dwellers left the nightmare of urban living for a peaceful rural setting. Crime had shot up astronomically in those last years, citizens had been inordinately taxed, and public services had deteriorated to minimal levels.

A large wooden structure was their destination. Saxon entered through two huge swinging doors, the women close behind him, the argumentative Trolls jostling one another in their eagerness to squeeze inside.

Jenny searched her memory of the books in the Family library, but she could not recall any reference to a building such as this. Rows of bleachers rose along all four walls, practically to the roof. The center of the floor was occupied by a square arena, or pen, with walls ten feet high. Access to this enclosed area was gained via two sturdy gates, one in the north wall and one in the south.

Saxon motioned for the women to follow as he climbed the steps of the bleachers, the wood warped and split, in need of a thorough repair job. When they were as close to the pen as they could get, and above the ten-foot wall, Saxon told them to be seated.

Nadine was with them. She maneuvered through the Trolls and sat next to Jenny.

"Have you any idea what this was?" Jenny asked.

"Not for sure," Nadine admitted. "I've

speculated it might have been a cattle pen, or
auction area, or even an arena for holding some type
of entertainment, like a small rodeo, but I just don't
know."

Jenny noted they were sitting directly above
the gate in the south wall of the pen. The floor of the
pen was bare earth. She detected patches of white
here and there, littered all over the dirt floor. What
were they? she wondered. She leaned forward for a
better look, then recoiled, shocked at her grisly
discovery. May the Spirit preserve them! Those pale
things were bones! Human bones!

Saxon was still standing, watching, waiting for
the Trolls to finish filing into the building. He
glanced down at the women. "You did well this
morning," he told them.

Nadine knew the nature of the next episode,
realized she could not prevent it from happening,
and averted her eyes in shame.

The Family women were edgy, aware an un-
pleasant event was going to transpire, but uncertain
of how it would unfold, unsure of what action they
should take.

Jenny looked at Angela, recalling Nadine's
words: "You will be thrown, alive, into a pen of
ravenous wolverines." Angela apparently remembered the warning too, because she was deathly
pale, her tiny hands gripping the edge of the
bleacher. What can I do? Jenny asked herself. What
could she possibly do to stop Angela from being
killed? There had to be something!

Saxon grinned. "Now we come to the best part
of the day." He paced back and forth in front of the
women as he addressed them. "Some of you might
be wondering what this is all about," he said,
unaware Nadine had divulged the terrible secret of
the bone-filled pen. "I'm going to tell you."

Jenny focused her attention on the gate in the
north wall, positioned opposite the bleachers they

were in. That gate was closed, but she knew it would be the means of ingress for the star attractions.

"More years ago than any Troll can remember, a raiding party went north into new territory," Saxon was saying, still pacing. "They did not find women, but they found something much better. A pus head and an animal Trolls had never seen before fought each other. Both died. When the raiding party found them, the two were dead. But close to the body of this dead animal were two young. Our men caught them and brought them back to Fox." Saxon observed Jenny was not paying attention, and paused. "Are you listening to me?" he asked her.

Jenny, preoccupied with reflections on Angela's impending fate, nervously glanced up at him. "Of course," she assured the giant.

"Good. You must learn from this." Saxon turned, continuing his measured back-and-forth walk.

The Trolls were quiet now, waiting, expectant.

"We didn't know what these animals were called, not until Nadine joined us. We did learn these animals are strong, the toughest animals anywhere, tough like the Trolls. We have a saying. You've heard it. Life to the strong and death to the weak." Saxon said the words proudly. "The Trolls must be strong, not weak. We do not want weak Trolls." He stared at the women. "We do not want weak females either."

From across the pen, behind the north gate, came a throaty growl.

Saxon grinned devilishly. It was time! "The Trolls wear the hide of the bear," he stated, drawing out the suspense, savoring their manifest fear. "Our bearskins are a mark of our courage, our strength. A Troll must prove himself to get the bear hide, must show himself worthy. I don't want you to think the Trolls are unfair." He stopped, his body inches from Angela, his hands draped behind his back.

The growling was louder.

Saxon nodded his head at the north gate. "Those animals we caught mated. Several litters have been born since then. The first pair are long dead. The don't seem to hold up well in captivity, and it's hard finding enough food for them. They can't get enough. Lucky for them, and us, we found a way to feed them and rid ourselves of weak ones at the same time. Would you like to see how?"

The women's eyes were riveted on the north gate. The animal behind it was scratching on the wood, hungrily pushing against the gate, attempting to force it open. The gate was secured with a metal latch on the pen side. A rope, tied to the latch, hung from the hands of a Troll in the bleachers immediately above the entry.

"Life to the strong and death to the weak!" Saxon suddenly shouted.

The Trolls, on cue, responded: "Life to the strong and death to the weak!"

Without warning, Saxon spun, grabbed Angela by her shoulders, bodily lifted her from her seat, and tossed her into the pen.

Ursa, Saphire, and Mary screamed.

Angela landed hard, tumbling into the dirt. She gamely jumped to her feet, aware of pain in her left ankle.

Saxon made a waving motion with his right hand.

The Troll with the rope flicked his wrists and the latch opened. Snarling, a male wolverine bounded into the arena.

Jenny, without really realizing what she was doing, leaped up and vaulted over the top of the pen wall.

An instant later, from the west side of the pen, a large Troll with a Bowie knife in his left hand followed suit, as two more wolverines charged through the north gate.

20

Hours earlier, three Trolls departed Fox on a hunting trip, bearing north. Two of the Trolls carried bows, the third a Ruger 77 bolt-action rifle.

Blade, hidden in a strand of trees a hundred yards from the fence, saw them leave and promptly backed into the underbrush, putting more distance between the town and himself, insuring any watchers in Fox would not detect any movement as he turned north and went in pursuit of the hunting party.

This was the break he was waiting for!

Hickok, Geronimo, Joan, and the three from Badger—Cyde, Cindy, and Tyson—were with the SEAL. The transport was parked a mile west of Fox, hidden in the woods at the side of the highway. They had stopped there for the night, safe, though crowded, from prowling predators. Blade had decided to get a good night's rest, and make their move on Fox the next morning. During the early morning hours before sunrise, as he slept fitfully, he formed a plan. At daybreak, after issuing final instructions to Hickok and Geronimo, he carefully crept as close to the Troll camp as he dared. The first part of his scheme involved getting into Fox undetected. Unfortunately, he had to leave the Commando with Hickok. The Carbine would attract undue attention if he carried it into Fox. The Trolls had guns, but he seriously doubted they owned any firearm similar to the exclusive Commando.

Now, as he jogged in a northerly direction, hoping to reach a vantage point ahead of the Trolls, he worried about Jenny. Was she still alive? The situation, he reflected, was ironic. Only days ago, at the prospect of his leaving the Home for the Twin Cities, Jenny had cried in his arms as he offered words of encouragement. With her gone, he now appreciated how useless his optimistic outlook had probably sounded.

The forest northwest of the town was relatively thick, the ground level. He made good time, dodging trees and bushes, his moccasins absorbing most of the noise as he ran. The Bowies jiggled against his hips and the Vega holsters flapped as he moved. He was wearing a green shirt for camouflage and faded jeans.

To insure success, he wanted to be at least a mile from Fox when he jumped the Trolls. If there were a struggle, if the Troll with the rifle managed to bring his weapon into play, anyone in Fox might assume the hunting party had bagged a deer.

He hoped.

The sun was already high and hot, sweat coating his body.

Blade was surprised when the forest abruptly ended. A hill, covered with boulders, rose in his path. He spotted a well-worn trail weaving up the hill to his right and he swerved, running at his maximum speed, alert for any sounds behind him, aware the Trolls couldn't be far behind. A third of the way up the slope he found the location he sought, and he ducked behind a massive slab of stone.

None too soon.

Moments later, the three Trolls emerged from the trees. They were using the trail, engaged in animated conversation.

". . . . miss the testing! It isn't fair!" The Troll with the Ruger was speaking.

"It's your fault," the tallest of the Trolls reminded him.

"Yeah," agreed the other. "You're the one who made Saxon angry. You knew he wanted the blonde."

"What an idiot!" the tall Troll snapped.

"How was I supposed to know Saxon was standing behind me when I said it?" protested Ruger. "I don't have eyes in the back of my head, you know."

"You don't have brains in your head either," grumped the third Troll.

"Saying you wanted the blonde first!" The tall Troll laughed. "Dumb! Dumb! Dumb!"

"Because of you," the third Troll said, pressing his compliant, "we'll miss the testing and the feeding. Just because we were talking to you!"

"So Saxon sends us after game!" The tall Troll was obviously disgusted with the state of affairs. "Some day Saxon will go too far!"

"Don't let him hear you say that," Ruger advised.

"I hate hunting," the tall Troll, walking behind Ruger and their companion as they climbed the hill, groused. "It's so damn boring!"

Blade, perched on top of the slab of stone, grinned and launched himself into the air, catching the Trolls off guard, slamming into the first Troll and bowling him over, knocking him against the two following on his heels. All three Trolls tumbled to the hard ground.

"Look out!" one of the Trolls shouted as he fell.

Blade had calculated his leap, landing on his right shoulder on a patch of grass, rolling and coming to his feet with his Bowie knives drawn and ready.

The first Troll was nearest, on his hands and knees, pushing erect, his bow lying out of reach.

Blade buried his left Bowie in the Troll's throat,

crimson gushing over his arm. He released the knife, the terrified Troll frantically clutching at his destroyed neck.

Ruger was already on his feet, the rifle in his hands, hurriedly drawing the bolt back, chambering the next round.

Blade reached him in one bound, kicking his right leg up and out, battering the rifle aside. He swung the right Bowie in a wide arc, again going for the neck, feeling the keen edge bite deep as it severed the windpipe.

The tall Troll was coming at Blade, a knife held low in his left hand. "You bastard!" he screamed. "I'll gut you!"

Blade gauged the distance, performing a feat he'd practiced countless times, sweeping his right arm all the way back, then forward, putting his entire body into the throw, the Bowie covering the three feet between them and imbedding in the Troll's chest, penetrating the heart.

The Troll, stunned, stopped, staring in amazement at the hilt of the knife. He glanced at Blade, grinning weakly. "Neat trick," he commented, before falling on his face.

Blade surveyed his handiwork. The tall Troll was still, but Ruger and the other were flopping and jerking spasmodically.

His plan was coming together nicely.

Blade bent over the tall Troll and removed his tunic and cloak, his nose balking at the rank odor from the Troll's body. Didn't the Trolls believe in bathing? He retrieved his Bowies, wiped the blades on the green grass, replaced them in their sheaths, removed his belt, and placed the big knives on the ground. Now came the hard part. Holding his breath, he pulled the tunic on over his broad shoulders, squirming as much from the tight fit as the stench. He adjusted the bear hide as best he could, rolling his pants up his legs until the jeans were obscured by the tunic. Next, he donned the cloak, fixing the Vega holsters so the guns were over the tunic but under the cloak. He strapped the Bowies around his waist, then removed the dagger from his calf and the one from his wrist and tucked them under his belt, out of sight. He was ready.

The trail the Trolls were following was apparently one used frequently by other Trolls over the years. It was clearly defined, enabling Blade to easily return along it to Fox. He reached an open area between the woods and the north fence and hesitated, hoping his disguise would hold up under close scrutiny. Lowering his head, he walked across the field, keeping his eyes on the fence, heading for the gate in the center of the barricade. What if there was a password? he wondered. What would he do then?

The sun was scorching the earth, rising in the morning sky.

Blade stopped at the gate, looking both ways, expecting to be challenged by guards.

He couldn't believe it!

The gate was unattended.

Maybe, he reflected as he opened the rickety wooden gate and stepped through the portal, the Trolls felt secure in Fox, exactly as the Family believed they were safe in the Home before the Trolls showed them the error of their ways. Possibly no one had ever attacked Fox.

Blade paused, studying the decayed structures, listening. He knew Fox was crawling with Trolls; he'd seen them earlier when he was spying, waiting for his opportunity to nab a bearskin. So where were they at now?

In the distance, from the east, came a great shout and the sound of cheering.

"What in the world?

Blade turned, making for the uproar. The streets were completely deserted. He could scarcely credit his good fortune. Whatever was distracting the Trolls was a godsend. Thank the Spirit!

One of the buildings drew his attention.

Blade walked to the front door, puzzled. Unlike the others, this edifice displayed signs of modest repair efforts. The door was intact, the windows covered with crude curtains. A hole in the wall was boarded over. Why? Why this one building only?

Fox was still devoid of life.

Blade opened the door and entered, carefully waiting for his eyes to adapt to the subdued light before he closed the door and stepped across the room, startled to discover a desk and two chairs neatly arranged against the far wall. Someone, evidently, was utilyzing this office on a regular basis. But who? And for what purpose?

On the oaken desk, meticulously stacked in separate piles, were several books and papers.

Blade picked up the papers and moved closer to one of the windows. These papers were written by someone named Aaron, random notes about a facility he operated and criminals he was rehabilitating. Several entries were fascinating: one concerning the evacuation and the failure of their transportation to arrive, and another detailing the prospects of survival for Aaron's charges if they could not relocate or find women. One item, in particular, stood out like the proverbial sore thumb: "If we are left on our own, must find women. None left in town. *Must find women!*"

Blade leaned against the wall, insight flooding his mind. Now, at least, he understood the origin of the Trolls and comprehended their motivation for stealing women. One detail still eluded him, however. Why were they called Trolls? He walked to the desk and set the papers in their original position.

Outside, all was quiet.

Blade sorted through the books, seven in all. The majority dealt with psychology: *Abnormal*

Psychology, Experimental Psychology, Psychological Testing, Current Psychotherapies, Counseling, Adjustment and Mental Health, and something titled *My Nympho Aunt*. Four drawers fronted the desk. He crouched, opening each drawer, discovering more papers, pencil stubs, and dusty paper clips. In the lower right drawer, hidden in the back under a pile of papers, was another book. There was a candle on the desk, unlit, and he wasn't about to light it even if he could. Too risky. He stood and returned to the nearest window, holding the thin book aloft to catch the available light.

There was the subdued sound of a commotion to the east, slowly drawing closer.

Blade grinned, amused by his latest find. It was a child's book, the cover torn, the pages ragged, entitled *The Three Billy Goats Gruff*. He couldn't recall this one being in the Family library. The book was cutely illustrated, and he flipped the pages, reading the simple print. When he came to the first mention of the troll, he paused, astonished. "It can't be," he inadvertently muttered.

But it was.

The plot was straightforward enough. Three billy goats wanted to cross a bridge. Under this bridge lived a nasty troll. The troll was not inclined to allow anyone across *his* bridge. The first two billy goats tricked the troll into permitting them to pass. But the third goat, the biggest and the strongest, confronted the troll and defeated him, strolling across the bridge. On the page where the goat beat the troll, scribbled in childlike print, faint, almost indistinguishable, were some personal comments added by a reader long, long ago: "*Stupid book. The troll should have won. It was his bridge!*"

Blade lowered the book, musing. Was it possible? Was this kid's book the key to the Trolls' identity? His imagination rambled. Had one of the early occupants of the state facility liked this book, and for whatever bizarre reason identified with the troll? Had this person prevailed upon his fellows to call themselves the Trolls? Possibly, after Aaron's demise, this criminal assumed the mantle of leadership.

"We'll just never know for sure," Blade said to himself.

An abrupt clamor came from the surrounding streets.

Blade tossed the book onto the desk and quickly crossed to the door. What was going on? He eased the door open several inches and peered out.

A great mass of Trolls was moving down one of the streets, talking and laughing.

Blade's curiosity was aroused. He saw them enter a large building and disappear. Were the Trolls holding a meeting? This required further investigation. He slipped outside, shut the door, and walked toward a building with two swinging doors, each twenty feet high and half as wide. Why so big? he wondered. Probably, before the war, machinery and vehicles had utilized it as an entry and exit point.

Somewhere, a bird was chirping.

Blade reached the swinging doors, glanced both ways, and entered the structure. He memorized the layout, his tactical training ingrained, noting the packed bleachers, the central pen, and four gaping squares high up on each wall, busted windows, the edges lined with spikes of pointed glass.

Most of the Trolls were already seated.

Blade hefted the cloak, covering his head as many of the Trolls did, hoping his hair, visible above his forehead, would give him away. He took a deep breath and climbed into the bleachers, bearing left.

The Trolls were obviously excited, concentrating on the pen and jabbering happily.

Blade caught snatches of conversation as he

ascended the bleachers: "... watch them crack the bones ..." "... Wolvie will make mincemeat out of her ..." "... a waste of good flesh ..."

An expanse of vacant bleacher arrested his attention, and he sat down, glad the Trolls were ignoring him. He studied the crowd, sweeping the arena, his gray eyes widening in alarm when he spotted the Family women and the giant Troll. Instinctively, his left hand crept toward the Bowie on his left hip, his mind racing. What was transpiring? Were the women in danger?

The colossal Troll was talking to the women, the words too faint for Blade to gather their meaning.

He didn't like this! He didn't like this one bit!

The Trolls were whispering and fidgeting.

Why?

Blade stood, his blood rushing, forcing himself to casually move down the bleachers in the direction of the women. If something did happen, he wanted to be as close as possible. The Trolls might be superior numerically, but before he would allow harm to befall the women, he would give a good accounting.

To the delight of the Trolls, and to Blade's consternation, ominous growls emanated from behind a gate in the north wall of the pen.

Blade experienced a sinking feeling, certain he wouldn't reach the women before something terrible happened.

He was right.

Twelve rows still separated him from them when the huge Troll raised his head and yelled: "Life to the strong and death to the weak!"

The Trolls, galvanized by the phrase, followed his lead: "Life to the strong and death to the weak!"

Blade surged ahead, bowling Trolls from his path, prompting angry outbursts and curses.

The giant suddenly gripped Angela and threw her into the pen.

No! Blade was six rows from them when Jenny stood and jumped after Angela.

Damn!

Blade changed direction, making for the pen, realizing the north gate was open, glimpsing a large animal crouching on the earthen floor.

Jenny!

Blade knocked the remaining Trolls aside and dove into the pen.

21

"I still don't think your friend was too bright," Clyde asserted testily. "Only a dummy would go into Fox alone."

"Like I told you before, old-timer," Hickok replied, "my pard can take care of himself."

They were waiting at the SEAL: Hickok leaning against the transport, Clyde squatting against a nearby tree, Tyson and Cindy on the ground at his side, and Geronimo on the roof of the vehicle, keeping his eyes and ears peeled for trouble. Joan was asleep inside.

"Don't you think he should have returned by now?" Cindy asked.

Hickok shrugged. "He'll take as long as needs be," he told the girl. Inwardly, he was uneasy and worried. Blade's plan, initially, had sounded okay; he would find a way to sneak into Fox, ascertain the location where the women were being confined, and return. Later, under cover of darkness, they would stealthily enter Fox and free the women. Now, Hickok wasn't so certain of the scheme. Too many variables.

"That sure is some vehicle," Clyde commented, admiring the SEAL. "I can't thank you enough for letting us ride in it."

"Doesn't sound like those others, though," Tyson absently said, engaged in poking holes in the earth with a stick.

"What others?" Hickok asked, surprised.

"Oh, must of been a year ago. . . ." Tyson began.

"Longer than that," Clyde corrected his son.

"It was at night," Cindy explained. "We were spending the night in a house not far from the highway, and we heard them go by and saw lights on the front of the vehicles."

"Are you serious?" Hickok demanded, disturbed by the implications.

"Sure am," Clyde confirmed. "Shocked us something awful. We ran to the highway, but they was out of shouting range. There were five or six of 'em, coming from the direction of Fox. Jeeps, I believe, is what they called 'em before the war."

Functional jeeps? Hickok glanced up at Geronimo and they exchanged puzzled expressions.

"I think I've finally caught up on my beauty sleep," Joan announced, stepping from the SEAL. She stretched, yawning. "Never imagined how delicious jerky and water could taste."

Hickok chuckled. She had consumed dozens of venison jerky strips and drunk two full jars of water since her rescue.

"Pardon my appearance." Joan grinned, walking over to Hickok and kissing him on the left cheek. "I know I'm a sight in the morning."

"You're prettier than a sunrise," Hickok flattered her, taking her right hand in his.

Tyson snickered.

"You think something's funny, boy?" Hickok faced him.

"He doesn't have any respect," Clyde hastily stated.

"Never did," Cindy added.

Tyson was smirking.

"You wipe that smug look off your face," Hickok warned him, "or I'll cram it down your throat, whelp!"

Tyson, duly impressed, resumed digging in the dirt.

"My, aren't we touchy today?" Joan teased Hickok.

"It's a rule I have," Hickok stated, ignoring her mocking tone. "Only my friends can make fun of me."

"Words can't hurt you, silly," Joan gently chided him.

"Sometimes," Hickok stated, "words can be as deadly as my Pythons."

"You're just too sensitive," she said, hugging him.

"Hickok? Too sensitive?" Geronimo had overheard. "Don't let it get around or it will spoil his reputation."

"As a fierce fighter?" Hickok bragged on himself.

"Nope," Geronimo replied, shaking his head, his eyes twinkling. "As having rocks for brains."

Tyson gave vent to uncontrollable mirth.

Hickok glared at Geronimo. "Thanks, pard."

"Any time!" Geronimo promised.

Joan giggled. "Don't blame him. You were asking for it."

"Hey, old-timer." Hickok opted to change the subject. "How many Trolls you reckon there are?"

"I don't know for sure," Clyde responded. "My best guess is sixty or seventy."

"That many, huh?" Hickok nervously tapped his silver belt buckle, fretting over Blade.

"What's eating you?" Joan asked him.

"He's worried about Blade," Geronimo interjected before Hickok could answer.

"Aren't you?" Hickok queried, looking up at Geronimo.

"Of course," Geronimo affirmed.

"I can't stand this waiting," Hickok stated, beginning to pace.

"There's nothin' you can do, son," Clyde told Hickok. "Your friend had the right idea. We should stay here until he gets back."

"What if he doesn't get back?" Hickok countered. "We'd have no way of knowing if something happened to him."

"What else could we do?" Joan asked. "We all can't sneak into Fox."

"I know," Hickok muttered. He wheeled, facing them. "I don't know why, but I feel uneasy, like something's not right."

"Maybe you should change your profession from Warrior to Empath," Geronimo joked, grinning.

"I'm serious," Hickok snapped.

"Well, if you feel that way, let's do something," Joan suggested.

"We have our orders," Geronimo reminded her.

"What were our orders?" Hickok questioned him.

"You know what they were," Geronimo stated.

"Humor me, pard," Hickok urged. "What were our orders exactly?"

"Blade told us," Geronimo said, sighing, "to stay with the SEAL until we heard from him. If he doesn't return, we were instructed to go to the Home for reinforcements."

"Ahhhh." Hickok nodded. "But he didn't say the SEAL had to remain here, did he?"

"What are you getting at?" Geronimo asked. "As if I don't know."

"Me too." Joan grinned.

"Blade told us to stay with the SEAL," Hickok said, hooking his thumbs in his belt. "So if the SEAL were to drive into Fox, we'd have to go along, wouldn't we?"

"He'll clobber you for disobeying orders," Geronimo predicted.

"Won't be the first time he's been ticked off at

me," Hickok noted. "Here's the bottom line. I don't believe in pussyfooting around. Every moment our womenfolk are in Fox increases the odds they'll be harmed. . . ."

"So you propose to waltz right in and kindly ask the Trolls to hand over their captives?" Geronimo inquired, interrupting.

"I propose we create a diversion," Hickok replied.

"A diversion?" Clyde stood. "How do you mean?"

"We do something to attract the Trolls to us," Hickok explained. "We divert them long enough for my pard to find our women."

"Sounds dangerous," Cindy commented.

"You can stay here with your father and brother," Hickok recommended.

"Miss a chance to get even with the damn Trolls?" Clyde clapped his hands and eagerly rubbed the palms together. "No way!"

"I'm going where my paw goes," Cindy declared.

"I think the idea is dumb," Tyson opined, "but I'm with you."

Hickok stared at Joan.

"Don't expect me to stay out of this," she told him. "I owe the Trolls. And, like I said before, I never should have left the others. I should be with them, protecting them. Let's do it!"

"That leaves you." Hickok gazed up at Geronimo.

"Before I give you my answer," Geronimo said, "I have a question for you."

"Shoot, pard," Hickok prompted him.

"How is the SEAL going to get from here," Geronimo asked, pointing at the clearing they were in, "to there?" He pointed in the general direction of Fox.

"You can drive, if you want."

"Me?" Geronimo laughed. "I wouldn't touch this thing with a ten-foot pole."

"Well." Hickok hitched at his belt. "I reckon that leaves me."

Geronimo groaned.

"What's wrong?" Joan asked.

"I forgot. You weren't there when Hickok drove the SEAL." Geronimo sadly shook his head, his dark hair waving. "You had to see it to believe it."

"I don't get it," Joan said, perplexed. "Hickok told me last night he's driven the SEAL. How did he describe it . . ." She paused, remembering the words. "Poetry in action."

Geronimo almost fell, he laughed so hard.

"So maybe I exaggerated a mite," Hickok grudgingly admitted.

"A mite!" Geronimo snickered. "If lies were horse manure, you'd be a mountain of it!"

"Did you lie to me?" Joan faced Hickok.

"I kind of stretched the truth a bit," Hickok conceded, uncomfortable under her probing eyes.

Geronimo was trying to compose himself. "Well . . . I . . . I . . . guess I'll go along, if only to pick up the pieces."

"Pieces?" Tyson repeated.

"Okay." Hickok motioned toward the transport. "Let's mosey along! We haven't got all day."

Clyde, Cindy, and Tyson walked to the SEAL.

"What did he mean by pieces?" Tyson asked Hickok.

"Ignore the varmint," Hickok replied, making a show of glaring at Geronimo. "Didn't you know all Injuns love to make fun of white folk?"

"You better believe it!" Geronimo agreed, still laughing. "Us red folk appreciate what natural comedians you white folk are!"

22

He found them standing near the moat, south of the drawbridge. "Plato, Rikki," he greeted them. "Why the gloomy faces?"

"We were discussing the Alpha Triad, Joshua," Plato answered.

"The Spirit will preserve them," Joshua declared.

"We hope so anyway," Rikki amended.

"I still think I should be with them," Joshua said to Plato.

"What would you do if you were with them?" Rikki asked.

"I'd want an opportunity to converse with the Trolls, to prevail upon them to release the women, to relate the essential spiritual relationship of all creatures."

"You really think Trolls are capable of appreciating the higher realities of life?" Plato quizzed Joshua.

"All creatures respond to love," Joshua stated positively.

"Only sincere, caring people can reciprocate genuine affection," Plato said, disputing Joshua's contention.

"So you believe all creatures respond to love?" Rikki queried Joshua.

"I do," Joshua confirmed.

"Then," Rikki winked at Plato, "the next time

you come across a mutate, run up to it and give it a big hug. Let me know how it responds."

"Trolls aren't mutates," Joshua argued. "They're persons, like us."

"Not like us." Rikki shook his head. "I happen to think we smell a lot better than your average Troll. Did you get a whiff of the one we caught?"

"I'm shocked by your attitude," Joshua said, frowning. "Are all Warriors so callous?"

"I can't speak for the others," Rikki replied, "only myself. I believe in the reality of the Spirit, Joshua. I believe in love. But I'm a Warrior, and I'm conditioned to confront the dangers of our everyday existence, to protect our Family and this Home. I can't go into a fight worrying about possibly killing a brother or a sister, a fellow cosmic child of the Creator. It's either them or me, and I can guarantee you, if I have anything to say about it, it won't be me!"

"I'm thankful I'm not a Warrior," Joshua said quietly. "I am repulsed by violence."

"The Elders are wise," Plato interjected. "We would not permit you to become a Warrior. It is diametrically opposed to your very nature. You are an excellent Empath. Be happy with that."

"I think I will make myself useful," Joshua stated, turning. "I will pray for the Alpha Triad, for their success and safe return."

Plato sighed, watching the flowing water. "They'll need his prayers. They'll need all the help they can get."

23

"There it is!" Clyde exclaimed.

Fox was up ahead, several of the weather-battered buildings visible through the trees.

Hickok was driving, Geronimo in the other bucket seat, and Joan sat on the console between them. Clyde, Cindy, and Tyson were in the back seat.

"What's the plan?" Joan asked Hickok.

The gunman braked the transport and glanced at Geronimo. "Do you have any suggestions?"

Geronimo shook his head.

"What? Why not?"

"I'm still trying to recover from the shock of getting here alive!"

"Will you be serious?" Hickok requested.

"This was your idea," Geronimo stated. "I thought you had it all worked out."

"Not quite," Hickok acknowledged.

"How much did you work out?" Joan inquired.

"Getting here."

"That's it? The extent of your big plan?" Joan looked at Geronimo. "I'm beginning to see what you mean."

"I've been here before," Clyde spoke up. "I might be of help."

Hickok twisted in his seat. "What's the layout like, old-timer? Do they have patrols and guards?"

"They have guards," Clyde recalled. "Posted at the gates."

"What gates?" Hickok questioned.

"Well, it's like this." Clyde leaned forward and gestured with his hands as he spoke. "This road cuts through the town, sort of divides it. The Trolls, though, only use the northern part. They've fenced it in and put gates in the middle of each side. We've seen guards at the gates, but never saw a patrol, just hunting parties and raiding parties. You can't see it, but on the other side of these trees is a big field. It's on the west edge of the town. To the north of Fox is more deep forest, and to the east some hills. That's about it."

Hickok pondered the information.

"What now, mighty mind?" Geronimo asked.

"I don't like the looks of the highway ahead." Hickok evaluated the terrain. "Some of those buildings are awful close to the road. The Trolls would be on us before we saw them coming." He turned and surveyed the trees to their left. "Clyde, do you think we could get the SEAL through those trees to that field you mentioned?"

"Might be a close fit in places," Clyde answered. "But you should be able to make it."

"Good." Hickok slowly accelerated, easing the vehicle off the highway and into the woods, avoiding the tree trunks. Limbs scraped against the SEAL's body as the transport brushed by.

"I take it you now have a plan?" Joan queried Hickok.

"Yep."

"And it will work?" Geronimo quipped.

"Piece of cake," Hickok stated. "We drive out in the center of the field and wait for the Trolls to see us."

Everyone watched Hickok, waiting for additional details. Finally, Joan broke the silence.

"That's it?" she asked, incredulous. "That's your plan?"

"Isn't it a stroke of genius?" Hickok nodded,

grinning.

"You know," Tyson said to no one in particular, "I'm beginning to see why the one with the dark hair, Blade, is in charge of you guys."

"You're lucky," Hickok warned Tyson, "I've got my hands on this steering wheel."

"What are all those?" Cindy questioned, pointing at the dashboard.

Hickok glanced to his right. She was indicating a row of toggle switches in the center of the dash. These switches were not mentioned in the Operations Manual. There were four of them, each with a single letter etched beow it: M, S, F, and R. Blade intended to ask Plato about them upon their return.

"Beats me," Hickok admitted. "Just don't touch them. Don't touch anything in here unless I tell you otherwise."

"Getting back to this great plan of yours," Joan interjected.

"Yes?" Hickok squeezed the transport between two saplings.

"How is waiting in the middle of a field going to help Blade?"

"Easy," Hickok replied. "If we park in the field, we're bound to draw the Trolls to the west fence. They'll be curious, but a mite afraid because they've never seen anything like the SEAL."

"And with most of the Trolls watching us," Joan completed the line of reasoning, "Blade will be free to find Jenny and the others and maybe even sneak them out of Fox. I'm impressed! You're not as dumb as I thought you were!"

"Ouch," was all Hickok said in response.

"What happens if the Trolls charge the SEAL?" Clyde queried.

"We get the hell out of there," Hickok answered. "I was told this critter is bulletproof, so we shouldn't be in any danger."

"Look!" Cindy shouted, gesturing with her left arm. "The field!"

Hickok stopped the vehicle. They could see the field through the trees. "Hold onto your hats," he advised, and drove the transport out of the protective cover of the foliage onto the exposed open field.

"Who's wearing a hat?" Tyson asked.

The SEAL was forty yards from the west gate, the dilapidated structures clearly visible.

"I still say the Trolls will charge us," Clyde stated, worried.

Hickok halted the vehicle, leaning forward and peering through the windshield. "Where are the guards at the gate?"

"I don't see any sign of life." Geronimo was studying the western fence and the buildings.

"They'll see us, any moment," Joan assured them. "Wait and see if they don't."

They didn't. Time passed, and nary a sound or movement from Fox.

"What's going on here?" Clyde demanded. "This ain't right."

"You're telling us, old-timer," Hickok agreed. "Any ideas?"

"They're holding their annual Troll picnic and wilderness frolic," Geronimo suggested, "and no one is home."

"They had to have spotted us by now," Joan stated. "What gives?"

"That's what I'd like to find out," Hickok said, twisting the key, turning the engine off.

"You shouldn't of done that!" Clyde nervously declared.

"Relax," Hickok ordered. He faced Geronimo. "You with me?"

"You'll require someone to cover your butt," Geronimo replied.

"Don't forget me," Joan told them.

"I want you to stay with the SEAL," Hickok directed.

"Not on your life."

"Why not?"

"You know why. I'm a Warrior too, and you're not going to pamper me just because . . ."

"You'll be safer here," Hickok said, interrupting.

"There is nothing you can say or do," Joan gravely informed him, "to prevent me from coming along. I owe those women in there."

"I don't know. . . ." Hickok hesitated.

"She has a point," Geronimo said, siding with Joan, "and you know it."

Hickok sighed, resigned to the prospect. "Okay. But I can't understand what I see in such a contrary female!"

"What about us?" Clyde inquired.

"You three stay inside until we get back," Hickok said.

"Why can't we come?" Cindy implored.

"Too dangerous," Hickok explained. "Besides, we don't have enough guns to go around."

"I have my own gun." Clyde hefted his rifle, a Sako Classic Sporter in 30-06 caliber. "And I'm going along too. I've hated the Trolls for more years than I can remember. I won't pass up this chance to get even!"

"How many rounds you have, old-timer?" Hickok asked.

Clyde lifted a small leather pouch from the floor. "About forty. Don't use the rifle much anymore, except for emergencies. We kill our game with the bow and the spear." Those two weapons, along with their other meager possessions, were piled in the rear section of the transport.

"You can come," Hickok told Clyde.

"What about us?" Cindy inquired.

"You two stay here with the SEAL," Hickok

directed.

"That's not fair!" Tyson protested, pouting.

"Get your spear," Hickok said, glancing at Tyson, then at Cindy, "and your bow, and prepare for the worst, just in case. If the Trolls manage to get by us, they'll attack the SEAL."

"And you want us to defend it?" Tyson questioned hopefully.

"As long as you can," Hickok said. "But if too many Trolls attack, if you see it's hopeless, both of you hightail it out of here. Understood?"

Only Cindy nodded.

"Understood?" Hickok repeated, looking at Tyson.

"I don't like running," Tyson grumbled. "But I won't let the Trolls get Cindy either!"

"There's hope for you yet, boy," Hickok stated.

"Let's get to it," Joan urged, holding the Commando in her lap. Four extra clips were thrust in her pockets.

"All set," Geronimo announced, clutching the Browning. He had strapped a bandoleer across his left shoulder.

"You'll need this." Cindy retrieved the Henry from the storage area and passed the gun to Hickok.

"Do you see that ammo belt back there, to your right?" Hickok guided her.

"Here it is!" Cindy swung the Henry's ammo belt around, almost clipping Tyson.

"Hey! Watch it, stupid!" Tyson groused as he ducked aside.

"Sorry." Cindy giggled.

"Thanks." Hickok leaned forward and secured the ammo belt directly above his cartridge belt for the Pythons.

"You look like you're going to a war," Cindy joked.

"We are," Hickok reminded her. "Let's do it." He opened his door and slid out, Geronimo doing likewise on his side.

Joan followed Hickok, pausing at the door, waiting for Clyde.

"You two kids take real good care of yourselves," Clyde said to his children.

"We will, papa," Cindy promised.

"You protect your sister," Clyde ordered Tyson.

"Tyson and I will be fine," Cindy stated. "Just watch out for your own self."

"If something should happen to me . . ." Clyde began.

"Don't talk like that!" Cindy didn't want to hear it.

"Okay."

Joan watched as Clyde kissed Cindy on her cheek. He went to exit the vehicle, paused, then quickly kissed Tyson.

"Don't worry," Joan assured the anxious teens. "I'll take care of your father."

"Sometime this year!" Hickok announced.

Hickok locked the doors, pocketed the keys, and smiled at Tyson and Cindy. "You use this lever to close the windows," he demonstrated as he spoke, reaching in the open driver's window, "and this latch to open the door. . . ."

"We've seen you do it a bunch of times," Cindy informed him.

"Good. I've locked the doors, so if you roll the windows up and someone tries to get it, winter will get here before they get inside."

"We'll do fine," Tyson said, his eyes on his father.

"Be seeing you, pard," Hickok stated. He joined Joan, Geronimo, and Clyde, crouched in the full grass ten feet in front of the vehicle. Behind him, Cindy and Tyson clambered into the bucket seats, Cindy on the driver's side, Tyson on the other, and stuck their heads out the windows.

"They're good kids," Clyde said proudly.

"Sure are," Hickok confirmed. "Now let's get to business." He motioned for Geronimo to bear right. "Fan out. Form a skirmish line." He waved Joan and Clyde to his left. "Stay low. Move in on the gate. Go!"

"The Spirit be with us," Joan offered, moving away. She winked at Hickok and blew him a kiss.

The three Warriors and the aged farmer advanced across the field until they were ten yards from the gate. Hickok raised his left arm and rested on his right knee, signaling a stop. There was still no sign of life in Fox. What the blazes was going on here? Had the Trolls abandoned the town? If so, why? Where the heck was Blade? It didn't make sense!

Hickok gripped the Henry and risked standing erect, scanning the fence and the buildings.

Nothing.

The others warily followed his lead, converging on the closed gate.

"If the Trolls have left," Joan whispered as they joined together, voicing her innermost fear, "and they've take the women, what will we do?"

"It appears like any other deserted town," Geronimo observed.

"Only it smells worse," Clyde corrected.

"We search the town," Hickok ordered. "Look for any sign of Blade and the women."

"All you can hear is the wind," Clyde marveled.

"Wait a second!" Geronimo froze, his head cocked.

"What is it?" Clyde asked.

"Quiet!" Geronimo snapped. He walked to the gate, opened it, and stepped inside, the others on his heels.

"Let us in on it," Hickok said.

"Sounds. Faint." Geronimo was pacing in a circle, testing the intensity and the distance. "Lots of voices. Yelling."

"Where?" Hickok asked.

Finally Geronimo was certain. "That way." He pointed. "They must be inside a building," he speculated.

"All of them?" Joan queried skeptically.

"Let's find out," Hickok said, leading the way along a narrow street, bearing east. Several blackbirds flapped on the roofs overhead.

"I'll get my revenge for Bess yet," Clyde stated, bringing up the rear.

Hickok's senses were primed, his eyes never still, as they made for the subdued din. Two rats scurried across the road ahead. A pile of human feces littered a doorway.

The clamor was louder.

The street they were on ended at a large structure, as rundown as the rest, with two great swinging doors, both closed.

"It's coming from in there," Geronimo whispered, saying the obvious.

Hickok stopped at the corner of the last building before an open, paved lot between them and the swinging doors. He didn't like the setup. They would be vulnerable as they crossed to the doors, and anyone inside would spot them in an instant.

The uproar was increasing.

"You stay put," Hickok directed. "I'm going to peek inside and see what the blazes is going on."

"I'll do it," Joan volunteered, and before he could prevent it, she was jogging toward the doors, hunched over to present a smaller target, the Commando at the ready.

Blast! Why did she do it? Hickok asked himself. She was trained better than that! What was she trying to prove? He kept his eyes glued to those swinging doors, sweat forming on his brow.

Joan was halfway.

"She'll make it," Geronimo assured Hickok,

noticing his pale expression.

Pandemonium erupted inside the structure with the doors.

"No!"

Hickok was in motion before the word died on his lips, running after Joan, throwing caution to the wind, a round in the Henry's chamber, his moccasins pounding on the pavement.

Joan was thirty feet from the swinging doors.

"Joan!" Hickok shouted, knowing those inside the building would not be able to hear him, hoping to stop her before she reached the doors.

Twenty feet now.

Why wasn't she stopping? Was she that worried about Jenny and the rest?

Fifteen feet.

The swinging doors suddenly burst open, disgourging a veritable horde of Trolls, dozens upon dozens.

Coming directly at Joan.

"*Joan!*" Hickok screamed, raising the Henry to his shoulder. "*Joan!*"

He was too late!

24

The wolverine, according to a book in the Family library entitled *North American Mammals*, a volume used frequently by the children in the Family school as a reference guide, was once considered the most ferocious animal on the entire continent. Wolverines would attack bears and cougars, and their voracious appetites earned them the nickname "glutton." They would consume anything they could catch and slay. Armed with razor teeth and claws, they were rulers of their wilderness domain. Usually dark brown, with lighter patches on the head and shoulders, they could reach a weight of fifty pounds and attain a length of five feet including their bushy tail. Wolverines were the bane of trappers, feared by hunters, and, except for grizzly bears and the later-appearing mutates, the most dreaded animal in the north woods, to be avoided at all costs.

Unless, Blade reflected as the tableau momentarily froze after he leaped into the arena, you had no choice.

Like right now.

The wolverines, a large male, a dusky female, and an undersized stripling, reacted first. They picked their prey and attacked, instinctively going after separate targets.

On the bleachers above, his revolver in his hand, Saxon grinned as he watched. Initially apprehensive when the newcomer entered the pen, he calmed down when he realized there wasn't a man alive who could take a wolverine one-on-one. So what chance did this guy have against three, all ravenous, all hating humans? None. He chuckled as the wolverines closed in, the one the Trolls called Wolvie making for the imposter, Momma going after Jenny, and Runt bounding toward the planned main course, Angela.

Blade's first thought was for the women. Jenny was nearest, twelve feet away, backed against the pen wall as Momma bore down. The Bowie in his left hand was useless at that distance; he crouched, drawing the right Vega, praying his aim was accurate for once, ignoring the wolverine coming after him, sighting and firing.

The Vega bucked and boomed and Momma twisted, snarling, only three feet from Jenny, her rear legs tensing for the killing leap.

Blade fired again, and once more, the slugs ripping into Momma's skull.

Jenny involuntarily screamed as the wolverine tumbled and slammed against her. She tripped as she desperately attempted to avoid the hurtling body, and panicked when the wolverine landed on top of her. "No!" She kicked and punched and struggled to her feet, only to shudder at the gaping, oozing wounds as the animal's brains flowed from the shattered cranium.

Momma was dead.

Saxon fumed. The bastard had a gun! He aimed his revolver, furious one of his prized pets was gone.

Blade had pivoted, his right arm extended, wanting to be sure, the smallest wolverine only inches from Angela. His finger was tightening on the trigger when two events occurred simultaneously; there was the sound of a shot somewhere above him and his right shoulder exploded in pain, and the largest wolverine crashed into his chest, slashing and tearing.

Jenny, horrified, saw the Vega fly from Blade's fingers as he went down under the onslaught of the wolverine. She ran toward him, but abruptly stopped when Angela's petrified shriek filled the arena.

Runt and Angela were on the ground, its steely jaws clamped on her right wrist, its claws gouging her body.

Jenny wavered, torn both ways. Who should she assist? The man she loved, or her friend? She watched as Blade heaved upward, the Bowie in his left hand flashing, driving into the wolverine over and over, making her decision easier. Blade could handle himself. Angela was another matter.

Runt was trying to sever Angela's wrist, his teeth grinding against the bone, blood spraying over her terrified face.

Jenny, racing toward them, frantically searched for a weapon, anything, and spotted a human thigh bone in the dirt of the arena floor. She scooped it up on the run, and raised it over her head as she came up behind the wolverine.

Saxon, relishing the spectacle, laughed.

Angela's struggles were growing weaker.

Runt, sensing victory, released the wrist and raised his head, prepared for a lunge at her pulsing throat.

"No!" Jenny shouted, hoping to distract the brute, sweeping the bone down, connecting with the wolverine's head.

Runt spun away from Angela, hissing, enraged by excruciating pain. He jumped aside as this new human swung her club again, his muscular body held close to the ground in the classic wolverine attack posture.

"Angela!" Jenny yelled. "Get up!" She wanted Angela to reach the pen wall, just six feet away, to reduce the area she must defend. If they could get their backs to the wall, the wolverine would not be able to try a rear assault. As it was, the creature was slowly circling them, growling, biding its time, watching the tip of the club.

"Angela! Do you hear me?" Jenny goaded, her eyes on the wolverine.

Angela was almost limp. Her head wobbled as she tried to nod, to acknowledge Jenny's directions.

"Angela! Please!"

Runt snarled, frustrated.

Jenny's arms ached. The wolverine was between them and the pen wall, still circling.

Angela moaned.

Jenny wanted to risk glancing at Blade, to see how he was faring, but she was too afraid to look away from the wolverine for even an instant.

"Jenny?" Angela groaned, on the verge of fainting, fighting to remain awake. She rolled over, onto her stomach, placed her hands under her chest, and pushed, trying to rise.

"Angela!" Jenny warned. "Stay down now! Wait until it comes around again."

Angela, only dimly conscious of the words, concentrated and heaved, reaching her knees before she completely blacked out. She pitched forward, away from Jenny, toward the wolverine.

"Angela!" Jenny screamed, lunging to catch her.

Too late.

Runt pounced, his lightning reflexes unbelievably quick, his pointed teeth ripping into Angela's neck and rending the flesh apart, blood gushing over his facial fur as he greedily gulped the raw, tender meat, his fiery stare fixed on Jenny, as if giving notice he would brook no interference with his meal.

Jenny backed away, repulsed, gagging, feeling her limbs loose their strength, knowing there was nothing she could do. Dear Spirit! No!

Someone was laughing.

Jenny looked up into a sea of smirking faces. The Trolls were packed to the edge of the bleachers, crammed together, craning for a glimpse of the action in the arena. With Runt temporarily occupied, they shifted their attention to Wolvie and his antagonist.

Blade's tremendous stamina and superbly conditioned physique were enabling him to hold his own against the sinewy power of the frenzied wolverine. So far. Despite the gunshot wound, his right arm still functioned. He had grabbed the wolverine's throat as it sprang at him, his right hand buried in the pliant folds of skin, and he steadfastly refused to relinquish his grip no matter how ferociously the animal struggled. They tumbled and rolled on the floor of the pen, the wolverine churning its legs, lashing him with its curved claws, while Blade repeatedly thrust his Bowie into the furry, bulky body, seemingly to no avail.

Both combatants were covered with dirt and caked with blood.

The Trolls started cheering the wolverine, shouting encouragement and waving their arms, some jumping up and down.

"Go, Wolvie! Go!"

"Tear the sucker up!"

Blade was jarred by the brutal impact of colliding with the arena wall, his head cracking against the wood. Wolvie took advantage of his slight disorientation and jerked free of his grip, just as he plunged the Bowie into its side one more time. The wolverine growled and pulled away, taking the knife with it, the blade still imbedded in its ribs.

"Kill the bum!" came from one of the Trolls.

Blade hastily scrambled to his feet, catching his breath, debating his next move. The wolverine, fortunately, seemed winded too. Maybe all his stabbing had finally taken effect. Whatever the cause, he had a brief respite to consider his options. If he drew his other Vega, he risked being shot again by someone in the bleachers. He still retained his other Bowie, but he must have pierced the wolverine a dozen times already and the damn thing was still on its feet. No, he needed a method guaranteed to succeed.

The wolverine was panting, gathering itself for another charge.

Blade wondered if he would have time to shed the heavy cloak, and as he reached for the leather tie string secured at the base of his neck, eager to toss the cloak aside and free his arms for maximum effectiveness, inspiration struck.

Wolvie was inching toward him.

Would it work?

Did he still have them on him? Or were they dislodged during their conflict?

There was no time to check. It would be now, or never.

The wolverine rumbled deep in its chest, craving this human more than any prey in its life.

Blade waited, his hands near the tie string. Everything depended on his timing. Too early, and he would only slow the animal; too late, and he would miss entirely and be at the wolverine's mercy.

The assembled Trolls were hushed, expecting the familiar rush and the shrill shrieks of agony as the victim was disemboweled.

"Get 'em, Wolvie!" one Troll shouted encouragement.

The wolverine made its move, three leaping bounds and it launched itself into the air, its mouth open, the gleaming teeth visible, saliva drolling over its gums.

Blade was in motion with Wolvie's first leap, yanking on the tie string and releasing the cloak. He held the cloak with both hands, gripping the top border, and swept the bear hide around, placing it directly in the path of the oncoming wolverine.

Wolvie couldn't stop. The beast hit the cloak

dead center and dropped to the ground, enfolded in
the cloak, tearing the skin in an effort to extricate
itself.

In moments it would be loose.

Blade hurriedly searched his waist for the
daggers. They were both still tucked under his belt,
jammed together over his right hip. He whipped
them from their respective sheaths, one in each
hand.

The wolverine managed to cut an opening in the
cloak. It poked its narrow head through the slash,
getting its bearings.

Now!

Blade jumped, landing on the wolverine's back.
The beast twisted to confront him, still confident in
its superior ability, its front paws imprisoned under
the bear skin.

Saxon was the only Troll to immediately grasp
Blade's intent, and he tried to bring his revolver
into play. His arm was still rising when he saw
the imposter bury the daggers in Wolvie's eyes,
actually sink the keen blades to the hilt in the
wolverine's eye sockets.

Blade vaulted beyond the range of the
wolverine's death throes and ran toward Jenny. She
was standing not far from where the final wolverine
complacently gorged on Angela, her face blank,
apparently in deep shock. He reached her side and
glanced up at the astonished Trolls, most of whom
were staring at the dying Wolvie, unwilling or
unable to accept what they saw.

"Jenny! Snap out of it!" Blade shook her.

"Blade?" Jenny looked at him, dazed, uncom-
prehending, unaware of their precarious predicament.

Blade knew the Trolls would channel their
collective revenge in his direction at any moment,
once the reality of the two dead wolverines hit home.
He needed a distraction, something to buy him time.

But what?

The smallest wolverine was savoring its feast, ripping chunks of bloody, dripping meat from Angela's body and wolfing them down. It was lying with its back to Blade and Jenny, engrossed in its feeding, not considering them much of a threat.

Blade's mind whirled. How heavy was the last wolverine? Maybe thirty pounds, maximum. The pen walls were ten feet high. He could do it, but speed was essential!

"Blade?" Jenny absently repeated.

Blade ran to the wolverine and stooped over, his powerful hands encircling the ten-inch tail.

Runt grunted in surprise as his tail was clasped in a vise of iron and he was hauled from the arena floor.

Blade surged upward, spinning his body, his momentum carrying the bewildered wolverine in a wide revolution. He spun and spun, gathering speed, the surrounding pen a blur as he dug his heels into the ground, his arm muscles bulging.

"Look at that!" a young Troll yelled.

"What's he doing?" another asked.

Saxon was vainly endeavoring to sight his revolver on the man, but he was reluctant to fire for fear of striking Runt.

Blade angled his body closer to the western wall of the pen. He needed to be as close as he could get to the wall when he gave the Trolls the shock of their lives.

Some of the Trolls, those nearest the edge of the bleachers, perceived their dilemma and attempted to back away from the arena. Those standing in the rear rows, however, were pressing forward, striving for a better look, ignorant of the activity in the pen.

Blade was at his limit, going as fast as he could go. He arched his broad back and elevated the wolverine as high as he could swing it, then released his hold on the tail.

To the complete consternation of the startled Trolls, Runt came sailing over the pen wall and landed among them in the bleachers.

The Trolls went crazy, screaming and screeching and falling over one another in their precipitate haste to remove themselves from the immediate vicinity of the thrashing, snapping wolverine.

Runt, enraged because of his interrupted repast, was biting and clawing everything in sight.

The Trolls broke, en masse heading for the swinging doors and escape.

With one notable exception.

Saxon, his revolver in his right hand, jumped from the bleachers into the arena below, his smoldering eyes and compressed lips indicative of his simmering fury. The man was holding the woman Jenny, hugging her close and whispering words in her ear. Saxon came up behind them and stopped eight feet away. He pointed his revolver at the man's back.

Blade heard the click of a hammer being drawn and he spun, his left hand going for the remaining Vega.

"Better not," Saxon grimly advised, "or you're dead."

Blade froze, his fingers inches from the automatic.

"Slowly take the gun from the holster," Saxon directed. "Use two fingers and hold it by the butt. Very carefully," he stressed.

Blade complied, dangling the Vega between his thumb and forefinger.

"Toss it," Saxon ordered, wagging his gun to their right, "as far as you can."

Blade threw the Vega. Jenny was still in shock, staring at Angela's grisly remains.

"Think you're pretty bright, don't you?" Saxon asked.

Blade shrugged.

"Well, you've reached the end of your rope," Saxon declared. "I'm going to personally finish you off."

"I'm scared," Blade taunted him, wondering if the giant would simply shoot him and be done with it.

"You will be," Saxon promised, "by the time I'm done with you." He smiled and holstered his revolver.

"You planning to crush me with your bare hands?" Blade asked derisively.

"I see you like big knives." Saxon nodded at the Bowie on Blade's right hip. "You used the other one real good on Wolvie."

"Wolvie?"

"The second wolverine you wasted," Saxon explained.

"Hope it upset you," Blade goaded him.

"It did," Saxon grudgingly admitted. "But like I was saying. You like big knives. I like big knives." His right arm disappeared under his cloak and came out bearing the machete. "So I'll tell you what we're going to do. You use your big knife, there, and I'll use mine. Fair enough?"

Blade drew his right Bowie. "You surprise me," he conceded.

"I'm not a damn backstabber," Saxon said angrily. "I like to see the fear in their eyes when I snuff 'em."

Blade took several steps toward the massive Troll, who towered over him by at least a foot.

"By the way," Saxon said, playfully twirling the machete in his palm, "what's your name?"

"They call me Blade."

"Saxon," the Troll stated. "Now let's get to it. I can't wait to slice you into itsy-bitsy pieces."

So saying, the giant closed in.

25

Hickok fired as he ran, aiming for the head, closing the distance, intent on reaching Joan's side before she was overwhelmed by the surging Trolls. She had dropped to her knees as the doors opened, the Commando chattering, the heavy bullets shredding the Troll ranks, flesh bursting and blood spurting as the astonished Trolls absorbed the initial onslaught.

"What do we do?" Clyde asked Geronimo. They were still at the corner of the last building. "We didn't count on this!"

"You do what you want," Geronimo told him, and charged from cover, the Browning booming.

The flabbergasted Trolls recovered quickly and tactically responded to this unexpected ambush; they spread outward, deploying their forces to the right and left of the swining doors. Stacks of bodies piled directly in front of the doors as Joan mowed down the Trolls still spilling forth from the bedlam inside.

Hickok concentrated on any Trolls posing a threat to Joan. He saw a grizzled Troll raise a rifle to his shoulder, aiming at her, and he snapped a shot into the Troll's brain. Another Troll ran at Joan, a sword upraised. Hickok shot him twice.

Geronimo, coming up fast, noted Hickok's efforts to protect the woman he loved. He also noticed the gunman was heedless of his own safety; a Troll with a bow took a bead on Hickok, and

Geronimo exploded his chest with a blast from the shotgun.

Clyde held back, slightly timid. He provided supporting cover, shooting at random, snickering, delighted at experiencing his long-deferred revenge.

Hickok reached Joan's side. He was beginning to believe they would break the Trolls, would compel them to retreat and scatter, when Joan suddenly stopped firing.

"Out!" she shouted, reaching behind her for one of the extra ammo clips.

Hickok shot a Troll attacking with a spiked club and pivoted, aiming at another bearded enemy, this one with a hatchet. He hastily squeezed the Henry's trigger, appalled when the hammer clicked. He was out too! How could he allow himself to lose track of the rounds fired? There was no time to reload. He dropped the Henry and drew the Pythons, both Colts simultaneously, forcing his aching, injured shoulder to obey his mental commands.

The Troll with the hatchet shrieked as he closed the gap.

Hickok shot, the right Colt only, the bullet slamming into the Troll's forehead.

Joan was frantically tugging on the spent clip, still in the Commando. "It's jammed!" she yelled. "The damn thing's jammed!"

Hickok stepped between the Trolls and Joan, the Pythons held low, at waist level. He would insure she was safe until she could switch clips.

With the Commando inoperative, the Trolls regained their momentum, closing file and advancing, retaliating against the greatest threat, the woman with the machine gun.

Geronimo reached Hickok and Joan. "Reloading!" he alerted them, and dropped to one knee, extracting fresh rounds from the bandoleer and feeding them into the Browning.

The Trolls, seeing only one opponent effectively

armed, voiced a collective war cry and attacked.

Hickok stood firm, shooting targets as rapidly as they presented themselves: two Trolls with rifles, another with a pistol, a fourth with a shotgun, one fleet of foot who managed to get within six feet with an axe, three more Trolls charging as a group. Arrows spun by his head, and bullets buzzed through the air, resembling angry hornets in flight. A spear cleaved a furrow in his left thigh.

Geronimo reentered the fray, four quick blasts from the Browning decimating a row of approaching Trolls. A slug nicked his left cheek, drawing blood. An arrow clipped his right ankle.

The Trolls had gained the advantage.

"Reloaded!" Joan suddenly shouted, the fresh clip finally in the Carbine. She heaved erect as Hickok dodged aside, and she cut loose with the Commando, bowling the Trolls over. They screamed and plunged, littering the ground with the dead and the wounded, pools of crimson dotting the pavement.

One Troll, smarter than his peers, had hung back, hidden just inside the swinging doors. He was armed with a metal-tipped lance, and as his beady eyes surveyed the carnage the woman was wreaking, he galvanized his burly body into action. Sheltered by the shadows, he hefted the heavy lance, judging the distance. He shuffled backwards several steps, then raced forward, his right arm swinging the lance back, then up and out.

Hickok, crouched by Joan's right side, caught a blur of motion as the Troll emerged from the building into the light of day. He automatically sent a bullet into the Troll's brain, even as the lance left the Troll's hand and hurtled through the air.

"Look out!" Hickok cried, diving, attempting to put his body in front of Joan's.

Joan, intent on dealing death to the Trolls, caught the flashing gleam of the lance out of the corner of her right eye. She heard Hickok's warning and whirled.

The lance, on course, descended from its apex, the tapered, sharpened point piercing Joan's left side, puncturing her lung. It passed completely through her body and impaled her to the ground.

"*No! No!*" Hickok scrambled to her side.

Joan was attempting to speak; blood dribbled from the corners of her mouth. She was on her back, her lips close to his face.

"*No!*" Hickok felt a drop of her blood spatter against his left cheek. He saw the Commando on the ground at her feet and he scooped the Carbine into his hands. "*No!*" Hickok rose and spun, the Commando bucking as he depressed the trigger. He began walking toward the Trolls, sweeping the Carbine back and forth, back and forth. He hardly noticed the havoc he caused: the torn and mangled bodies covering the pavement, the screams of agony and destruction, the frenzied efforts of the remaining Trolls to escape the mayhem. He held the trigger in, his mind attuned to a singular activity: sweeping the Commando in an arc, back and forth, back and forth.

"Hickok!"

Hickok disregarded the voice, still firing.

"Hickok!"

Hickok advanced, keeping the trigger pressed, unaware of all else.

"Hickok! It's me!" Geronimo stepped in front of him and gripped him by the shoulders. "It's me! The gun's empty! Do you hear me? The gun's empty!"

Hickok stopped, disoriented. He stared at the smoking Carbine.

"The gun's empty!" Geronimo repeated. "The Trolls are gone."

Hickok scanned the area. Sure enough, except for the dozens of bodies all over the place, the Trolls had withdrawn.

"Are you okay?" Geronimo asked. He was sporting a nasty wound on his right side.

"Fine," Hickok mumbled. "Piece of cake." Then he remembered. He turned and raced to Joan, aghast at the sight of her pale face and the red puddle at her feet.

"Joan!" Hickok knelt by her side. "What do I do?" He glanced at Geronimo. "Should I remove the lance?"

Geronimo sadly shook his head.

"Joan!" Hickok stared into her beautiful blue eyes, his own watering.

Joan grinned weakly. She licked her dry lips and managed to raise her right hand.

Hickok tenderly took her hand in his. "Don't move," he advised her. "Stay as still as possible."

"It's no use," Joan said, her voice a wavering whisper.

"Don't talk like that!" Hickok stroked her forehead, tears streaming down his face.

"We sure gave it to them," Joan stated proudly. "Didn't we?"

Hickok nodded, his throat bobbing.

"You've got to find the women," Joan declared urgently. "Jenny, Mary, Ursa, and the rest."

"We will," Hickok promised.

Geronimo was standing guard, his back to them, scanning for danger. His own eyes were misting over.

"Get them to the Home, safe and sound," Joan said.

"We will," Hickok assured her. "Don't worry."

"You know," Joan began, a faraway look in her eyes, "this would happen now, after I finally find someone I care for. Murphy's Law strikes again." She smiled.

"Please," Hickok begged her. "Don't talk. If we can remove this thing. . . ."

Joan reached up and touched the tip of her right forefinger to his lips.

"Take care, lover," she told him.

"Joan . . ."

"It's been fun." She began coughing.

"Don't talk!"

Joan shook her head. "Doesn't matter. I'll be waiting for you in the mansions on high."

"Please . . ."

"Tell me you love me," she urged him.

"I love you."

Her eyes abruptly widened, her body stiffened, and she gave vent to one last, lingering breath. Then she was gone.

Hickok raised his tear-streaked face to the heavens.

"*NOOOOOOOOOOOOOoooooooooo!*"

26

Saxon was toying with Blade. The giant knew he had the longest reach, and the machete added to his leverage, the Bowie being fourteen inches shorter. He swung the machete again and again, almost lazily, displaying his contempt, forcing Blade to back away.

For his part, Blade was using this game to gather his energy. After the battle with the wolverines, he was winded, tired, and feeling the loss of blood from the wounds covering his body. The wolverine's claws had caused considerable damage. He glanced at Jenny, still staring mutely at Angela. What was the matter with her? Was it shock?

Saxon caught the glance, and promptly misinterpreted it.

"Don't worry about her," the giant teased. "I won't harm her. I'm saving her for myself." He grinned lecherously.

"You'll never have her," Blade rejoined harshly.

"Think so, eh?"

"I know so," Blade confirmed.

Saxon bore down, his blows coming faster now, his playfulness gone.

Blade parried his opponent's thrusts and slashes, continuing to retreat across the arena, away from Jenny.

"I must admit," Saxon spoke even while

250

fighting, "you are a worthy foe. No one has dared face me in years."

"You know what they say. . . ." Blade managed to retort as he ducked beneath a sweeping blow.

"No." Saxon chuckled. "What do they say?"

Blade scurried away from another stabbing thrust. He paused, smiling, strangely appreciative of this colossus of a man. "The bigger they are . . ."

". . . the harder they fall," Saxon finished for him. "Yes, I've heard that one."

"I don't suppose," Blade said lightly, "I could prevail upon you to surrender?"

"What?" Saxon laughed. "Do you hear that?" he asked.

For some time, from outside the swinging doors, came the sound of gunfire and screaming and yelling.

"That's my men," Saxon stated. "Finishing off whoever was with you."

"It could be the other way around," Blade reminded him.

Saxon glanced in the direction of the combat, his brow furrowed. "You could be right," he mused. "We don't have machineguns. The Watchers do, but we have a pact with them."

"Watchers?" Blade said. "What are the Watchers?"

Saxon shook his head. "Sorry. I really must get outside." Without warning, he flipped his machete at Blade.

Blade twisted, avoiding the machete, off balance, his back turned toward the giant for only an instant.

It was enough.

Saxon leaped, pouncing on Blade from behind, wrapping his mighty arms around the Warrior. He lifted Blade from the floor and applied pressure, squeezing, exerting his stupendous brute force.

Blade, caught in a steel vise, struggled and

heaved, attempting to trip the giant and drop them to the ground. He surged against Saxon's restraining arms until his own biceps and triceps bulged, to no avail.

"Why fight it?" Saxon hissed through clenched teeth. "Make it easy on yourself."

Blade tossed and pitched, trying to butt Saxon with his head and kick him with his legs.

Saxon laughed.

Blade could feel the pressure building in his chest. He could easily imagine it caving in if he couldn't break free.

Jenny was showing signs of life, looking around her, her green eyes blinking rapidly.

Blade's face was reddening, his arms weakening, the sustained conflict taking its toll on his physique.

"You should never mess with the Trolls," Saxon stated, straining even more.

Blade remembered his Bowie, still clutched in his right hand. A vital spot, a death stroke, was out of the question; they were out of his reach. But there was one option. . . .

"Blade!" Jenny was running his way, horrified at what she saw.

"I think I'll have her for supper," Saxon gloated.

Blade focused, aligning the Bowie. He gripped the handle and drove the blade upward, through the tunic, and into Saxon's groin, slicing into the gonads and twisting the knife.

Saxon screeched and released Blade. He stumbled backwards, his hands groping his bleeding groin.

Blade dropped to the arena floor. He quickly hiked the tunic and found one of the Solingen throwing knives.

Saxon was doubled over, whimpering. His hands grabbed the Bowie and pulled, and he

screamed as the knife jerked loose. He looked up at
Blade. "I don't believe it!" he said, moaning.

Blade slowly stood, the Solingen hidden behind
his right leg.

"Don't leave me like this," Saxon pleaded. "The
pain! The pain!"

"I could take you prisoner, back to the Home,"
Blade told him.

"Don't leave me like this," Saxon repeated. He
looked down at the blood oozing from his ruined
testicles. "Don't leave me less than a man."

Blade nodded once, understanding. The Soligen
was up and on its way in the blink of an eye.

Saxon flinched as the thin blade penetrated his
sloping forehead. His eyes closed and he toppled like
a jumbo tree in the forest, his head striking the
ground first, driving the knife even deeper.

"Blade!"

Jenny reached him, tossing the thigh bone
aside. She hugged him and buried her face in his
shoulder.

Blade held her, allowing his nerves to relax.
Outside, all was quiet. What had happened? he
wondered. He detected movement in the bleachers
and tensed, then smiled when he recognized the
Family women—Lea, Mary, Daffodil, Ursa,
Saphire—and an elderly woman he did not know.

Or did he?

"Bless you, Blade," this woman said. "Thank
you for saving us from hell."

"Do I know you?" he asked her.

"Know me? You used to sit on my lap and eat
my cookies."

"Nadine!" Blade realized, grinning. "Wait until
Plato sees you."

"Wait until I see him." Nadine smirked. "I'll
probably wear the poor dear out the first week I'm
home."

27

The mop-up took the remainder of the day.

They searched the entire town, but any remaining Trolls had vanished into the woods, taking the other women prisoners with them. Of the Trolls involved in the battle, only five were still alive. Blade placed them in one of the buildings, and gave them a jar of water and several strips of venison. He couldn't afford to take them to the Home; there wasn't enough room in the transport for all the Family members as it was, and it would be slow going, with several of the women forced to march outside the vehicle, guarded by the Warriors.

Cindy and Tyson conferred, deciding they still wanted to go to the Home, although they were inexpressibly saddened by the death of their papa. Geronimo had found Clyde slumped against the building he had stood near during the fight, an arrow through his chest and a deep gash over his left eye.

Runt, Ursa told them, had escaped. In the confusion and the din, sensing his chance, he had jumped from the bleachers, found a sizable hole in the north wall, and departed the company of detested man for good, instinctively yearning for the scents and sounds of the natural element he'd been denied confined in a cage, the deep forest.

Hickok, morose, inconsolable, wrapped Joan in several discarded, and relatively clean, cloaks. They placed her body in the rear section of the SEAL. She would receive the honor of a Warrior's burial in the Family plot.

Blade, after collecting his weapons, joined the others. They were huddled around a fire near the SEAL. The sun was setting, the horizon a vivid display of reds and pinks and yellows.

"I'll never let you out of my sight again," Jenny said, her arms around him. "I can't believe we're together, we're alive, and we'll be safe in the Home within a few days."

"Did you doubt I'd find you?" Blade asked her.

"I was beginning to wonder," she confessed.

Blade sadly stared at the transport. He knew Hickok was in there, slumped over Joan's lifeless body.

"I feel so sorry for him," Jenny stated, seemingly reading Blade's mind.

"So do I," Blade replied gloomily.

"He'll recover," Jenny predicted.

"How would you feel if I was the one lying in there?" Blade queried.

Jenny didn't respond.

"You know," Blade mused aloud, "just a few days ago Plato was telling me how hard life can be, how these hardships are intended to mold our character. If he were here right now, I'd ask him how Joan's death is supposed to mold Hickok's character."

"One thing's for sure," Jenny concurred, kissing him on the lips.

"What's that?" he asked.

"One thing life definitely isn't," Jenny mused, "is a piece of cake."

"Maybe," Blade grinned, despite his sorrow, "it all depends on how you slice it."

GET FREE BOOKS!

You can have the best fiction delivered to your door for less than what you'd pay in a bookstore or online. Sign up for one of our book clubs today, and we'll send you *FREE* BOOKS* just for trying it out...**with no obligation to buy, ever!**

If you love fast-paced page turners, you won't want to miss any of the books in Leisure's thriller line. Filled with gripping tension and edge-of-your-seat excitement, these titles feature everything from psychological suspense to legal thrillers to police procedurals and more!

As a book club member you also receive the following special benefits:
- **30% off all orders!**
- **Exclusive access to special discounts!**
- **Convenient home delivery and 10 days to return any books you don't want to keep.**

Visit www.dorchesterpub.com or call 1-800-481-9191

There is no minimum number of books to buy, and you may cancel membership at any time.
*Please include $2.00 for shipping and handling.